"Do you play, too?" Emmett asked, sounding shocked that I knew my way around the game.

"I used to. Years ago."

"Wow, I never would've guessed. I mean, you're so . . ." He gestured to my light pink maxi dress, neatly curled hair, and glossy pink lipstick, struggling for an adjective that wouldn't offend me.

"Girly? Dainty? Out of shape?"

"The first two." He appraised me again with renewed interest. "Why did you stop? Playing, I mean."

I shrugged and looked away, the universal signal for *Not even worth discussing*. I didn't like to admit it, to myself especially, that I'd stopped playing because of some stupid, ignorant comments made by a couple of gossipy soccer moms who didn't even know me. I'd not only quit sports, but changed my entire image on top of it, all because I wanted people to stop assuming I was somehow maladjusted and in need of female guidance. No, I'd much rather Emmett get to know me as I really was—someone who'd been raised by two men but was just like any other girl. Only with a different type of family from most people.

"A great story of an underdog finally coming out on top as she learns to love each flaw she has, one at a time."
—*RT Book Reviews* on *Faking Perfect*

any
other
girl

rebecca phillips

KENSINGTON PUBLISHING CORP.
www.kensingtonbooks.com

KENSINGTON BOOKS are published by

Kensington Publishing Corp.
119 West 40th Street
New York, NY 10018

All Kensington titles, imprints, and distributed lines are available at special quantity discounts for bulk purchases for sales promotions, premiums, fund-raising, educational, or institutional use.

Special book excerpts or customized printings can also be created to fit specific needs. For details, write or phone the office of the Kensington sales manager: Kensington Publishing Corp., 119 West 40th Street, New York, NY 10018, attn: Sales Department; phone 1-800-221-2647.

KENSINGTON and the K logo are Reg. U.S. Pat. & TM Off.

ISBN-13: 978-1-61773-882-1
ISBN-10: 1-61773-882-4

First Trade Paperback Printing: February 2016

10 9 8 7 6 5 4 3 2 1

Printed in the United States of America

First Electronic Edition: February 2016

ISBN-13: 978-1-61773-883-8
ISBN-10: 1-61773-883-2

any other girl

chapter 1

I didn't set out to flirt with someone else's boyfriend at Miranda Lipton's party. But I did it like I did a lot of things—without even thinking about it, as spontaneous and subconscious as breathing. The incident itself probably would've gone virtually unnoticed if the boyfriend in question had been anyone other than Braden Myers, and if the "someone else" had been anyone other than my best friend.

"I'm gonna miss you," Shay said, squeezing me into an impulsive, coconut-scented hug. We were standing in Miranda's main floor bathroom, primping in front of the mirror above the double sinks. Our second-to-last week of school had ended just three hours before, and since then we'd hit Starbucks for Frappuccinos, gorged on deep-dish pizza at Mario's, and then walked to Miranda's house in the warm June sun to help her set up for tonight's party. Most of the junior class planned to end up there tonight, eager to take a one-night break from studying and blow off some steam before final exams started on Monday. But for now, it was just us girls.

"I'll miss you too," I said, hugging her back. "It's just for a couple months, you know. I'll be back before school starts again."

"I know." She pulled back and took a swig from her

bottle of vodka cooler, one of several currently sitting in the fridge. Miranda's parents had left this morning for an out-of-town wedding. "Summer's boring without you around, though."

I laughed and sipped at my own cooler. Shay had said the same thing last summer and the summer before that. She always acted sentimental in the week or so before my parents and I left to spend the season at our cottage on the lake. We had been best friends for only two years, but we'd been inseparable since the day we'd met in the spring of freshman year when we both turned up in Mrs. Lockhart's after-school study group for math. There, we'd bonded over our mutual failure to comprehend polynomials.

"What do you think?" I stepped back from the mirror and turned from side to side, inspecting myself from each angle. I didn't have much of a tan yet, so my white off-the-shoulder dress didn't set off my skin tone as much as I'd hoped. "Does this make me look washed out?"

Shay glanced at me through the mirror as she brushed her glossy black hair. "You look like Marilyn Monroe with those fake eyelashes on. Only you're thinner. And not blond."

I smiled, pleased. *Seven Year Itch* was one of the first classic movies I'd ever seen, and I often went for the Marilyn look—wavy hair, parted on the left. Curve-hugging dress. Thick eyelashes. I liked to stand out.

"My God, Kat," Cassidy Boveri said when Shay and I joined her and Miranda in the kitchen. "This isn't a nightclub."

I just laughed and slid up on the counter, bare legs dangling off the edge. Cassidy used to bother me back in freshman year when my reputation made me basically friendless, but all that changed when I started hanging around with Shay. Everyone liked her, which meant they had to like me, too. Or at least tolerate me like Cassidy tried to do, even though it pained her. She still hadn't let go of the grudge she'd been holding against me since the eighth grade when her boyfriend dumped her at the Halloween dance so he could start going out with me.

"I think she looks hot," Shay said, grabbing a Cheeto from the bowl on the counter and popping it into her mouth.

"We all do," Miranda said, ever the neutral peacemaker. "And speaking of hot," she added, a grin unfurling on her freckled face, "is Man Candy coming tonight, Shay?"

Shay washed her Cheeto down with a gulp of cooler, trying to appear nonchalant. But I knew her well enough to see past the act. Braden Myers was more than just man candy to her. They'd been dating for about a month. Not long enough to become serious, but it was obvious how much she liked him. Braden was a senior at Nicholson, a huge high school across the city from ours, and she'd met him at a basketball game. The rest of us had only seen him once when we all went to the movies together a couple weekends ago, but once was enough to stick him with the "Man Candy" nickname. He was a lean, muscular jock, like Shay, but whereas she was short and dark, Braden was tall, blond, and fair. And pretty damn hot.

"Yeah, he'll be here," Shay said, and then she shot me a private look, reminding me of what we'd discussed earlier. About how if the mood struck her, she planned to lure Braden into an empty bedroom so they could advance their relationship to the next level. Not the *final* level, but at least the one that came after kissing. For her, it was a huge step.

Several bottles of vodka cooler and bags of munchies later, the party was in full swing. I stuck close to Shay until Braden showed up around ten, then I headed off to circulate. The house was packed and stuffy, the music deafening. In the dining room, I paused at the table to join a group of guys playing quarters. All the chairs were taken, so one of the guys—Chris Newbury—pulled me down on his lap. I wrapped my arm around his shoulders and made myself comfortable, only vaguely aware of the judgmental stares coming from a cluster of girls sitting in the attached living room. *Let them stare.* I felt buzzed and happy and carefree, immune to rumors and whispers.

"You want to go somewhere?" Chris breathed wetly in my ear after losing his fifth consecutive round of quarters.

"Oh look!" I said, craning my neck toward the kitchen. "There's Shay. I'd better go say hi."

I hadn't actually seen Shay, but I needed some kind of diversion. I was good at making diversions.

"Wait," Chris said as I slid off his lap and shouldered my way out of the dining room. He said something else, but I didn't quite catch it over the music. I could guess, though. The word *tease* was attributed to me often, along with various other unflattering terms.

The house was an oven, the mass of bodies blocking any breeze the open windows may have created. I could feel my dress sticking to the sweat on my back. *Gross.* Craving fresh air, I made my way through the kitchen and outside to the deck where half a dozen people were gathered around on the patio furniture, smoking. So much for fresh air.

"Kat."

I turned at the sound of my name and saw Braden "Man Candy" Myers leaning against the deck railing, alone. I walked over to him, relishing the feel of the light breeze against my skin. "What are you doing out here all by yourself?" I leaned next to him, peering out at the tiny backyard and the distant downtown lights beyond.

"Have you seen Shay? She went inside to use the washroom and never came back."

I presented him with one of my toothy, full-watt smiles. "There's a big line in there."

He smiled back, and I felt myself light up inside the way I always did when a guy responded to my attention.

"Mostly girls, right? You girls take forever in the bathroom."

I let out a big gasp, pretending to be offended, and he laughed. The sound of it made the light inside me glow brighter. "That's because we actually take the time to wash our hands afterward," I teased.

"Hey, I wash mine." He held up his hands, which were big and powerful-looking.

I playfully swatted them back down, and an uneasy expression flickered across his face in response to the contact. He shifted a few inches to the right, away from me, and glanced toward the door like he was wishing for Shay to appear.

Undeterred, I continued to tease him. "I bet you spend just as much time in front of a mirror as any girl. You don't just roll out of bed looking like that."

"Yeah, well . . ." He scratched the back of his neck, which looked flushed in the dim light coming from the kitchen window.

"Stop being so modest. I'm sure you hear compliments like that all the time." I turned and leaned my back against the railing, aware of the way the moonlight played on the bare skin of my shoulders and cleavage. "Shay is a very lucky girl."

He laughed nervously. "So, uh, are you ready for exams next week?"

I threw back my head and laughed, even though his question wasn't even remotely humorous. Vodka coolers and warm summer nights made me giddy. "Oh, come on, Braden." I said, sidling closer to him and poking him in the shoulder with my finger. "This is a party. It's almost summer. Exams are *so* not what I want to be thinking about right now."

His throat moved as he gulped, like he was imagining what, exactly, I *did* want to be thinking about. I peered up at him through my fake eyelashes and grinned, slow and mysterious. If he were any other guy, he probably would have drawn closer at that point, intrigued by the endless possibilities in my smile and eager for more.

But not Braden. He shifted again, uncomfortable, and started backing away. "Well, I'm going to go, um, find Shay."

"Okay," I said, confused. What was his problem? Why was he acting so eager to get away from me? I rewound our short conversation in my head, trying to pinpoint something I'd said or done to offend him. Nothing. I'd acted like my typical bubbly self. Then again, Braden didn't know me very well—in fact, it was the first time we'd ever spoken to each other for longer than a second—so he wasn't exactly familiar with my effusive personality. The guys (and girls) I went to school with and saw on a regular basis were all used to it. No one took me too seriously.

But Braden—going by the scandalized look on his face as he walked away from me—wasn't accustomed to assertive girls who modeled their appearance after retro actresses and liked to stand out in a crowd. Shay, after all, was none of those things.

Shay. For whatever reason, I felt a sudden, intense need to go look for her. Call it intuition, or premonition, or whatever the hell people called it when they were struck with that ominous sense of foreboding. I just knew I had to find her, and soon.

The kitchen was even more congested, and it took me a few minutes to get through. As I maneuvered around the bodies, Cassidy Boveri's strident voice rang out from somewhere behind me. "Classy, Kat. Real classy."

Distracted, I didn't bother to look back and ask what she meant.

In the dining room, the guys were still playing quarters at the table, though their coordination had decreased significantly since I'd left. As I passed, Chris Newbury made a grab for my arm, but I dodged him and headed for Miranda, who was mopping up a spill on the living room hardwood.

"Where's Shay?" I asked when she straightened up, a wad of paper towels in her hand.

"She just left with Braden," Miranda told me.

"Left? I thought we were spending the night."

She shrugged. "I thought so too."

I dug out my phone to see if Shay had texted me. She hadn't, so I sent her a text, asking where she was and what was going on. What had Braden said to her to make her ditch me without explanation? What exactly did he think had happened between us out there on that deck?

Shay never did text me back.

I wasn't used to being invisible. Especially not in the loud, crowded hallways of Brighton High. The cacophony of voices, footsteps, and bursts of laughter seemed almost subdued on the first day of final exams.

No one paid any attention to me as I walked away from Mr. Porter's English class, my wrist sore from the three-hour exam I'd just written. Cassidy brushed past me like I didn't exist. I knew where she was going—to meet up with Shay outside the main doors. From there, they'd probably hit Starbucks and then maybe study together for their next exam. That was what Shay and *I* would've done, anyway, if last Friday night hadn't happened and she was still my best friend.

Friday night. It had been three days, but knots still formed in my stomach whenever I thought about the uneasy look on Braden's face, and Shay's disappearance, and the fact that she'd ignored my texts and phone calls all weekend. Worst of all, it was due to one giant misunderstanding, which she refused to give me a chance to explain away.

I had every intention of heading to my locker next, but instead of turning left at the end of the hall, I turned right and followed Cassidy. Intent as she was on escaping, she didn't notice me skulking a few feet behind her. I trailed her all the way down the stairs, across the lobby, and out into the hot sun where Shay waited on a small patch of grass near the sidewalk.

"Shay," I said, but my voice was lost in the roar of a passing transit bus. Brighton High was located in one of the busiest areas of the city, surrounded by restaurants and coffee shops. That came in handy for fast-food runs during lunch hour, something else Shay and I used to do together.

"Shay," I repeated louder, and she glanced up. Immediately, the welcoming smile she'd had for Cassidy dropped into a scowl at the sight of me.

"Seriously, Kat?" she said, shaking her head like she couldn't quite believe I had the nerve to seek her out after she'd avoided me all weekend. "You seriously want to do this right now? Here?"

I glanced around. Students were still teeming out of the main doors like ants, squinting as the afternoon sun hit their faces. Several of them eyed us with interest. A lot of people had been at that party Friday night, had heard what I had done to Shay, my supposed best friend.

My *only* true friend, really. They'd waited a long time for a confrontation like this. Waited to see me, Kat Henley, shameless flirt and supposed boyfriend stealer, get what was coming to her, at last.

"Please, just listen to me," I said, reaching out to touch Shay's arm. She stepped back, closer to Cassidy, who leaned toward her in support and gave me the same look she'd been giving me since Shay had brought me into their group, the one that said *I'm a much better friend than you.* She was loving this more than anyone.

Suddenly, I remembered what she'd said to me at the party. "*Real classy.*" She'd seen me, I realized. Seen me talking to Braden outside. Maybe he hadn't been the one to tell on me, after all. "You have it all wrong, Shay."

She folded her bare, caramel-colored arms over her chest and smirked at me. "Oh, *do* I? Tell me, then, Kat. What exactly do I have wrong?"

I opened my mouth to speak then closed it again, unable to come up with an acceptable answer. Maybe there wasn't one. To me, the way I'd acted with Braden wasn't any different from the way I'd acted with Chris Newbury in Miranda's dining room, or the rest of the boys at school—just harmless, playful flirting. Shay knew how I was, knew about my reputation when it came to boys, but she'd always accepted me at face value. She'd believed in me . . . until I gave her a reason not to.

"We were just talking," I said, frustrated tears throbbing at the backs of my eyes. "It wasn't anything more than that, I swear. You *know* me, Shay. I act like that with all the guys. It's no big deal."

Shay wasn't like me. She didn't relish the weight of many sets of eyes on her. She didn't seek attention or enjoy an audience. I knew her anger at me had completely taken over when she thrust a finger in my face and started yelling at me in front of everyone.

"No big deal? Braden isn't just some random guy at a party, Kat. He's my boyfriend. *My boyfriend.*" She turned her face to the side and blinked a few times. She hated crying. "I can't believe I was actually stupid enough to trust you."

"You *can* trust me," I said quickly. Pleadingly. "I'm your friend, Shay. You know I'd never—"

"Even after hearing what everyone said about you, I gave you a chance." Shay spoke over my words like I hadn't even uttered them. "And this is how you pay me back for two years of friendship? By flirting with my boyfriend the minute I turn my back? Screw you, Kat." She turned and stormed away, leaving me there on the grass, the center of everyone's attention just like I always craved.

Their gazes made me feel ashamed. Naked.

"You know," Cassidy said as we both stared after Shay, who was disappearing quickly down the sidewalk, her black ponytail swinging behind her. "I'm glad you're going to be at your cottage for the summer, Kat. I think we all need a break from you." With that, she turned and went after Shay, catching up to her at the crosswalk.

Together, they crossed the busy street and headed toward the Starbucks on the corner, arm in arm. I watched them go as the crowd milled around me, already back to whatever it was they'd been doing before the drama started. They gave me a wide berth as I stood there, half in shock and unable to move. Like I was some kind of disease. Like my very presence was stressful and exhausting, something people needed a vacation from.

Summer couldn't get here fast enough.

chapter 2

The only time my parents ever fought was when we were packing to go somewhere.

"Bryce, we don't *need* the bread maker," Dad said, trailing Pop into the kitchen, his face pink with exasperation. "It's just two and half months. We'll buy loaves of Wonder Bread at the corner store."

"Wonder Bread?" Pop said, aghast, as if Dad had suggested we dine on rat poison all summer. "That stuff's not even *bread*. It's loaded with preservatives. Besides, Kat can't go a day without my oatmeal bread. Right, Kat?"

"Sure." I was sitting at the small table in our small kitchen, painting my nails Bubblegum Pink and trying to stay out of it. All I could think was, *I'm getting too old for this.*

"Besides," Pop said as he unplugged the bread maker and coiled the cord with uncharacteristic neatness and speed, "we also don't need socks, and you packed ten pairs. It's summer, Mark. Time to trade in the power suits for shorts and sandals."

Dad sighed and ran his hands through his perfectly groomed black hair. "Fine, bring the bread maker. Bring the food dehydrator too, while you're at it. You never know when we might want a batch of preservative-free beef jerky."

"Exactly," Pop said, hugging the bread maker to his chest with the kind of affection he reserved for two things: me and his vast collection of kitchen appliances.

Ignoring him, Dad turned to me. "All ready for tomorrow, Katrina?"

I nodded and swiped another layer of Bubblegum over my pinky nail. When it came to packing for our annual summer-long stay at our cottage on Millard Lake, my technique lay somewhere in the middle of both my fathers'—economical and practical like Dad, bringing only what I needed and maybe a few "just in case" items, and excessive and sentimental like Pop, wanting to transfer all the bulky, unnecessary objects of daily life to our new location. And unlike both of them, my packing had been done two days ago. I may have been getting too old to spend summers in the middle of the woods with my family, two hours away from the city and my life there, but that didn't mean I wasn't anxious to get away.

"You *did* arrange for Mrs. Adamson to feed the fish this weekend, right?" Dad asked Pop, whose expression immediately shifted into that wide-eyed *uh-oh* look he used whenever he got sidetracked and forgot something crucial. Dad sighed again with an added fingers-pressed-into-forehead *You give me a headache* gesture. "Bryce. Seriously."

Pop started making excuses, something about having to resolve an unexpected plot hole in his latest novel before we left tomorrow. I took that as my cue to retreat. Hearing my parents bicker made me feel slightly panicked, like a tiny pinprick had appeared in the safe, reliable bubble around the three of us, threatening to let in the tainted air. I knew it was normal, knew *they* were normal, but this once-a-year squabble-fest never failed to cast a pall over the beginning of summer. Luckily, they were always fine and back to their happily married selves once we got to the cottage and settled in.

In my room, I settled on the edge of the bed and carefully texted my cousin Harper, using the very tips of my fingers so as not to smudge my flawless manicure.

T-minus 12 hours until Operation Best Summer!

Her reply arrived in less than a minute.

Yay! OBS is almost in effect. Can't wait to see you.

Same here. We'll be there around 10AM to clean and unpack. Goody's for first dinner?

Of course. Best summers start with Goody's.

I smiled. *Best summers start with Goody's.* It was the slogan we'd made up months ago, in our early stages of planning for the summer. Goody's, a kitschy, run-down diner that hadn't been renovated since its heyday back in the fifties, was the only restaurant within miles of our little summer cottage community. Considering my undying love of everything retro, Goody's appealed to me. It appealed to my cousin less, but she tolerated it every year because they had the best burgers in the world. And because she loved me and there was nowhere else to go.

Operation Best Summer (OBS) first originated at the end of *last* summer as the two of us sat together on my dock, waxing nostalgic about how next year was our last official summer together before Harper headed off to college and her mom sold their cottage, which was just a two-minute walk through the woods from ours. Right then and there, over melting ice cream cones from Goody's, we swore that our last summer would be the *best* summer, one that would surpass all the other amazing summers since our family started vacationing there when I was eleven and Harper was twelve. We sealed the deal by touching our ice cream cones together like champagne flutes during a wedding toast. Since then, we'd exchanged thousands of phone calls and texts, plotting ways to go out with a bang. One thing we conclusively agreed on was that it had to begin with a burger and song B6 on Goody's ancient jukebox, "Yakety Yak" by The Coasters.

Harper and I couldn't talk long because she still hadn't started packing (her mother, Carrie, was Pop's older sister, and the procrastination gene ran deep with them all). Through the walls of our undersized condo, I could still hear my dads bitching at each other in the kitchen. From the sounds of things, they'd moved on from bread makers and doomed goldfish and were debating the best time to hit the road tomorrow morning.

"It takes hours to clean and air out the cottage," Dad argued. "The earlier we leave, the better."

"And hit Friday morning rush hour?" Pop said. "We'll get there quicker if we leave after eight."

I sat there staring at the poster above my bed, a black and white shot of Lauren Bacall, circa the nineteen-forties, my favorite era. Dad had introduced me to old movies when I was about ten, but *Dark Passage* was the one I remembered the best. Not because it was particularly suited to my ten-year-old tastes, but because during one of the Lauren Bacall scenes, Dad had commented offhandedly, "Women looked so classy back then." I didn't learn what *classy* was until a couple years later, but when I did, I understood what he meant. Lauren was classy, feminine, and intriguing, everything I knew I could be. From then on, I strived to be more like her.

"You just hate getting up early. Admit it."

"That has nothing to do with it. I just think—"

Okay, time to end this. I tore my eyes away from Lauren's sultry gaze, walked over to the window, and let out a piercing screech I was sure most of the building heard. Two seconds later, both my fathers stood in my bedroom doorway, their faces leached of color.

"What's wrong? What happened?" Dad demanded, rushing to my side as Pop hastily scanned my room as if expecting to find one of the nasty aliens he wrote about in his science fiction books.

"Oh, I . . ." I took a deep breath and placed my hand on my chest like I'd seen old actresses do when they'd "had a fright." "I thought I saw some guy getting jumped down there, that's all. But it was just his friends playing a trick or something."

Dad peered out my window, which faced a busy city street. "Katrina," he said warily. "There's no one getting jumped down there."

I shrugged and moved away from the window, satisfied that I'd accomplished what I set out to do—distract them. Distracting people in a theatrical way was what I did best. "Well, they left," I said, blowing on my still-sticky nails.

"You scared the hell out of us," Pop said, still searching my room for invisible threats, just like he used to do when I was little and claimed my walls were inhabited by a tiny troll who wanted to steal my breath. Dad liked the classics, but Pop preferred creepy old Stephen King movies.

"Sorry," I said, feeling guilty for frightening them. Only rarely did I need to unleash my many diversionary tactics on my dads. Normally, they were meant for other people, a ploy to deflect attention *away* from my dads.

"We're just glad you're okay," Dad told me.

He stood in front of me, lifting my chin with his index finger until our pale green eyes met and held. *Celery eyes,* my aunt Carrie called them. Unfortunately, eye color was one of the only visible features I'd inherited from Dad, whose dark good looks epitomized the straight-female lament *Too bad he's gay*. Mostly I resembled Pop—brown-haired and average with a tendency toward plumpness.

"And good job on screaming like we taught you," he added, smiling.

I grinned and flung out my arms in a *ta-da* kind of way. One of the life lessons my dads drilled into my head on a semi-daily basis was, "When you're in trouble, scream, even if you're not sure." But they'd never said, "When you're sick of listening to your parents fight about small appliances and rush hour traffic, scream, even if you're not sure." Still . . . it *had* gotten them to stop bickering.

Fake crisis averted, my parents left me alone and went to bed, our safe bubble strong and intact once again. I fell asleep shortly after, visions of sparkling water and made-from-scratch burgers and unobstructed sunsets fighting for top position in my head.

Dad won at least part of the argument and we left bright and early the next morning, beating rush hour by a good ninety minutes. I went with Pop in his car, a Volvo station wagon he'd had since I was young enough to need a car seat. Dad followed us in his BMW, hauling little things like groceries and towels. The Volvo carried our luggage and whatever kitchen appliances Pop had smuggled in. In the rear view mirror, I could see the top of our blender sticking out of an open box.

"So I think I'll make Victor and Lydia start working *with* this new group instead of *against* them," Pop was saying as he drove. "Especially now that Lucien is gaining strength."

I turned a page in my *Style* magazine. "Mmm hmm."

As usual, Pop ignored my obvious lack of interest and

kept talking, using me as a sounding board to work through potential plot lines in his latest book. I didn't mind. Even though I was only vaguely aware that Victor and Lydia were the protagonists of his series and that Lucien was some sort of evil alien kingpin set out to destroy humankind, I was proud of my dad's writing success. My other dad was vice president of business development for an IT company and was successful in different ways. He made more money than Pop, but Pop enjoyed his job more. He was writing Book Six at the moment, and his modest-but-loyal fan base kept clamoring for a release date.

"You feeling okay, Noodle?"

I glanced up from my magazine, my hand flying automatically to my hair, smoothing it down. When someone asked me if I was feeling okay, I usually took it to mean, "You look like crap." But today's hair style—luxurious waves parted to one side, inspired by Rita Hayworth in *Gilda*—still felt as neat as it had this morning after a thirty-minute tryst with the curling iron.

"I'm fine," I said, going back to my magazine. "Why?"

His wide brown eyes followed Dad's BMW as it roared past us on the highway. Pop shook his head with amused exasperation before turning back to me. "You've been really quiet. That's not like you."

"I've been up since five a.m. and you won't let me drink coffee." My parents didn't know what had happened between me and Shay. I was too ashamed to tell them that I'd lost yet another friend over my inability to restrain myself.

"It's bad for you." He said this so often, the words had turned into one of those customary, mindless phrases, like *Have a nice day* and *Be careful*. "Besides, you're always a bundle of energy even without caffeine. I thought you'd be thrilled about summer break starting."

"I am." I *was* thrilled. For two and a half months, I'd be free. No whispers or rumors or name-calling or dirty looks. Just my family and several acres of green space where I could revert to my childhood self and let loose.

"I am, too," Pop said, veering onto the exit ramp for Erwin, the small, nowhere town that bordered Millard Lake. "I plan to spend the summer sitting on the deck with my laptop and making you oatmeal bread in the bread maker I was smart enough to pack."

I laughed and put my magazine away, choosing instead to gaze out the window. We were getting closer. Through the trees I could see snatches of lake water glinting in the morning sun. In spite of what it would do to my hair, I opened the window and let the pine-scented breeze wash over my face.

Pop slowed down as we passed through Erwin proper, which took all of three seconds, and then turned onto the gravel road that led to the cottages. Dad's BMW was parked neatly in our oversized driveway. He wasn't in it, which meant he was probably inside, seeing how our little summer haven had faired during the long, cold winter.

Pop parked the Volvo and we both climbed out, immediately taking deep, synchronized breaths. Trees, vegetation, water, and not much else. Heaven. Operation Best Summer had officially begun.

chapter 3

Our cottage wasn't much to look at from the outside. Or the inside, for that matter. A thousand square feet with only two bedrooms, it wasn't much different in size from our condo in the city. But whereas our condo was modern and sleek, the bungalow-style cottage was thirty years old and rustic-looking. Ugly oak paneling covered the entire front wall of the house, and the living room and bedrooms all had this hideous fuchsia carpeting that had been there forever. The previous owners had been kind enough to install beautiful oak hardwood in the kitchen, which sort of drew the eye away from the faded laminate countertops and ancient appliances. My dads had planned to do one major renovation each year, but not much had changed in the six years since they'd bought the place.

"We didn't buy it for its looks," they'd say every summer when I complained about the lack of progress. "We bought it for *that*." And they would gesture toward the huge yard and shimmering lake visible through the living room window.

I saw their point. The only person who spent much time indoors during the summer was Pop. His writing career was the reason a summer cottage was doable in the first place. Unlike Dad, who had to commute back to the

city during the week for work, Pop could do his job anywhere, anytime, all the while keeping a watchful eye on
me. And making me oatmeal bread.

"Give me a hand with this, would you, Kat?" he said,
struggling to unload his illicit box of appliances from the
back of the Volvo.

I paused in my inspection of the scraggly front lawn
and went over to help. Shooing him away, I hoisted the
box and balanced it on my hip. I may have had a propen-
sity for flab like Pop, but I'd also inherited Dad's impressive upper body strength. Well, three years of boxing
lessons may have helped.

"Pop, how much did you *bring*?" I asked, peering
down into the giant box. Along with the blender I'd noticed earlier, I saw a food processor, a waffle maker, an
electric can opener, and that blasted bread maker. My
arm muscles were burning.

"Just the essentials," he called from the back seat
where he was gathering up his e-reader and laptop bag.
He backed his way out and looked at me over the roof
of the car. "I know you and your father are content to
live off Pop Tarts and grilled hotdogs, but I'm sorry,
you're getting fresh fruit smoothies at least four times a
week."

I carried the box into the cottage where, coinciden-
tally, Dad was unpacking a grocery bag filled with
processed, non-perishable goodies in the kitchen. The
house smelled musty and stale, the way it always did the
first day. He must have gotten there at least fifteen minutes before us because all the windows were open and
the counters and kitchen table looked shiny and dust-
free. He could not abide dust.

"Everything seems to be in good working order," he
told us, opening the old fridge to show us the working
light inside. Going by experience, it would be hours un-

til it got cold enough to put food inside. "The septic tank and well look good, too."

"How long have you been here?" I asked, depositing the box on the scratched pine table. The cottage had come mostly furnished, and most of the furniture was just as old as the house. The only things we'd bought new were our beds. Dad couldn't abide used mattresses either.

"A half hour. You guys are slow."

"I always go the speed limit when I have Noodle in the car with me," Pop said as he unloaded his prized appliances. Dad gave him the same affectionate exasperated look Pop had given *him* when he sped past us on the highway. There would be no more petty bickering, I knew. All the grievances they'd had with each other last night had been swiftly forgiven, the slate wiped clean.

"Damn it!" Dad said as he searched frantically through the shopping bags. "I forgot to bring a box of light bulbs. And the one in the bathroom is burnt out. Shit."

"I'll run to the corner store and get some," Pop said.

"The corner store doesn't carry light bulbs, remember? We looked last year when the oven light died. I think there's something wrong with the voltage in this house." Dad sighed impatiently. "I really don't feel like getting back in the car right now and driving into town. Katrina," he said, turning to me. "Go see if your aunt Carrie has some spare light bulbs."

"They're not here yet," I told him. "Harper told me they wouldn't be in until around noon."

"Hmm. How about the McCurdys?"

"No *way*," I said. The McCurdys had a son my age who was a complete douchebag. He'd likely twist my asking for bulbs into a dirty joke and torture me with it for the rest of the summer.

"The Cantings?" Pop suggested. "They live here year round."

"Yes! They're bound to have some extra bulbs."

They looked at me sprawled on the scratchy arm chair at the edge of the living room, massaging my upper arm muscles.

I frowned. "What? Now? Can't I wait until we actually need light in the bathroom?"

"You've been stuck in the car for two hours," Pop said, arranging the waffle maker just so next to the toaster oven. "Go. Exercise is good for you."

Sighing, I dragged myself up and began the ten minute walk to the Canting cottage, suppressing the urge to run down the winding gravel road at top speed like I used to. Instead, I walked slowly, slapping mosquitoes off my neck and admiring the way my pink toenails looked against my white flip-flops.

A small black car sat in the Cantings' driveway. *Odd,* I thought. Mr. and Mrs. Canting owned a red truck . . . or they had the last few years, anyway. I walked up to the door and knocked. A minute later, the door swung open and a heavyset blond woman appeared behind the mesh screen. She was neither Mr. nor Mrs. Canting.

"Hi!" I said, unleashing my full I-still-wear-my-retainers-every-night smile.

Blondie looked back at me, straight-faced and unimpressed.

"I was wondering if I could borrow a light bulb."

She peered at me as if I'd just requested one of her kidneys. "Sorry?"

"A light bulb. See, our bathroom light burned out and the corner store doesn't sell them, so—"

"The Reeses don't arrive until tonight," she said abruptly. "I don't know where any light bulbs are, dear."

"I'm sorry . . ." *The Reeses? As in peanut butter cups?* It seemed we had some sort of disconnect. "Um, where are the Cantings?"

"Who? Oh, the previous owners? I think they died. Well, he died, and she moved. That's what Mrs. Reese said anyway."

It was like she was speaking a different language. Mr. Canting, with his cowboy hat and pickup truck and cigars, was dead? My eyes filled with tears. The Cantings were a nice couple, accepting of my dads even though they were well into their seventies and probably rabidly conservative.

"I'm sorry," I repeated, clearing my suddenly tight throat. "Who are you, again?"

"Oh," Blondie said, lifting her hand, which I'd just noticed contained a dusty wad of paper towels. "I'm just here to clean."

"Oh," I said, echoing her. "And the Reeses are . . . ?"

"The new owners. They arrive tonight." She peered at my moist eyes and then bit her lip as if contemplating something. "A light bulb, you said? Let me go see if I can find one for you."

"No, no, you don't have to—" I said, but she was already gone, ambling down the hallway toward the kitchen. Now that she wasn't blocking my view, I could see that the house was clear of all Mrs. Canting's ceramic dog statues and doilies. I felt another rush of sadness.

Blondie returned a couple minutes later and handed me a grimy light bulb. "Here you go. I took it out of the range hood above the stove. A bit greasy, but it works."

"Thanks." I smiled at her tremulously and got a tiny one in return. Then she shut the door in my face.

Holding the non-greasy end of the bulb between my fingers, I walked back to our cottage. Dad was in the detached garage, unearthing the lawn mower, and Pop was digging in the trunk for the last of the luggage.

I walked up to him and said, "Mr. Canting is dead."

He jerked his head out of the trunk and stared at me

in much the same way he had last night when I'd screamed in my room. "What? Oh my God, should we—Mark!"

"Not *now*," I said quickly before he called 911 and ran over to the Canting house with a first aid kit. "I mean . . . yes, now, but not over *there*, at this very moment. He died at some point over the past ten months and Mrs. Canting sold the cottage to the Reeses."

"The Reeses?" Dad said as he walked up to us, his T-shirt soaked with sweat. "As in Pieces?"

Dad's mind always went straight to chocolate, just like mine.

"I don't know," I said with a shrug. "But whatever they are, they arrive tonight."

During lunch (PB&J on chemical-laden Wonder Bread with a fresh fruit smoothie to balance it out), a knock sounded on the screen door and Harper burst in, all smiles. I squealed and jumped up from the table, attacking her before she even had a chance to speak.

"You look great, Kat," she said, pulling back to examine my outfit of white shorts and a pink halter top that matched my nails. "Very retro."

I grinned and took my turn studying her. We'd last seen each other about six months ago, over Christmas, but Harper looked exactly the same: long dirty-blond hair, blue eyes, and slim, athletic build. People always seemed surprised when they found out we were related.

When we were done with our little reunion, my dads came over to greet Harper, too.

"How was your drive, sweetheart?" Dad asked, wrapping her in a hug.

"Long," she said with a sigh. "Eight hours of non-stop Celine Dion. Mom likes to torture me."

Pop made a face as he leaned in to receive his own hug. "That's child abuse."

"Exactly, Uncle Bryce. You make sure to tell her that."

"I will, when I see her. Where is she?"

"Unpacking," Harper said. "I kind of ditched her. I guess I should go back and help."

"Dinner tonight, right?" Dad said, gathering up our lunch dishes.

Harper looked at me, eyes twinkling, and I knew exactly what she was thinking. *Best summers start with Goody's.*

"Um, Dad, I think we're going to walk down to Goody's for a burger later. Harper and me."

"Harper and *I*," Pop corrected automatically.

"Is that okay, Uncle Mark?" Harper called both my dads *uncle* even though she was only technically related to Pop.

"Of course," Dad said. "But tell your mom to come over. We have some steaks in the cooler."

"I will." She mouthed the letters *OBS* at me and then left, the screen door swinging closed behind her.

I spent the afternoon setting up my small room, putting clothes in drawers and posters on the walls. At five, I redid my *Gilda* hair until it hung in soft waves and then sprinted through the woods to my cousin's cottage. Aunt Carrie was out front, hosing down her wilted flower garden.

"Come give me a hug, beautiful," she said when she saw me. I did as she asked, breathing in her customary vanilla scent. Being around Aunt Carrie always made me crave cake. "So good to see you."

"Same here," I said, noticing the marked increase of gray in her light brown hair. Carrie was fifty-three, the oldest of Pop's five sisters and by far my favorite.

"See you later, Mom!" Harper said as she emerged from the cottage and took my arm, pulling me away.

"Be back before dark," Aunt Carrie reminded us and went back to her hosing.

The walk to Goody's took exactly eighteen minutes. We'd timed it one summer. As we hiked up the gravel road, Harper and I caught each other up on the things we hadn't fully discussed over the phone during the last six months.

"So how was the last week of school?" she asked, threading her slender arm through mine. "As bad as you predicted?"

"Worse. Shay wouldn't even *look* at me."

"Kat." She sighed and looked down at her feet. "If I say something honest, promise you won't get mad?"

"Since when do I get mad at you for being honest with me? It's what you do."

"Okay," she said, picking up the pace a little. "Friends don't like it when you flirt with their boyfriends. I don't blame Shay for being pissed at you."

I rolled my eyes. Harper had always felt an affinity for Shay because she had more in common with her than she did with me, her own flesh and blood. They were both fit, athletic types who preferred running around on a soccer field to strolling around the mall, shopping for clothes. Not to mention they both had to deal with me.

"We were just *talking*," I said, not very convincingly. Okay, so maybe I *had* stepped over the line. Some guys just brought out the temptress in me, but it didn't mean anything, really. "I had no idea he'd assume I was trying to seduce him and then go blab to Shay about it."

"Kat, I've seen you talk to boys. You have this way of making them feel good about themselves. Important."

She bumped my hip with hers. "You're very charming, you know. Even when you're *not* flirting, you're flirting."

I thought about earlier, when my smile had driven Blondie to swipe a light bulb already in use and hand it over to me. Maybe it worked on females, too.

"It's the reason for your bad track record with boys, you know," Harper said, her gaze following a tiny squirrel as it shimmied up a tree at the side of the road. "Guys don't like it when you flirt with other guys either."

"No, it's because every guy I've ever dated has been incredibly insecure," I said. "Not my fault."

She shook her head at me. "Oh, Katty."

"Oh, Harpy."

Laughing now, we approached the two-lane road at the end of the gravel and looked both ways. Cars flew down that road at reckless speeds, and if a person wasn't careful, they could end up as flattened as the assortment of wildlife that was brave enough to attempt crossing.

"Clear," I shouted, and we took off across the road, careful not to lose a flip-flop on the way like Harper had done last summer. Three more minutes and we were coming up on Goody's, a small, ramshackle beacon of light and grease.

When I swung open the heavy wooden door and walked in, I couldn't help but stagger back and shriek, "What the *hell*?"

Harper stepped in behind me, her eyes as wide as mine undoubtedly were. Goody's had vanished. The grungy black and white floor tiles had been replaced with shiny dark hardwood, the ripped padded booths had turned into small round tables, and the sticky, laminated menus were thick, creamy paper. Everything familiar was gone, exchanged for . . . whatever this was trying to be. And the jukebox . . . where was our jukebox?

Sherry—owner, operator, and all-around Jill-of-all-trades at Goody's—appeared in the empty dining room, dressed in her usual uniform of black pants and a checked shirt. At least *one* thing had remained the same.

"Sherry, what happened?" I demanded.

"Oh, hey! Welcome back, girls," she said, walking over to us and grabbing a couple menus off the stack near the cash register. "Just two?"

We stood there gaping at her until she explained herself. Renovations had taken place over the spring, apparently, in an effort to make the diner "classier" and "more accessible" to customers—which was weird because the vast majority of Goody's customers consisted of people who summered at Millard Lake and long-haul truck drivers.

In other words, she'd sold out.

"The jukebox?" I asked hopefully as she led us to a table.

She shook her head. "Sold it."

Harper and I looked at each other in disbelief. No more singing along to "Yakety Yak" as we waited for our burgers and shakes. No more shabby, vintage ambiance. The food, Sherry assured us, was pretty much the same, with a few added dishes. At least we still had that.

As we waited for our orders, I ran my hand over the smooth, clean tablecloth (tablecloth!) and wondered what it meant when the place that was supposed to kick off the best summer ever wasn't the same place we once knew.

chapter 4

The next morning, I got up extra early. After gobbling down a bowl of cereal, I threw on a pair of jeans and a hoodie, located my heavy black boots, and headed out to the garage.

The sun had barely cleared the horizon, and the air felt chilly and damp. I breathed in, enjoying the fresh, unadulterated scent as I unlocked the garage door and pulled it up. The detached garage, installed by the previous owners, was home to a lot of things—the lawnmower, bikes, tools, and anything else one might need over the summer.

Taking up most of the small space, however, was the sole reason I'd dragged myself out of bed at the butt crack of dawn: my Yamaha Raptor Sport Quad ATV.

I'd started trail riding a couple years ago, after Dad had taught me the basics. At first, I wasn't sure I'd like riding. Zooming along the bumpy terrain on a loud, dirty ATV sounded more suited to the younger me, before I'd abandoned soccer cleats and mud for makeup and sundresses. *A sundress would be a disastrous fashion choice for this*, I thought as I secured my goggles, helmet, and gloves. When I was ready, I rolled the ATV onto the driveway and checked it over. Dad had de-winterized it for me yesterday evening, testing the tire pressure and lubing the drive chain and whatever else he needed to do. I didn't know much about the mechanics of it all—I just loved to ride.

I pressed the start button and then cringed, knowing the engine noise would probably wake my parents. Dad wouldn't care, but Pop always worried when I was out riding. According to him, all-terrain vehicles were even worse for my health than Pop Tarts and coffee. For one, they could potentially kill me outright. But so could a lot of things.

When I got to a steady roll, I let out the clutch, shifted into first, and gave it some gas. *Slow and easy at first*, I heard Dad say in my head. *Get a feel for it.* By the time I reached my favorite riding path in the woods, I felt confident enough to speed up a bit. Soon, I could feel the familiar lightness in my chest, pure joy bubbling up as I traversed the jagged earth, my body lifting and twisting to absorb the impact. My laughter echoed through the confines of my helmet, and for a moment I felt completely, utterly, unabashedly free.

I was so absorbed in my adrenaline rush of freedom that I barely noticed the flash of red up ahead on my left. At first glance, I assumed it was some kind of animal. A deer or maybe even a black bear, both of which I'd encountered now and then on my rides. But deer and bears didn't wear red tank tops, and I'd never hit an animal the way I was pretty sure I was about to hit this human.

Frantically, I mashed the hand brake, but it was no use. The human was running toward me, oblivious, out for a nice, early morning jog in the serene woods. As I barreled closer, I had just enough time to register that the jogger was actually a young guy before swerving sharply to the right, missing him by a couple feet. The ATV came to a stop inches from the base of a tree, and I immediately twisted around, searching for him. He who had appeared out of nowhere had disappeared. Maybe I *had* hit him, and his body was lying in a nearby shrub, mangled and bloody. My heart in my throat, I threw the ATV in reverse.

Relief coursed through me when I spotted him in the exact spot we'd nearly collided moments before. Instead of peacefully running, he was half bent over and panting like someone who'd just narrowly escaped death—which he probably had.

"Are you okay?" I asked through my helmet. My face felt like it was on fire. Not only had I almost flattened a guy like a fox on the highway, I'd almost flattened a *cute* guy who looked no older than nineteen.

He just stared at me, his blue, blue eyes taking in my outfit and helmet before finally resting on the only body parts of mine that were exposed—my eyes, which were no doubt wide and panicked behind their goggles. He stood up straight, yanked out his earbuds, and gave me a look that could only be described as murderous.

"Maybe you should pay attention and watch where you're going," he snarled at me over the loud rumble of my engine.

I jolted slightly on my seat. It wasn't often I got yelled at by a guy. My dads didn't believe in yelling, and I'd never tolerated it from boyfriends. Girls were a different story, but I could handle that. Getting yelled at by a total stranger for something that was only partially my fault? That wasn't gonna fly.

"How could you not see me?" I replied loud enough for my voice to penetrate the helmet and the engine noise.

"I was watching my footing so I wouldn't break an ankle." He glared at me again, and even as I burned with indignation, I couldn't help but notice when a lock of his wavy brown hair fell across his forehead.

"How you could not see *me*?" he asked. "I'm wearing bright colors. Maybe you shouldn't ride that thing if you can't follow simple safety rules."

"Maybe *you* would've heard me coming if your music wasn't so damn loud," I said hotly. Before he could come back with another smartass reply, I shifted out of neutral and went on my merry way, leaving the jerk to stew in the trees all by himself.

I rode back to the cottage with my knees shaking and my blood racing. The trembling in my limbs didn't let up until after I'd shed my bulky clothes, took a shower, and dressed in a pair of pink capris and a white tube top. *Much better*, I thought as I smoothed my hair into a ponytail in front of the bathroom mirror. In this outfit, no one would ever suspect that I'd been inches away from plowing someone down. In this outfit, I looked innocent. Demure.

Feeling calmer, I headed over to Harper's cottage. The cool, dreary weather still hadn't cleared, so we hung out in the kitchen, making pancakes. Aunt Carrie didn't share her brother's passion for appliances, so their counters were always a lot less cluttered and easier to work on than ours. As we mixed ingredients together, I tried not to think about how this was the last summer I'd ever spend with my aunt and cousin at the lake. Because whenever I did, I wanted to cry in the batter. They'd been spending summers there even longer than we had. Aunt Carrie and her ex-husband Lawrence had bought the cottage outright, and she'd acquired it during their messy divorce four years ago. Actually, she'd gotten the cottage *and* Harper, because Lawrence no longer gave a crap about either.

Shaking off my sentimentality, I told them all about what had happened earlier in the woods. It felt good to get it all out, like confession.

"My God, Kat," Harper said, horrified. "You could've killed him."

I loved my cousin, but her steadfast insistence on keeping me in check freaking annoyed me sometimes. "I know, but I didn't."

"Who was he?" Aunt Carrie asked from the couch where she was curled up with her coffee and a book.

"No idea." I opened a container of blueberries and dumped some in the batter.

"Didn't you say there were new people moving in?" Harper asked.

Duh. Of course. Obviously, he had to be one of the infamous Reeses, who'd taken over the Cantings' cottage. I wondered if they'd noticed the missing light bulb yet. "So, yeah," I said, handing the mixing bowl to Harper so she could start the pancakes. "I think I might have gotten off on the wrong foot with the new neighbors."

The three of us sat down to eat, filling our plates from the huge platter of pancakes and fruit in the middle of their small table.

"Heard from your aunt Beth lately, honey?" Aunt Carrie asked me as she speared a strawberry from the fruit tray.

"Not since Christmas. You?"

She shook her head, chewing. "You know how she is . . . always on the go, too busy to return her big sister's calls."

I nodded even though I didn't really know "how she was." I barely had any contact with Aunt Beth. She'd lived in England all my life and I'd only met her twice. Once when I was six, when she came to visit for a couple weeks in the summer, and once when I was twelve, when my dads and I went to London on vacation. Well, theoretically I'd met her three times, but I never counted that first time, seeing as I was just an embryo.

Aunt Beth was Pop's second youngest sister . . . and also my egg donor. When my dads decided they wanted a baby, she was the one who'd selflessly offered up her eggs for implantation. Growing up, my friends were always fascinated and slightly confused when I told them I was biologically related to *both* my fathers. Back then, I loved telling the story of how I came to be. It made me interesting. Unique. Of course, once my classmates and I hit preteen age and had some sex education under our belts, the first question asked was always something like, "Wait, so your father had sex with your *aunt*?" To this, I always rolled my eyes. For one, Dad was one hundred percent gay and always had been. For another, how weird would *that* be? The person who'd carried me and ultimately given birth to me hadn't been my aunt. For that part, they'd used a woman named Valerie from a surrogacy agency who wasn't genetically related to any of us. My friends usually lost interest after I started explaining to them how the fertility clinic had used one father's sperm and the other father's sister's eggs, mixed them in a dish like pancake batter, and then inserted the concoction into the surrogate. Of course, that was back when I was still comfortable discussing my dad's sperm. *Shudder.*

So yes, my aunt Beth was technically my "bio mom" too, but I'd never thought of her like that any more than she thought of me as her daughter. She was simply the woman who'd bravely and generously donated her eggs so that my dads could realize their dream of having a child who was biologically connected to both of them. And the surrogate? She was a vessel, nourishing me and keeping me safe until it was time to hand me over to my real parents. I'd never wanted or needed a mother. My dads had always been enough. And I had Aunt Carrie, who always said *she* would've been my donor if it hadn't taken her ten years and several thousand dollars' worth of fertility treatments to have Harper. Harper and I often joked that we were too competitive to share her eggs anyway.

After brunch, Aunt Carrie took the leftover pancakes over to my dads while Harper and I took off for the lake. The sun had finally made an appearance and was quickly burning off the clouds. Maybe later it would get nice enough to lie out on my dock and start working on our tans.

Harper and I walked along the rocky shoreline, talking and jokingly looking for pretty stones like we used to when we were smaller. My room at the cottage was still filled with jars of interesting rocks, summer relics that lived there year-round. I didn't take home souvenirs at the end of August like some people. To me, summer only existed at the lake.

As we approached the McCurdys' dock, I almost grabbed Harper's arm and turned back. Nate McCurdy was standing at the edge of it, holding his cell phone up to the sky as if trying to get a signal. *Idiot*. Nate and his family had been coming to the lake as long as we had; he should've known how incompatible Millard Lake and modern technology could be.

"Try standing on your head while singing 'Jingle Bells'," Harper called to him.

Great, I thought. *Now he's going to speak to us.*

Nate spun around, almost dropping his phone in the water. "Oh hey, ladies." He recovered quickly, presenting us with his signature smarmy grin. Yes, he was the kind of teenage boy who called girls *ladies*, which was likely part of the reason why he never got any. Nate was good-looking, if you liked the gelled-hair preppy type, but he was just too douchy to take seriously.

"Hey, McTurdy," I said, resurrecting the nickname I'd given him when we were twelve. It was still funny.

"Hey, Hurricane Katrina. How's it blowing?" At this, he cracked up.

"You do know that Hurricane Katrina killed almost two thousand people and left millions homeless, right?" I reminded him for the millionth time. I didn't like being referred to as a devastating natural disaster. Especially hours after I'd almost killed the new neighbor with my ATV.

"Who are you trying to call, McCurdy?" Harper asked, crossing her arms as she peered up at him from the shore. "Your girlfriend?"

I snorted. Any girlfriend Nate had ever managed to snag turned out to be short-lived. Not that it stopped him from trying. He'd been working on charming Harper and me for years, but we were too smart and self-respecting to fall for it.

"Why, are you jealous?" Nate said, slipping his phone into the front pocket of his board shorts and moving closer to us.

"More like sympathetic," she replied. "Toward her, I mean."

I snorted again, even louder. Normally, Harper was pretty shy, but Nate brought out the snark in her.

"For your information," Nate said, sitting on the edge of the dock, facing us. "I was trying to text Emmett to let him know that the bonfire was officially on for tonight."

"Who's Emmett?" I asked.

Nate smirked, like he enjoyed dangling scraps of bait for us to nibble on. "Emmett's the guy who moved into the Cantings' cottage. I met him earlier while I was looking for some dry kindling in the woods. I mentioned that I planned to have a bonfire tonight if the weather cleared up and told him he should come. He said okay. Seems like a cool guy."

Harper looked at me and raised a blond eyebrow. Emmett. The cute guy who'd yelled at me in the woods that morning was named Emmett. And he was going to McTurdy's summer-kick-off bonfire on the beach, an annual event that Harper and I never missed because his mom always bought enough s'mores provisions to feed a small army.

"We're looking forward to meeting him," Harper said, the corners of her mouth twitching. "Aren't we, Kat?"

My mind flashed on those blue, blue eyes, burning with anger and aimed directly at me. I swallowed. "Yeah. Can't wait."

chapter 5

"He probably won't even recognize you," Harper assured me that evening while we were in my yard, batting around the soccer ball. "You're, like, covered head-to-toe when you ride."

"True," I said, gently tapping the ball with the inside of my foot and then flicking it toward her. "But he did see my eyes, and they aren't exactly a common color."

She stopped the ball with her knee and then kicked it back almost simultaneously, making me run for it. Once upon a time, Harper and I had been pretty evenly matched during these casual scrimmages. But I'd quit playing at twelve while she continued on. She was hoping to play for her college next year. Still, I'd never really lost my competitive spirit.

"Getting kind of rusty there, Henley," Harper taunted me as I ran, out of breath, back to my position.

"Shut it, Griggs."

The game was *on* when we started calling each other by our last names. Laughing, I hauled my foot back and booted the ball as hard as I could, sending it flying over her head and down the green wooden stairs to the lake. A moment later, we heard a dull splash.

I looked back at my cousin. "Rusty, you say?"

She stuck her tongue out at me and then went to retrieve the ball. The second she was out of sight, I collapsed on the grass, exhausted. I *was* rusty. Feeling forgotten muscles throb from disuse made me miss soccer all the more. As usual, the longing came with a side dish of resentment when I thought back to the reason I'd quit in the first place.

Before we got our condo in the city, we'd lived in a small town called Oakfield, about twenty minutes away. My dads had left their cramped apartment downtown and moved us to suburbia because they figured that was what a kid needed—a regular house and grass and yard sales and good, safe schools. But one thing Oakfield didn't have was a lot of diversity in its residents. The town mostly consisted of traditional families, moms and dads and kids. We were the only "dads and kid" family in the entire town, and eventually I started noticing. Not only were we different, but some people *treated* us like we were different. It made my dads sad.

When I was around four or five, I figured out a way to help. Whenever I saw someone staring or heard someone make a hurtful comment, I'd do whatever I could to divert their attention off my dads and onto me. I'd start dancing, or singing, or faking an injury, or pretending to be a horse. Anything to turn their heads my way. As time went on, I started seeking attention even when my dads *weren't* getting stared at. Like during my soccer games, for example. I'd monopolize the ball and act aggressive toward my teammates, which usually resulted in the coach kicking me off the field for a time-out. It was during one of those time-outs that I overheard Mrs. Jolley say to Mrs. Fiedler, "Someone needs a lesson on how to act like a proper young lady."

"Two fathers and no mother," Mrs. Fiedler replied with a tsk. "No wonder she's so rough with the other kids."

That was my last season on the team. I quit sports, developed an interest in my looks, and started emulating the refined, elegant women I saw in Dad's black-and-white classics. Like Lauren Bacall, whom I'd adopted as my personal icon. I became the consummate girly girl, and no one called me rough or boyish or claimed I needed a maternal influence ever again. My dads were more than capable of raising a "proper young lady," and I was proof.

Summer, though, was different. At the cottage, surrounded by the people who'd known me all my life, I let that rough little tomboy punch her way through.

"Hey," Harper said, startling me as I lay half-comatose in the grass. "On your feet, Henley. It's go time."

I groaned. "Shouldn't we start getting ready for McTurdy's bonfire?"

"I am ready," she said, looking down at her black Nike shorts and tank top. Fitness wear. She was hopeless.

"Come on." I hoisted my body into its upright position and brushed grass off my butt. "Let's at least change into something less sweaty."

I sent her to her cottage to shower and I did the same, changing into a short, white sundress with spaghetti straps. Attempting one of my vintage hairstyles in the humidity was pointless, so I brushed my hair smooth, letting it flip up on the ends, and added a thick white ribbon to match my dress. The entire ensemble made me look innocent in a slightly naughty way, just like I'd hoped. Satisfied, I headed over to Harper's.

When I entered the cottage, my dads and aunt all turned away from their cribbage game to stare at me.

"Oh Kat," Aunt Carrie said, clapping excitedly. "You look like Natalie Wood in *West Side Story.*"

"Stay away from the water," Dad said with a snicker. When I gave him a blank look, he added, "Natalie Wood drowned."

"Okay then," I said. Clearly, they'd gotten into the wine already. "Where's Harper?"

"Hiding from you," Pop told me, placing his cards face down on the table. "She thinks you're going to make her wear a dress."

Aunt Carrie laughed. "Harper doesn't even *own* a dress."

My cousin emerged from her room then, wearing black denim shorts and a slightly dressier tank top than the Nike one she'd had on earlier. It was a start.

"Midnight curfew, Noodle," Pop said as we got set to leave.

"You too, Harper," Aunt Carrie chimed in, and they went back to their crib board.

Outside on the deck, Harper rolled her eyes. Sometimes our parents forgot that we were seventeen and eighteen, practically full-grown adults. It didn't help that Pop still called me *Noodle*, a pet name he'd christened me with when I was a baby for reasons even he'd forgotten. Oh well, I much preferred being called after a pasta than a catastrophic hurricane.

We walked to the McCurdys' via the road instead of going the beach way like earlier. As we passed their cottage on our way to the lake, we could see Mrs. McCurdy through the kitchen window, busy with something at the counter. Probably assembling the ingredients for s'mores. Nate's father was nowhere to be seen, but that wasn't unusual. He was an obstetrician and worked nonstop. The odd time he *did* have a day off, he spent it fishing. Due to this lack of help, Mrs. McCurdy was overwhelmed to the point of indifference, which meant Nate and his three younger brothers regularly got away with murder. And underage drinking.

When Harper and I stepped into the clearing a few yards to the right of Nate's dock, the bonfire was blazing and he had already passed around cans of beer from his not-so-secret stash in their cottage's crawl space. The only person who didn't have one in hand was Nate's eleven-year-old brother, Keaton, who was still innocent enough to be content with roasting marshmallows and lighting sparklers in the fire. He was currently doing a combination of both.

"Ladies," Nate bellowed when he saw us. "It's about time. Come on over! I saved a spot on my log just for you."

Finn and Declan, his fifteen-year-old twin brothers, chortled appreciatively. Nate was a horrible influence on his siblings. Keaton was the only sweet one left, and it was only a matter of time before he ended up corrupted, too.

I moved toward the log on the other side of the bonfire, messing up Nate's blond, perfectly-gelled hair on the way. Harper followed, and we sat down next to Zoe and Gabriella, two local girls who'd been hanging around the past couple of summers. They didn't like Harper and me because we were "summer people" and not true Erwin dwellers. Nate and his brothers were summer people, too, but they got away with it because they were male and cute.

The pissed-off dude from earlier—Emmett—wasn't there. My body lightened in relief. I wasn't eager to test Harper's "he won't even recognize you" theory.

Keaton came over to say hello and show off his clever innovation—a marshmallow stuck on the end of a sparkler. That could only end messily.

"Hey, Buster, how was fifth grade?" I asked him.

He grinned. He loved it when I called him Buster. He thought it sounded tough, but it was actually a reference to Buster Keaton, the silent film star. "It was fun," he said, sticking the marshmallow sparkler in the fire. "But I'd rather be here."

I nodded and looked out at the calm, inky water in front of me. The small island situated in the middle of the lake looked like a smudge of gray against the dark sky. All along the shore, fragments of light peeked through the thickets of trees, the only indication of the various cottages nestled in their midst. I took a deep breath, inhaling the aromas of spruce and pine and mud and wood smoke. "Me too," I told Keaton.

As I spoke, footsteps sounded on the rocks and angry Emmett appeared. Only he didn't look angry as he stood there in the clearing, hands stuffed in the pockets of his shorts. He looked self-conscious. Unsure. Like he wanted to jump into the lake and swim far, far away.

"Hey, man," Nate said, gesturing for him to join him and the twins on their log. When he did, Nate reached into the cooler next to him and handed him a can of beer. The way we were seated around the fire made me think of a gymnasium during a sixth-grade dance—boys on one side and girls on the other . . . only with a fire between us instead of a buffed floor.

Like a proper little host, Nate introduced Emmett to his brothers and then to Zoe and Gabriella, who subtly nudged each other and exchanged *Ooh, fresh meat* smiles. Then his gaze landed on Harper and me. "And this," he said with an exaggerated flourish, "is Harper and her cousin, Hurricane Katrina."

"Kat," I corrected, and Emmett nodded with barely a glance in my direction. I felt another wave of relief. Clearly, he hadn't made the connection between the girl sitting in front of him in the flouncy white dress and the helmeted psycho on the ATV who'd almost mowed him down that morning. Maybe I *had* been sufficiently disguised.

I glanced over at Harper, expecting to see a look of smug victory on her face, but she wasn't even looking at me. Her eyes darted between the fire and Emmett, one of which was causing her cheeks to turn uncharacteristically pink. My guess was the latter, as bonfires didn't usually make her fidget like she was wishing she'd taken more care with her hair and makeup. It appeared she was suffering from an acute case of lust-at-first-sight.

"So, Emmett, where you from?" Zoe asked, rearranging her legs so that her micro-shorts slid up higher. Apparently, the lust bunny had bitten her, too.

He mumbled, "Hyde Creek," which was a medium-sized town about halfway between my home city of Weldon and Erwin.

"Cool," Gabriella said brightly as if the news was just so fascinating. As if she didn't constantly rant about outsiders and how they rolled through Erwin in their fancy cars and acted like they owned the place all summer.

"So what was with the hardcore running in the woods this morning, dude?" Nate asked, reaching for the marshmallow bag and popping one in his mouth. "You on a track team or something?"

"No," Emmett replied. He rolled his still-unopened beer can back and forth between his palms. "Cross-country."

"What's the difference?" Finn asked.

"It just means I run on natural terrain instead of on a flat track."

"That sounds hard," Gabriella said as her gaze devoured the contours of his toned runner's body.

Emmett shifted uncomfortably, as if her blatant ogling bothered him. Figuring I owed him one for the ATV incident, I swiftly diverted everyone's attention away from him and onto me.

"What does a girl have to do to get some s'mores around here?" I said, standing up and craning my neck in the direction of the dock as if waiting for Mrs. McCurdy to appear with her boxes of graham crackers and chocolate—which I kind of was.

"Oh, yeah," Nate said. "I think Mom forgot to buy the stuff."

"She *forgot?*" I cried. Mrs. McCurdy *always* provided s'mores for our bonfires. What was going on? First Goody's, and now this. What else had changed without my knowledge?

"So, Emmett," Gabriella said, twirling one of her dark brown curls around her finger. "How do you like Millard Lake so far? Are you here with your parents?"

Emmett, who'd been looking at me during my s'mores outburst, dropped his gaze to the fire again. "Yeah. It's a nice spot."

"What does your dad do?" Zoe asked. Sometimes she and Gabriella acted like it was the eighteen hundreds and their parents wanted them to find a suitable mate and marry into a well-off family.

"He's in accounting," Emmett said, and then all of a sudden he stood up and handed his unopened beer to Nate. "I'm gonna take off now. There are some things I need to do."

"But you just got here," Gabriella said, pouting.

Emmett glanced around the clearing, his gaze never quite landing on any of us. "Uh, it was nice to meet you all," he said before turning around and loping easily over the rocks to the dock, where he disappeared into the night.

"Was it something we said?" Zoe asked in the awkward silence that followed.

Nate shrugged and took another gulp of beer, Keaton lit another sparkler, the twins went back to staring at Zoe and Gabriella, and I looked over at my cousin, who hadn't said a word in the past twenty minutes. She blinked at me like she'd just gotten whacked in the head with a bat and then let out a long, dreamy sigh.

Yep, it was official. My shy, sporty little Harper had just entered the beginning stages of a sweet summer crush.

chapter 6

For the rest of the weekend, Harper managed to insert Emmett's name into every single one of our conversations.

While making microwave popcorn: "Yeah, let's do extra butter. Emmett's really cute, isn't he?"

While sunbathing on my dock: "My shoulders feel burnt. Do you think Emmett has a girlfriend?"

While eating ice cream sundaes at the counter at Goody's: "Does this chocolate sauce taste different to you? I wonder if Emmett will go out with Gabriella."

That one in particular made me snort into my waffle bowl. Normally, Harper was too preoccupied with school and sports to bother with dating so the odd time she did like someone, she acted like a twelve-year-old with her first crush.

"Only if he's desperate," I said.

"What? She might be opportunistic and shallow, but you have to admit she's pretty. A lot prettier than me."

"Harper, you're gorgeous."

She licked some whipped cream off her spoon. "Right, because big noses and thin lips and flat chests are *so* attractive."

"You are. Embrace it. Guys are attracted to confidence too, you know."

"Says the girl who looks like a voluptuous nineteen-forties pinup model," she said, nudging me with her elbow. "Confidence has always come easy to you, Kat."

It didn't always come easy, but I understood why Harper struggled so much with her own insecurities, so I let it go. My self-esteem would probably be shaky too if one of my dads virtually dropped out of my life like Lawrence had dropped out of Harper's. He'd never been the involved-father type, even when he and Aunt Carrie were still together. I remembered how he always used to shoo us out of the room when we were kids, like our voices and happy giggles annoyed him. When Aunt Carrie finally left him after his third consecutive affair, it was a relief to everyone but Harper, who'd assumed the breakdown of her parents' marriage was somehow *her* fault. The way Lawrence treated her did little to dissuade her from the theory. Nowadays, she was lucky if she heard from him once a month.

Still, regardless of how Harper saw herself, anyone who didn't recognize her as the beautiful, great catch she was didn't deserve to clean the dirt off her Nikes. Even cute, grumpy Emmett.

On Sunday evening, Dad left to go back to the city for the week. I hated to think of him all alone in our condo in the evenings, eating greasy take-out and watching the Turner Classic Movies network without me. But knowing him, he'd spend most of his time at the office anyway, working overtime so he wouldn't have to take many calls over the weekend. Pop worked a lot during those five days too, partly as a distraction and partly because Dad wasn't there to remind him to step away from the computer every few hours and "join the land of the living." With Dad gone, that particular job had been reassigned to me.

The next afternoon, I slid open the screen to the deck and stuck my head outside. Pop sat in one of the plastic lounge chairs, his laptop propped on his legs. "Yoo-hoo," I called.

"Hmm?" He typed feverishly, his eyes never leaving the screen.

"We're out of milk," I told him as I stepped outside. "And paper towels. And bananas."

"Bananas?" he said vaguely, his fingers still dancing over the keys.

"You know, the long, yellow fruit I like to cut up and put on peanut butter toast? Pop?"

He stopped typing, finally, and let out a relieved sigh. "Sorry, Kat. I just *had* to get that sentence right. Now what were you saying?"

I moved closer and peered down into his mug of tea, which sat on the deck beside him. Still full. He hadn't so much as paused to take a drink since nine o'clock. "We need a few groceries," I said, picking up the cold mug. "And you need a break."

"Apparently I do," he said, squinting at the laptop screen. "I actually *typed* the word *bananas*."

Thirty minutes later, the two of us were strolling down the aisles of Erwin's one and only supermarket. The place was pretty deserted, even for a Monday afternoon.

"You feel like grilling some chicken breasts for dinner tonight?" I asked when we reached the paltry meat section. Erwin's stores weren't exactly famous for their large selections.

"Hmm?" Pop replied.

I knew from experience that it always took him at least an hour to emerge from the foggy, fictional land inside his head, so I never took offense to his occasional negligence. "Chicken," I repeated, steering him and the cart to the poultry display.

"Right. Do you want to grill some for dinner tonight?"

I patted his arm. "*Great* idea, Pop."

He didn't fully resurface until we hit the cereal aisle where I attempted to toss a box of Lucky Charms into our cart. "Over my dead body," he said, intercepting me and putting it back on the shelf. He replaced it with a box of Shredded Wheat. "There. This one has lots of fiber."

"Pop, why do you insist on feeding me so much fiber? It's not like I'm constip—oh!"

The front of our cart had just come very close to ramming into someone at the corner of the aisle. *Again?* I thought when I looked up to see a pair of blue, blue eyes staring back at me, wide with surprise. Again. I'd almost crashed into Emmett Reese. Again.

"Sorry," I said, backing up. My cheeks started flaming, mostly because I'd just remembered what I'd been about to say right before our near-accident.

Emmett continued to stare at me, perplexed, like he couldn't quite understand why people kept trying to take him out with large, wheeled objects. "It's okay," he said, letting go of the front of our cart, which he'd grabbed to avoid the impending collision with his more sensitive regions. "Um . . . Kat, right?"

I nodded and smiled, pleased that he a) wasn't yelling at me and b) remembered my name. "Good memory." I glanced at Pop, who was watching me with raised eyebrows. "Oh. This is my dad."

"Bryce Henley," Pop said, sticking out his hand. "Nice to meet you."

"This is Emmett," I supplied. "His family bought the Cantings' cottage."

Pop's expression turned grave. "It's a shame about Albert."

Looking slightly confused, Emmett nodded. As he did, a lock of hair slid down his forehead, obscuring his right eyebrow. The bright overhead lights of the store brought out all the different shades in his wavy hair—brown, lighter brown, blond, and even a few patches of auburn. *Women pay good money for those kinds of highlights*, I thought. "Sorry again," I said and then I whipped out my most dazzling smile, the one that always got me out of trouble with teachers.

"No worries." He shoved his hands into his pockets, turned as if to walk away, and then swiveled around to face us again. "Would you happen to know which aisle the baking soda is in?"

"Aisle three," Pop and I replied in unison. We knew the store better than the shelf stockers.

"Thanks," Emmett said before turning left in the direction of aisle three and then disappearing completely.

"Nice boy," Pop said as we started walking again. "What do you know about his family?"

I shrugged. "Nothing. That's the most I've ever heard him say." We rolled into the produce area and I made a beeline for the bananas. "Oh wait. His dad's an accountant or something."

"Interesting."

"And Harper has a crush on him."

"The accountant?"

"No," I said, digging for the ripest bunch of bananas. "Emmett."

"Ah. Even *more* interesting." Pop picked up a head of iceberg lettuce and examined it for brown spots.

"But she's too timid to do anything about it," I went on.

"Well, maybe she just needs a little push."

"Yeah," I said, looking in the direction of aisle three. "Maybe she does."

After dinner, I shut myself up in my room and, for the first time since we'd arrived, I turned on my cell phone. I'd sent six texts to Shay so far, the first four asking for a chance to explain and the last two begging for forgiveness. Each one had gone unanswered, which didn't exactly surprise me. The last time I'd seen her, she'd made it quite clear that she never wanted to speak to me again. It seemed she was fully on the bandwagon with the girls at school who thought I was a whore on some kind of devious mission to steal everyone's boyfriends. That was far from the truth. For one, I had no interest in stealing anyone's boyfriend. And two, I wasn't a whore, whatever that subjective term meant in their minds. Yes, I'd dated a lot of guys, but I'd never had sex with any of them. Usually, they dumped me before I had the chance to consider going that far. Harper was right. Boyfriends didn't like it when their girlfriends acted too friendly with other guys.

Even when you're not flirting, you're flirting, Harper had told me. I guess she had a point. I knew if I didn't at least *try* to tone down my excessive friendliness, senior year would be hell. I needed to fix my reputation, and the first step would be showing everyone that I was so redeemed, so transformed, that even Shay had decided to forgive me.

I had the rest of summer to convince her to do it.

My cell phone kept wavering in and out of connectivity, but I'd always found if I stood on the edge of my bed and held it up toward the far corner of the ceiling, I'd get at least one bar. Just enough juice to send a quick text.

Shay, please talk to me. Let me explain.

To my surprise, a response arrived two minutes later.

Nothing to explain. I'm blocking you now. Leave me alone.

I tried to send another text, another appeal, but the signal had been cut off once again. Frustrated, I threw my cell on the bed and flopped down beside it, tears stinging my eyes. One party, one misunderstanding, and our friendship was over. She had been one of my last female friends, the last one to disregard the rumors and give me a chance to prove myself. And I'd failed. Horribly.

At least I'll always have Harper, I thought, wiping the moisture from my face with my pillow. She was my cousin, sure, but also my friend. Possibly my *only* friend, depending on whether my classmates' negative opinion of me died out or gained traction over the summer.

After a while, I stopped crying and started formulating a plan. Harper just needed a little push, like Pop had said, and it was up to me to give her one. Maybe orchestrating someone else's relationship would stop me from constantly wrecking my own.

chapter 7

By ten o'clock the next morning, the plans were in motion. First, I called Nate McCurdy at his cottage to ask if he'd be willing to help. After a few lewd comments I chose to ignore, he readily agreed. Next, I talked to Harper. I had to propose a slightly edited version of my plan in order to get her on board, but hopefully she'd forgive me later if everything worked out.

The only thing left for me to do was convince Emmett.

At the lake, there were only two ways to effectively get in touch with people: call their landline or walk over to their cottage and see them. Since I didn't know Emmett's phone number, I slipped on a pair of flats and headed over there.

The first thing I noticed as I approached his cottage was that someone had ripped up Mrs. Canting's prized sunflowers. The second thing I noticed was the yelling. Two separate voices, one male and one female, trickled through the open windows and echoed across the yard. I couldn't quite work out the specifics of the argument, but it sounded like World War Three. For a second I considered turning back, but I really needed to secure plans for tonight and Emmett was the final corner piece I needed to complete the square. I was banking on his cooperation.

Determined, I crossed the driveway and stepped up to the door. Hesitating for only a moment, I knocked firmly on the weathered wood. The fighting ceased as if by magic, and the door was flung open to reveal a tall, red-faced man in a blue Polo shirt and shorts. "Yes?" he barked.

I gaped at him for a few seconds, speechless. He was breathing hard, as if he'd been interrupted in the middle of a workout instead of a screaming fight.

"Hi!" I said, attempting to muster one of my wide, toothy smiles. I couldn't quite manage it. "I'm looking for Emmett."

He glanced over his shoulder into the house where I could see an outline of either a young girl or a very tiny woman. "He's not here. I think he went out for a run."

"Oh. Right. Okay, I'll just come back later then."

"And you are?" he asked, his dark eyes sweeping over my beribboned ponytail and polka-dotted blouse like I was some kind of freak of nature. Or a time traveler from the fifties.

"Kat Henley," I said, thrusting my hand out.

He stared at it for a moment and then shook it briefly.

"I live a few cottages that way." I pointed in the direction of our cabin.

"I see. Well, I'll tell Emmett you came by." And with that, he backed into the house and closed the door behind him.

I stood there for a minute, trying to piece together what had just occurred. Obviously, that had been Emmett's father—he had the same multi-colored hair and perfectly straight nose. But he'd seemed so . . . abrupt. Unfriendly. I guess it wasn't very different from what I'd witnessed so far in his son.

"What are you doing here?"

Startled, I spun around and caught sight of Emmett standing a few feet away from the house and watching me with a vaguely panicked look on his face. He wore gray shorts and black sneakers and was naked from the waist up, unless you counted the ear bud wires dangling down his bare chest. They didn't cover much at all, however.

"Um," I said, looking everywhere but at him. "I was looking for you."

"What for?"

Behind me, the screaming had started anew. Quickly, I distanced myself from the door and moved closer to Emmett, all the while keeping my gaze trained above his neck and not on his defined, glistening torso. *Why does it have to be so hot today?* I wondered.

"A few of us are going to Goody's for dinner tonight," I said, finding my smile. "You should join us."

"I should?" He was still panting slightly from his run, and something about it made the tips of my ears feel warm.

I cleared my throat. "Definitely. It'll be me and my cousin Harper and McTur . . . uh, Nate . . . and some others." There *would* be others there, I was sure, but they wouldn't be sitting at our table. It would be just the four of us. But like Harper, Emmett didn't need to know *all* the details.

"I don't know," he said, raking a hand through his damp hair. As he did, a particularly loud burst of yelling filtered outside, making him wince. His cheeks, flushed with exertion, turned even redder.

"Oh, come on." My hand went up to poke him, but I caught myself and pretended to scratch an itch on my shoulder instead. *Don't touch. Don't charm. And most important, don't look down.*

"What's Goody's?" he asked.

"Oh, it's this little diner across the road from the entrance to the cottages. You must see it when you drive by. Great burgers. Made totally from scratch, even the buns."

It was weird, standing there talking about burgers while a brawl ensued in the background. The raised voices seemed wrong and out of place in such a quiet, peaceful setting. Like hearing someone curse in church.

"Look, Kat, you should probably go," Emmett said, his gaze flicking toward the cottage.

"Is everything okay?" I asked carefully.

He sighed. "Yeah. My parents are . . . well, this is normal."

Normal? Screaming fights at eleven o'clock on a beautiful summer morning at the lake was normal? I couldn't think of anything helpful to say, so I settled on, "I'm sorry."

"Don't be. Just go, okay? As you can hear, it's not the best time for me to have guests."

I nodded and turned to leave. As I reached the copse of trees, I glanced back at him again. He was still standing in the same spot, hands in his pockets and eyes on the ground. "So you'll come with us tonight?" I asked. "Seven o'clock?"

"Yeah, sure, whatever," he said impatiently as his parents' voices splintered the air. "I'll meet you guys there. Okay?"

Success. I nodded at him again and started picking through bushes and tree roots to get to the woods path.

"Careful going through the woods," Emmett called from behind me. "During my run the other day, I almost got flattened by some moron on an ATV."

I had to force myself to keep walking at an even, non-guilty pace. "Thanks for the warning!" I called back, grateful that he could no longer see my face.

I knew before the night even began that I'd made a huge mistake.

My first clue was when Nate showed up at Goody's smelling like he'd just bathed in a tub of beer. Apparently, he and his twin brothers had spent the afternoon out on the lake, pretending to fish while they polished off the rest of the cans from the bonfire the other night. *Idiots.*

My next clue was Harper's face when she spotted Emmett standing outside the restaurant and realized he was waiting for *us*. All I'd told her was that we were going to Goody's for dinner and that Nate and some other people might stop by, too. I'd neglected to mention Emmett's role in the proceedings. She looked at me, her expression vacillating between terror, excitement, and confusion.

When I smiled encouragingly at her, her eyes narrowed into slits. *You did this*, they said.

Awkwardness abounded when Sherry pointed us to a table and Nate quickly claimed the chair to the left of Harper's, forcing me to sit next to Emmett. The tables were small and round, so personal space and elbow room were basically non-existent. Harper sat on my other side, simultaneously blushing and shooting me dirty looks. Nate was acting even douchier than usual due to his beer-guzzling party earlier, and Emmett seemed embarrassed to be seen with us.

All I could do was try to salvage the evening before it veered off the rails and took us all with it.

"So, Emmett," I said, breaking several long moments of uneasy silence. "You live in Hyde Creek, right? What's that like?"

He looked at me the same way he had at the supermarket yesterday when I'd almost run him over with the cart—surprised and a bit bewildered. "It's okay. Where are you from?"

"Oh, my dads and I live in Weldon, right downtown."

I watched Emmett's face carefully as the words registered. People's reactions to hearing "my dads" for the first time ranged anywhere from curiosity to awe to disgust. If Emmett was going to act weird or offended, the matchmaking scheme of mine would fizzle out before it even got off the ground. Harper would never want to hang out with someone who disapproved of her favorite uncles. Neither would I, for that matter.

But luckily, all he did was nod and say, "Cool."

The waitress, a new girl named Cindy, arrived with our drinks and asked if we were all ready to order. Thankfully, we were.

The instant she was out of sight again, Nate reached into his shorts pocket and brought out a small bottle of vodka. "Anyone want to supplement their drinks?" he asked as he unscrewed the cap in full view of the entire restaurant. It was virtually empty, but still.

"Are you insane?" I whisper-shrieked at him.

He poured a large dollop into his Coke while Emmett watched in amazement, Harper buried her head in her hands, and I scanned the place for witnesses. Getting banned from Goody's was all we needed.

"Last chance," Nate said, glancing around the table.

We each shook our heads no. I wasn't opposed to alcohol and even indulged now and again, but never when I had to go right home afterwards. My dads would smell it on me from miles away, even scentless vodka. Harper never drank, and as for Emmett, he didn't seem like the risk-taking type. Either that or he thought we were all crazy and wanted to stay sharp and sober in case he needed to escape quickly.

By the time our food arrived, Emmett and Harper were barely speaking at all and Nate was a few sips away from full-on drunk. The more he drank, the more combative he became.

"Hey Emmett," he said in a stage whisper as he leaned toward him. "You know why these two refuse to go out with me?"

I leaned across the table to slide his vodka-and-Coke closer to me and out of his reach. "Eat your cheeseburger, Nate."

"Um, isn't she . . ." Emmett said, confused as he gestured to me, "out with you?"

Nate laughed. "Yeah, right. Kat made it *very* clear this morning that this was not a date. You know why? She thinks she's too good for me."

"Quit it," Harper snapped at him. "You're being an ass."

He ignored her. "Or . . . wait, I have another theory. Maybe a bit of all that gay rubbed off on her and she's not into guys at all. Is that the problem, Hurricane? Because I can think of a few ways to change your mind."

I dropped my French fry and gaped at him. "Seriously?"

"I don't think that's how it works," Emmett said wryly.

Okay, maybe he was decent after all. Or maybe . . . maybe *he* was gay. I'd never considered that possibility. Even though I'd been raised by same-sex parents, my gaydar was terrible. Case in point, I'd spent two months last year flirting with a cute guy who lived in my building, completely oblivious to the fact that he wasn't really responding to my advances. Finally, he just came right out and told me one day that he played for the other team. It was so humiliating.

"McTurdy, the reason Kat won't go out with you is because you're a jackass," Harper said, sounding more animated than she'd been all evening.

I nodded in agreement. Even though Harper was probably furious with me for setting this up without her knowledge, she still had my back.

"Well, fine by me," Nate said, lifting himself off the chair and reaching across the tablecloth for his glass. As he plopped back down again, his unfocused gaze skimmed over the pink crop top I wore with my floral lace skirt. "I prefer skinny girls anyway. Hey Harper, you up for it? Oh wait . . . I prefer really hot girls."

Nate had always been insufferable, but never to the point of nastiness. I would've liked to blame the vodka, but sadly enough, he could be just as douchy while stone-cold sober. In his mind, since Harper and I refused to spend our summers making out with him, we had to be either stuck-up snobs or lesbians. He was just that full of himself. I didn't care what he said about me—I'd heard worse around school—but he wasn't allowed to antagonize Harper like that.

"You're an asshole," I told him.

"Fair enough." He drained his glass and stood up. "This asshole has to go take a piss. Try not to miss me too much while I'm gone."

He staggered off to the washroom while Harper, Emmett, and I stayed put at the table and picked halfheartedly at our food. This had to be the most unsuccessful secret setup date ever attempted.

"This was a *great* idea, Kat," Harper said around her milkshake straw. "So glad you thought of it."

"Is he always like that?" Emmett asked.

She nodded. "Pretty much."

"Wow."

"Yeah," Harper agreed.

Wow indeed, I thought. At least Nate's repulsive behavior had gotten them talking—sort of—which was more than I'd thought was going to happen between them tonight. Perhaps my epic fail of a plan hadn't been a total waste of time after all.

chapter 8

During the week that had passed since the near-accident with Emmett in the woods, I was still too traumatized to get back on the ATV. But when Saturday morning dawned so clear and so beautiful, I could no longer fight the urge to suit up and ride. *This time,* I thought as I started the engine, *I'll pay better attention to my surroundings and keep my eyes peeled.*

As it turned out, the extra vigilance was unnecessary. I didn't spot anything in the woods aside from a few squirrels and a garter snake. The only time I paused was when I came across a small blue tent set up near the narrow brook that ran deep in the woods. People sometimes camped there so its presence wasn't unusual, but I slowed down a fraction in case someone suddenly popped out of it and stepped in my path. Luckily, no one did.

When I got back to the cottage, Harper was seated at my kitchen table, keeping Dad company while he drank his coffee and read the morning paper. He'd arrived yesterday evening, exhausted from a long week of work.

"How was your ride?" he asked, looking up from his newspaper.

"Peaceful." As I kicked off my boots, I noticed the gym bag by Harper's feet. "Did Erwin open up a health club over the winter or something?"

"No. I start practice with the soccer team this morning, remember?"

"Oh, right." To keep her skills up over the summer, Harper had joined a local women's soccer league. She'd badgered me to join, too, but I'd declined. Not only was I rusty and out of shape, but I saw summer as a time for relaxing, not adhering to a grueling practice schedule.

"I came over to see if you wanted to go with me," she said.

I filled a glass with water at the kitchen sink. "Sorry, but all I want to do right now is stand in a freezing cold shower."

"You're coming to our first game though, right? It's Monday evening." *You owe me,* her eyes said.

It was true. I owed her that and more after Tuesday night's disastrous "double date" at Goody's. Well, the night hadn't been a *total* loss. Harper's irritation with me all but disappeared when Emmett paid for our food and then offered to walk us back to our cottages. At that point, Nate was still in the bathroom, likely puking up everything he'd ingested in the last several hours. The decision to leave him behind was unanimous. The jerk deserved to be ditched.

As the three of us strolled down the gravel road to the cottages, Emmett must've been swept up in a sense of camaraderie because he was no longer the quiet, reticent boy we'd seen at the bonfire and during dinner. In fact, we'd been able to coax quite a bit of info out of him. I let my mind drift back to our walk home.

"Are you starting college in the fall, Emmett?" I asked him. Harper walked between us, so I had to lean around her to see him.

"No," he said, his eyes skimming my face before returning to the road in front of him. "I'm going to be a senior."

Like me, *I thought. Harper and I exchanged a surprised look. There was something in his demeanor—a hardened maturity—that made him seem older, like he'd been through a lot. Or seen too much.*

"And you're on the cross-country team, right?" Harper asked in her quiet, reserved way.

"For the past two years. My brother ran cross-country, too. He's the one who got me into it."

Brother? *As far as I knew, it was just him and his parents at the Canting cottage.*

Emmett obviously sensed our confusion because he added, "Older brother. Wes. He works on the oil sands out west and rarely comes home. He was supposed to fly home this summer to spend a couple weeks at the cottage, but"—he shrugged one shoulder and tilted his face away from us and toward the tree line—"he and my dad don't get along."

Harper nodded. She understood. "A change of scenery doesn't usually help."

"Exactly." He cleared his throat like he was working up to something. "I think my parents bought the cottage here because they thought quiet summers on the lake would strengthen our bond as a family. Or something."

"And is it working?" I asked.

He shot me a quick glance, eyebrows raised, as if to say What do you think? *I dropped my gaze, feeling a little stupid. Clearly, the new peaceful backdrop wasn't helping at all.*

I hadn't told Harper about that morning when I'd gone over to Emmett's cottage and heard his parents arguing. I figured it was his personal business, up to him to discuss when—or if— he chose to. He still barely knew us, after all, and he didn't come across as the type to blab about his family issues to anyone, even people he did know. I got the sense that he wanted me to pretend that morning had never happened, so I quickly got us off the subject of his parents and started talking about sports instead. Athleticism was the main thing he and Harper had in common, and just as I'd hoped, it got them talking about train-ing and injuries and various other things that were no longer a part of my vocabulary.

In fact, they were still gabbing away when they dropped me off at my cottage and continued down the road together without me. She'd just needed a push, after all. I was sure she'd have a bunch of juicy details to share with me in the morning, in be-tween thanking me profusely for bringing them together in the first place. But that wasn't what happened. In reality, Emmett had simply left her on her doorstep without so much as a de-parting handshake and neither of us had seen or heard from him since.

I shook my head to clear it. Maybe they *both* needed pushes.

"Of course I'll be at your first game," I told Harper as I refilled my water glass. "Though I'm sure the Erwiners are going to stare at us like we're circus freaks."

Harper grabbed her bag and stood up. "Great. I need my own cheering section."

"I'll bring my pom-poms," I promised.

She laughed like I'd made a joke and then waved at us on her way out the door. "Say good morning to Uncle Bryce for me."

When she was gone, I took her spot next to Dad at the table. "Where's Pop?"

"Sleeping in." Dad put down his paper and looked at me. "How many hours did he spend writing this week, Katrina?"

A wave of guilt hit me and I dropped my gaze to the placemat. Whenever Dad was gone, he relied on me to make sure Pop didn't waste away in front of his laptop. I'd been so preoccupied with my matchmaking scheme and hanging out with Harper that I hadn't done a very good job of monitoring Pop's well-being. I knew for a fact he'd skipped several meals and at least one shower in order to pound out a few extra thousand words. He always got like this near the end of a book. The story consumed him and he could think of little else until he finished it.

"He was working on an epic battle scene," I said defensively. "I didn't have the heart to interrupt him."

"His agent wants the book by September and he's feeling all this pressure from his readers . . ." Dad sighed and ran a hand over his face. "God, I think I liked it better when he wrote user manuals for a living."

"But he hated being a technical writer," I reminded him. "Writing this series makes him happy."

The corners of Dad's eyes crinkled as he smiled at me. "True. Now go take a shower before you scare someone with that helmet hair."

A couple hours later I was stretched out on my stomach on the dock, soaking up UV rays and reading a dog-eared romance paperback I'd left at the cottage years ago. It was my favorite time of day—the sun had finished burning off the morning fog, leaving behind a clear, brilliant blue sky. The lake was a sheet of glass, its stillness interrupted only by an occasional breeze or fallen leaf. Or in the case of that particular morning, the motor of a small aluminum fishing boat.

"Hey, Hurricane!"

I shut my eyes and muttered a four-letter word. I'd been hoping it would be Dr. McCurdy passing by in their boat on his way to catch some rainbow trout. No such luck. When I glanced up from my book, Nate was steering himself toward me. I watched as he killed the engine and floated the rest of the way, reaching an arm out to grab the ladder that hung off the end of our dock. The front of the boat bumped against the corner, shaking the boards beneath me. His father would kill him if he knew how his son treated his beloved boat.

"What do you want?" I asked, returning my gaze to the book. Harper and I had been avoiding him—or maybe he'd been avoiding us—since we'd ditched him in the washroom at Goody's.

"Look, Hurricane—"

"Kat."

"Look, Kat, I know you guys are pissed at me for the other night and I wanted to come over and tell you that I'm sorry."

I peered up at him through my big sunglasses. He sat on the boat's bench seat, shirtless and disheveled, his body swaying slightly from the small waves the motor had produced. For once, he wore an expression of what appeared to be genuine remorse, usually a foreign emotion for Nate.

"You acted like a complete dick," I told him, not quite ready to fall for his apology. "I asked you to go out to dinner with us so Harper and Emmett would feel less awkward, but you made everything even *more* awkward. All you had to do was sit there and behave like a normal human being, and you couldn't even get *that* right."

"I know," he said, hanging his head. "I shouldn't have gotten drunk beforehand, or brought that vodka with me. It was a stupid thing to do."

Okay, he was starting to freak me out. Nate *thrived* on doing stupid things. The summer we were thirteen, he'd tried to jump his bike over a huge patch of thorny bushes (he made it about halfway). The summer we were fourteen, he threw a water bottle filled with gasoline into a fire and almost burned the forest down. When we were fifteen, he convinced Keaton to eat some suspicious mushrooms he'd found in the woods, which luckily turned out to be just plain mushrooms and not the poisonous kind. Last summer, he "borrowed" his father's Lexus and backed it into a tree. His idiocy knew no bounds. My dads blamed it on "a lack of discipline and structure in the home." I blamed it on the fact that he was a boy.

"How about I make it up to you?" Nate asked, giving me a winning smile. "I'm having another bonfire tonight. You guys should come."

"No," I said, turning a page in my paperback.

"My mom bought the stuff for s'mores," he sang.

My mouth watered at the promise of warm, gooey chocolate. Then I thought about Shay and all those texts I'd sent, begging for her forgiveness. Everyone deserved a second chance at redemption, even McTurdy. "Okay, maybe. On three conditions."

"Shoot."

I put my book down and looked him square in the eye. "One—stop staring at my ass."

He tore his gaze away from my bikini-clad behind. "I wasn't," he lied.

"Two—apologize to Emmett for the way you acted on Tuesday night."

"Already did. I ran into him yesterday and invited him to come over tonight. He said he would."

Perfect, I thought. *Condition two might help facilitate condition three.* "And three—apologize to Harper and convince her to go tonight . . . all by yourself."

His smile drooped. "How am I supposed to do that? She hates me. I'll apologize, but it's you who needs to convince her, Kat. She always listens to you."

I picked up my book again. "Sorry. Those are the conditions."

For a moment, the only sound between us was the

rhythmic thump of the boat rocking against the side of the dock. Then Nate made a growling noise and said, "Fine. Is she at her cottage?"

"Yeah, she's probably back from soccer practice by now."

He pushed against the ladder and reached behind him to the motor. "I've always kind of liked her, you know," he said, his hand pausing on the switch.

"Harper?" I said, shocked. "You *like* her?" He had a funny way of showing it.

"Since that first summer." He grinned slyly. "She was, like, this older woman."

I laughed. "Yeah, a whole year older. Is that why you were acting like such a jerk the other night? Because you were jealous of Emmett?"

"Maybe," he said as if the thought had never occurred to him.

"How come you've never seriously asked her out?"

"Like I said, she hates me." Nate pulled a cord and the motor sputtered to life, effectively ending our conversation. "See you tonight!" he shouted over the racket, and then he pointed the boat in the direction of Harper's cottage.

Good luck, I thought, watching him go. Trying to push Harper and Emmett together was challenging enough, and he was a guy she *liked*. Convincing her to see Nate in a different light would take nothing short of a miracle.

chapter 9

"Remind me why we're doing this again?" Harper asked me as we picked our way along the shoreline.

"Because Nate promised to behave," I said, hopping over a slimy rock. "*And* provide s'mores."

"We could've made s'mores in the fire pit in your yard."

"Right. You think Pop would let me have unlimited access to sugar like that?"

Harper shook her head. "I can't believe my mom and your dad came from the same parents."

"I know." We discussed this all the time, how different Pop and Aunt Carrie were in spite of being raised in the same household. Aunt Carrie was a lot more laid back and go-with-the-flow. She was a high school teacher and a big believer in picking your battles.

We were the last to show up in the bonfire clearing. Emmett had already arrived and was sitting by himself on one of the logs, head bent as he stabbed a stick into the coarse sand below him. Zoe and Gabriella paddled in the water nearby, giggling and dunking each other and essentially putting on a show for the guys. But only the twins were watching, their mouths hanging open in dual expressions of awe. Nate was busy getting the fire going, and Emmett kept on drawing patterns in the sand like it was the only thing preventing him from dying of boredom.

"Ladies," Nate said when he saw us. His eyes literally twinkled in the glow of the fire as if he was silently congratulating himself on luring us there. I raised my eyebrows at him warily and went to join Emmett on the log. There was just enough space to the right of him for one person, and I immediately claimed that spot so Harper would have no choice but to sit on his other side.

"Hi, Emmett," I said cheerfully. "You're here for the s'mores too, huh?"

He sat up straight and threw his stick into the crackling fire. "Obviously."

Zoe or Gabriella let out another loud squeal from the water, and Harper rolled her eyes. To his credit, Emmett hadn't looked their way even once since we'd arrived. Either he had caught on to their utter shamelessness or he really *was* gay. I still hadn't decided.

With the fire suitably underway, Nate stood up and peered over at us. "Hey, Harper," he said, brushing off his hands. "Want to help me bring down the s'mores supplies?"

"I'll help you, Nate!" Zoe called from the water.

Nate ignored her.

"Um," Harper said, glancing at me.

Earlier, I'd told her what Nate had said that morning in his boat, how he'd liked her since that first summer. Her response had been to wrinkle her nose like she'd smelled decaying fish and make gagging noises, but she didn't seem *totally* against the idea.

"I guess so," she decided after a long pause, and slowly stood up to join him. Together, they walked up the steps to Nate's cottage.

"Nate's mom always gets the good chocolate," I said to Emmett. I felt slightly awkward, sitting so close to him without Harper. But getting up and moving to his other side would be weird, and it didn't seem like he was about to scoot over anytime soon. "Like this Swiss stuff that literally melts in your mouth," I went on, trying to distract us both from the fact that our thighs were touching. "So yummy."

He looked over at me, his lips turning up into a small smile. He didn't smile often, but when he did, it transformed his face and his demeanor. Smiling Emmett seemed lighter, more relaxed. And about ten times cuter.

"You know what?" he said, his gaze traveling over my hair, which was fashioned into a forties-inspired roll, and then down to my yellow, halter-style dress. "You look different every time I see you."

I couldn't stop myself from smiling back at him. "I like to stand out."

"Well, you definitely do," he told me, and once again I felt the tips of my ears grow warm.

We fell silent, each of us mesmerized by the growing flames in front of us. The smoldering wood sizzled and spit, throwing sparks into the air above. I struggled to think of something to say, something random and safe, and settled on, "What happened to the sunflowers?"

Emmett glanced at me again. "What?"

"The sunflowers," I repeated. "In front of your cottage. The ones Mrs. Canting planted. I noticed when I was over there the other day that they're gone. What happened to them?"

"Oh, those. My mom ripped them up. She thinks sunflowers are creepy."

"Seriously?"

"Yeah," he said, grinning even wider. "She says they look like giant black eyes, watching her."

I laughed. "I guess they kind of do."

His smile disappeared and he shifted his position on

the log. "Look, I've been meaning to talk to you about that day you came to see me. What you heard—"

I reached out to touch his arm, to stop him from talking, but retracted my hand at the last second. *No touching.* "You don't have to explain."

"I know, but I want to." He took a deep breath and exhaled it through his nose. "Like I told you, what you heard that morning was normal for them. My parents have been at each other's throats for as long as I can remember. I'm not sure when it started, or why, but it's always been this way. Sometimes they go months without fighting and everything's good, but then something will set one of them off and it'll start all over again."

"What do they fight about?"

"Everything. Work, money, chores . . . me. Sometimes they try to get me to take sides, and when I do, one of them will accuse the other of trying to turn me against them. They used to do the same thing to my brother Wes. That's why he moved away right after graduation and has hardly been back since." He stretched his legs out toward the fire. "I still have another year before I can escape, but I try to stay out of the house as much as I can. That's one of the reasons I joined the cross-country team, you know. When I'm running, all I can hear is my breathing. I don't have to think about anything other than where my foot is going next. It centers me. Quiets my mind."

I placed my palm on his forearm and squeezed. I couldn't help it; I was a hugger, a toucher, especially when someone was so clearly in need of a dose of positive human contact. He didn't stiffen up or pull away, so I assumed he didn't mind the offer of comfort.

"I can't believe I just told you all that," he said, sighing. "I don't usually talk about it, especially to someone I only met a week ago, but I figured I owed you an explanation after what happened. Thinking back on it, I was kind of rude to you that morning. Sorry."

I waved my free hand, brushing away the unneeded apology. "What about divorce?" I asked him gently. "My aunt Carrie and her ex-husband fought a lot too, and everyone was much better off when they separated." The mention of Harper's parents made me think of her, and I dropped my hand from Emmett's warm arm.

"They've tried separating twice already and got back together both times. I'm not sure why . . . it's like they hate each other." His eyes met mine again. In the dark, the blue of his irises seemed black like Mrs. Canting's creepy sunflowers. "Do your parents get along?"

I nodded. "For the most part, yes. They've been together for twenty-three years, since they were seniors in college, and they're still in love. They rarely fight, and I absolutely hate it when they do. I can't imagine listening to it all the time."

"You're lucky."

"I know." Even when Pop was being overprotective, or when Dad was away on a business trip instead of spending time with me, I never took for granted how fortunate I was to have them.

"Are you . . ." Emmett shifted again, running a hand through his hair in a gesture I'd come to recognize as nervousness. "Are you, um, adopted?"

It was a question I received often, so I never took offense at the personal nature of it. "No," I replied, and then went on to explain about Aunt Beth's egg donation, the surrogacy, and Dad's contribution to it all. "Most kids like me are either adopted or related to just one parent, but I'm biologically related to both my dads."

"That's so cool," he said. "I mean, that something like that is possible."

"It wasn't easy, but it was important to them."

"So how do you decide whose last name to use?"

That was another question I got often. My dads had been legally married for several years, but unlike most opposite-sex couples, they'd both kept their last names.

"That was the subject of one of their rare fights, so the story goes," I said. "Since Dad is technically my *father*, my other dad—I call him Pop to avoid confusion—argued that I should get *his* last name. So I'm Kat Henley, which is fortunate because my other dad's last name is Colvin. Kat Colvin sounds too cutesy, even for me."

Emmett smiled again. "At least your last name doesn't make people think of peanut butter cups."

"Mmm," I said, because I was thinking about chocolate again. Where were Harper and Nate? They'd been gone for at least fifteen minutes. Actually, where was *everyone*? Zoe and Gabriella and the twins had all disappeared, too. I'd been so preoccupied talking to Emmett, I hadn't even noticed their departure.

"Well," I said, stretching out my legs next to his. "I guess we should—" But before I had a chance to finish my sentence, heavy footsteps sounded on the stairs and Harper appeared, looking out of sorts.

"Harper, what's wrong?" I asked when I saw her face. She was frowning and looked close to tears.

"Nothing," she said, eyeing the lack of space between Emmett and me.

Flustered, I stood up and moved toward her. Up close, her eyes were red and puffy.

"Are you ready to go? Let's go."

"What happened?" I demanded. So help me, if Nate had done something to her, I'd make him wish he was never born.

"Nothing." Her eyes flicked to Emmett, who was still sitting on the log a few feet away, watching us.

I grabbed her arm and led her away, closer to the water. "Tell me," I whispered.

"It's nothing, Kat."

I refused to let go of her arm or leave until she spilled. She must have seen it on my face because she caved pretty quickly.

"Nate tried to kiss me in the kitchen and I wouldn't let him, so he got pissed and said he wasn't desperate enough to make out with me anyway. Then he found Zoe and started making out with her. That's what happened, okay? Satisfied? Can we go now?"

White hot rage bubbled in my stomach. "That son of a bitch," I snarled. "I'm gonna kick his ass." I started toward the stairs, murder in my heart, but Harper pulled me back.

"Just forget it, Kat. It's not worth it. He was just being Nate."

"No, he was just being a total shithead."

"Same difference," she said as Emmett came up behind us and asked if everything was okay. "We're fine," she replied. "Just leaving."

"I'll walk you guys home," he said.

The three of us headed toward the dark road, not even bothering to stop by Nate's cottage as we passed to let him know we were leaving. That jerk had officially run out of chances and it was only the second week of summer.

"Why do you guys even hang out with him?" Emmett asked as we walked.

I was in the middle, with him on my left and Harper on my right. Going by the undercurrent of disgust in his voice, he'd overheard our conversation earlier. I'd forgotten how voices tended to carry near the lake.

"I don't know," Harper said bitterly. "Habit?"

"He's always been kind of an asshat," I put in. "But mostly a harmless kind of asshat, you know? I'm not sure what happened to him over the past year, but this summer it's like he's reached a whole new level of asshattery."

"All I know is, that was my last bonfire at McTurdy's cottage," Harper said.

"Mine too."

"And mine," Emmett said, and a moment later, I felt his broad shoulder brush against my bare one. It was really dark on the road, the gravel uneven in spots, so I was sure it had been an accident. But my skin tingled nonetheless.

Just like last Tuesday, the two of them dropped me at my cottage first and then continued on to Harper's. But unlike last Tuesday, I didn't go inside right away to assure them maximum privacy. Instead, I stood at the edge of my driveway, watching them until they reached a curve in the road and disappeared.

chapter 10

To make up for neglecting Pop last week as he wrote himself into a stupor, I made it my personal mission to ensure he got plenty of fresh air and sunshine. The mission began at precisely six-thirty on Monday evening, when I sat down across from him at the kitchen table as he tapped away on his laptop and ignored the grilled cheese sandwich I'd made for him.

"Time to go, Pop," I said, rapping my knuckles against the table top.

"Hmm?" He glanced up at me without really seeing me. "Go where?"

"Harper's first game? Soccer? The Erwin Eagles?" I pressed my finger against his laptop screen and slowly began to push it closed. "Ring a bell?"

"Oh, right." He scooted his laptop closer to him and opened it back up. "Okay, just let me finish this one—"

"No. I haven't bugged you all day, so you owe me at least a couple hours of father-daughter bonding."

He stopped typing and looked at me for real, his forehead smoothing. "That I do," he said, smiling as he hit SAVE and shut the laptop. He stood up, grabbed his car keys and the cold grilled cheese, and ushered me out the door.

As we crawled down the gravel road in Pop's Volvo, I

spotted Emmett up ahead of us, alone and walking toward town. "Stop for a second," I told Pop, and then I leaned out the passenger side window and called Emmett's name.

He spun around, startled, as if bracing for yet another collision. That first run in the woods had traumatized him, obviously, and he didn't even know about my involvement in his near-death.

"Hey," he said, his face relaxing when he realized it was me. He walked over to my side of the car.

"Where you headed?" I asked him.

He stuffed his hands in his pockets and looked behind him. "Just taking a walk," he said, his eyes back on me. *They're at it again over there*, they told me.

"Well, why don't you come with us instead? We're on our way to Harper's game at the soccer field."

"Oh, no, that's okay."

"Come on. It'll be fun." I glanced over at Pop, who was scratching his stubbly jaw like he did whenever he was trying to work out a scene in his head. No help there. "We're not from here, so Harper needs her own cheering section."

Emmett deliberated for another few seconds before opening the door and climbing into the backseat. The station wagon was always a mess, so he had to move aside a pile of papers and junk before he could sit down. "Cool," he said, picking up the object on top—one of the bookmarks Pop's publicist had made for his last book launch. "You're a K. B. Marks fan, too? The Core Earth series is awesome. Can't wait for Book Six to come out."

I had to turn away and press my fist to my mouth to keep from laughing. K. B. Marks was Pop's pen name, a combination of my first initial, his first initial, and Dad's first name. Not many people knew the man behind the name. His paperbacks had no photo at the back, so he wasn't often recognized.

"Me either," Pop said with a completely straight face. He loved it when he came across a fan who unwittingly discussed his own books with him. Usually, he didn't bother to set them straight.

If Emmett only knew that Book Six was currently under construction just a few cottages away from his.

The Erwin Eagles played their home games on the town's one and only soccer field, which was located behind the town's one and only high school. When we got there, we found Aunt Carrie seated on the rickety-looking bleachers along with about a dozen other spectators, most of whom were fanning themselves with books or magazines or whatever else was handy. On the field, the Eagles were alternating between warming up and eyeing the visiting team for potential weaknesses as they kicked the ball around.

Pop, Emmett, and I made our way up the bleachers to join her. After introductions had been made, Pop sat next to his sister while Emmett and I settled on the bench below them, the distance between us much greater than it had been on the log Saturday night. Shortly after we sat down, I spotted Harper, number fifty-eight. She looked tough and strong in her black Eagles jersey. From the looks of things, she was probably the youngest on the team. I hoped the Erwiners were treating her well.

"So you like to read sci-fi, do you?" I asked Emmett while we waited for the game to start.

"Yeah," he said, squinting against the glare of the sun. "It's another escape thing, I guess. Why? Do you?"

"Nah," I said, glancing back at my dad, who was deep in conversation with Aunt Carrie. "I find it kind of boring."

"You'd probably like the Core Earth series, though. It's anything but boring."

I placed my finger on my lips, feigning interest. "Really."

"I own all the books. You can borrow them if you want."

I held back another giggle and wondered how long I could keep up the charade. "No need . . . we have them all at home."

He nodded, oblivious, and then turned his attention toward the field as a whistle sounded. The game was about to begin.

Harper was playing midfield, which used to be my position back when I played. But unlike me, she never hogged the ball or tried to be a hero. Her passes were smooth and precise, almost always reaching their target. When she helped her team score a goal in the first half, I reached into my bag and pulled out the pom-poms I'd made out of old magazines and tape that morning. I could feel Emmett staring at me as I jumped up and waved them around, yelling "Go, Harper, go!" at the top of my lungs. Actually, everyone was staring at me, even some of the players.

"You really do like to stand out, don't you?" Emmett said after I sat down again. He touched the magazine pages I'd spent two hours cutting into thin strips and shook his head at me, his expression one part amused and two parts embarrassed. He'd obviously had no idea what he was getting into, appearing in public with me.

Pop and Aunt Carrie were so used to my nuttiness, they'd barely reacted to my cheerleading routine.

Shortly before halftime, I started yelling for a different reason . . . at the ref. "Is he blind?" I grumbled to myself when the ref ignored me. "Number sixteen was clearly offside."

"Do you play, too?" Emmett asked, sounding shocked that I knew my way around the game.

"I used to. Years ago."

"Wow, I never would've guessed. I mean, you're so . . ." He gestured to my light pink maxi dress, neatly curled hair, and glossy pink lipstick, struggling for an adjective that wouldn't offend me.

"Girly? Dainty? Out of shape?"

"The first two." He appraised me again with renewed interest. "Why did you stop? Playing, I mean."

I shrugged and looked away, the universal signal for *Not even worth discussing*. I didn't like to admit it, to myself especially, that I'd stopped playing because of some stupid, ignorant comments made by a couple of gossipy soccer moms who didn't even know me. I'd not only quit sports, but changed my entire image on top of it, all because I wanted people to stop assuming I was somehow maladjusted and in need of female guidance. And that I was as much of a sell-out as Sherry, who had altered everything real and raw and special about Goody's just to appeal to the general masses. No, I'd much rather Emmett get to know me as I really was—someone who'd been raised by two men but was just like any other girl. Only with a different type of family from most people.

By the end of the first half, the Eagles were ahead three goals and I was worn out from cheering. Harper and her teammates spent halftime downing water and strategizing, but I did manage to catch her eye once. She waved, her gaze flickering to Emmett next to me. She hadn't said very much about their private walk to her cottage on Saturday night, and I wondered if anything had happened between them. And if she would've told me if something had. Until this summer, she'd never had anything like that to tell.

"Hey," Emmett said beside me. "I'm actually getting a signal here."

I waved back at my cousin, who watched us over the top of her water bottle as the coach lectured, and then I looked over at Emmett. He was holding his cell phone, scrolling through some texts he'd missed since moving out to the boonies. When he started typing a text of his own, I turned away and pulled out my own phone, hoping for a message from Shay, a change of heart. Nothing. I sighed and glanced over at Emmett again, who was still texting away. *Maybe he has a girlfriend back home,* I thought. That would explain his apparent lack of interest in the girls of Millard Lake.

"What's your cell number?" Emmett asked me once he'd finished texting whoever it was he'd been texting.

I told him without even thinking about it first. A moment later, a text appeared on my phone.

Hi.

Smiling, I typed back. **Who's this?**

He typed for a few seconds, his thumb flying across the letters, and soon my phone dinged again.

I'm the guy who's sitting next to the loud crazy girl who thinks she's a cheerleader.

I snorted.

I'm the enthusiastic girl with the remarkable team spirit who's sitting next to the quiet dull guy who thinks he's at a golf game.

You think he's dull?

OK, not dull . . . just introverted.

Compared to the girl, everyone is.

I grunted indignantly and elbowed him in the ribs. He ducked away, laughing, and I could feel the huge smile on my face even as I realized what I'd just done could be considered flirting. *Don't touch. Don't smile. Don't charm.* What was wrong with me? I couldn't act this way any-more, especially not with Emmett. If Harper ever looked at me the way Shay had, if her familiar blue eyes ever burned with disappointment and betrayal from some-thing I'd done to her, it would destroy me.

Emmett, whether he knew it or not, would be my practice subject. If I could stop myself from flirting with someone so irresistibly cute, I'd be well on my way to re-formed.

Luckily, I was saved from further temptation by my fa-ther's hand on my shoulder. "Hey Noodle, you just missed Harper's amazing pass."

My phone chimed again.

Noodle?

Instead of answering, I gave Emmett another indiffer-ent shrug, turned off my phone, and shifted my full at-tention to the field and my cousin . . . where it belonged.

chapter 11

For the most part, Erwin was the kind of town you passed through without stopping, barely noteworthy enough to locate on a map. Only two things inspired visitors to actually go there on purpose—the lake and the town's annual summer carnival.

It wasn't some dinky little fair. Erwin went all out. Rides, games, cotton candy, go-carts, live music . . . it was always the most exciting thing to happen all summer. The carnival usually set up sometime in July and stuck around for about a week, long enough for Harper and me to overdose on sugar and win at least five stuffed animals apiece. We'd gone every year—first with our parents and then just the two of us—since we'd started spending summers at the lake. A few times, we'd gone with the McCurdy brothers, but that wouldn't be happening this year. Instead, we kidnapped Emmett.

Well, not literally. We didn't force him to come with us, but it may have happened against his will. Kind of. And it was Harper's idea, not mine, to drive up to his cottage on Thursday evening, the opening night of the carnival, and lure him into the backseat of her mother's Subaru.

"Maybe we should've called first," I said as we idled in his driveway, staring at the dark cottage. Luckily, all was quiet in there. Probably because both his parents' vehicles were missing. "It doesn't look like anyone's home."

"How are we supposed to call first? We don't have his number."

All of a sudden, I felt acutely aware of my cell phone tucked into my purse and still bearing Emmett's name, phone number, and every single text he'd sent me at the soccer game the other day. I should've told Harper about them, even shown them to her just to prove how innocent our banter had been, but for some reason I hadn't.

"Right," I said, swallowing around a lump of guilt. "Let's go up and knock on the door."

Harper gripped the steering wheel like I was about to drag her outside bodily. "No! This is embarrassing. Let's just go."

"Harper. He's probably in there wondering who's out here lurking in his driveway and if they're about to break in and murder him. The least we can do is let him know it's us."

"You go, then. I'll stay here. If he sees he's outnumbered, he might call the cops. Or start shooting."

"Good point." I got out of the car and smoothed the skirt of my dress. In the spirit of the occasion, tonight's look had been modeled after Rachel McAdams in the carnival scene of *The Notebook*, one of my favorite movies. My red dress was somewhat different from hers, more summery, but I'd gotten the hair exactly right— loose and held back on one side. All I needed was my own Ryan Gosling.

I banged on Emmett's door for a good three minutes, the reverberation bouncing off the trees. Finally, just as I half-turned to yell to Harper that he wasn't home, the door flew open and there he stood. Wearing nothing but shorts. Again. And dripping. Again. But the beads of moisture falling from the ends of his hair and running down his chest were made up of water, not sweat. I knew because he smelled strongly of soap, like he'd just been in the shower.

"Oh," he said, pushing the screen open. "Hey, Kat."

Speak, I ordered myself. I could hear the engine of my aunt Carrie's Subaru, purring impatiently behind me. I wondered if Harper was staring with her mouth hanging open like a dumbass, too. "Hi," I said, rearranging my lips into a smile. "We've come to take you to the carnival."

"The what?"

"The carnival." I shook my head, at a loss to explain. "Just, um . . . dry off and meet us out here when you're ready."

He gave me a weird look and then pulled back, letting the screen slam shut between us. He didn't close the heavy wood door, though, which I assumed meant he'd be back. It also meant I could see the way his shorts just barely clung to his hip bones as he walked away. Not that I was supposed to notice.

I got back into the car, hoping my face wasn't as flushed as it felt.

"Is he coming?" Harper asked, and then she raised her eyebrows at me. "And was he just, like, half-naked or was that my imagination?"

"He was in the shower," I said, trying in vain to deflect my own imagination.

Emmett emerged from his cottage five minutes later, fully dressed and mostly dry, and climbed into the backseat. "Where exactly are you taking me?" he asked warily, like we really were there to abduct him.

"You'll see," Harper said, backing out of the driveway and onto the road.

The sky was just beginning to get dark, which made the first glimpse of the lit-up Ferris wheel all the more thrilling. Harper and I grinned at each other as she turned into the large parking area next to the fair-grounds.

"I swear this wasn't here yesterday morning when my mom sent me to the store for ant traps," Emmett said, gazing at the colorful rides the same way most people over the age of fourteen did—like he was suddenly a lit-tle kid again.

"It's a traveling carnival," I explained as we parked and exited the car. "It just got here today."

The midway was packed. It seemed like everyone in town had shown up, families and kids and teenagers and old people and tourists. At one point, as we shouldered our way to the ticket booth, I tripped over some woman's foot and fell backwards into Emmett, who was behind me. He caught and then righted me, his hands cupping my elbows. I glanced back to thank him, trying not to think about how warm and solid his chest had felt against my back.

"Where to first?" Harper asked once we all had our tickets.

"The Tilt-a-Whirl!" I suggested. It was my favorite.

"No way," she said. "You know what spinny rides do to my stomach."

Emmett caught my eye. "I'll go with—"

"Kat?"

I felt a hand on my forearm and spun around to see Sawyer Bray standing there, grinning and looking much taller and cuter than he had the last time I'd seen him. "Oh my God," I said, reaching up to hug him.

He was a local boy I'd known for years. We'd sort of dated for a couple weeks near the end of last summer, but it was all very casual. When the end of August had rolled around, I went home, he'd stayed in Erwin, we'd both moved on with our lives, and that was the end of our lit-tle romance. I'd never felt anything for him beyond general fondness, so I wasn't exactly broken up about it. In fact, I'd forgotten all about him until I saw him.

"I thought I might see you here," Sawyer said, hugging me tight. He smelled like aftershave and beer. "You look great."

"You look *tall*. And where did these come from?" I squeezed his new, bulky bicep muscles and grinned up at him. He'd matured quite nicely over the winter. He'd always been suitably cute with his curly dark hair and deep-set brown eyes, but the filled-out body made him look much less boyish.

"Hey, Harper," he said, nodding courteously to her.

Harper, never one for fake friendliness, nodded back and mumbled a grudging hello. The two of them had never gotten along; she thought he was conceited and annoying, and he thought she was an uptight stick-in-the-mud. The subtle hostility between them had only escalated when Sawyer and I started spending time together. He'd kept trying to pawn her off on his friends in a not-so-subtle attempt to get rid of her so he could spend some time alone with me, which my cousin did not appreciate.

But it was a brand new summer—Operation *Best* Summer, no less—so maybe we could all start fresh.

"Do you girls want to go throw some darts at balloons?" Sawyer asked. "I bet I can win you that giant stuffed dog wearing the sunglasses."

"Oh, um . . ." I looked over at Emmett, who had backed up a couple paces and appeared to be studying with intense fascination the price list on the side of the ticket booth. "This is Emmett," I told Sawyer. "He's new to Millard Lake this summer."

"Hey," Sawyer said.

Emmett nodded at him much the same way Harper had—tersely and with a hint of suspicion.

Sensing a kinship, she moved a few inches closer to Emmett. "Why don't you guys go ahead?" She shot me a significant look, one that said *I want to be alone with Emmett for a while.*

Emmett was looking at me too, but his expression was closed off. Almost bored.

"Okay," I said and let Sawyer pull me into the crowd.

We threw darts for a while, never quite busting enough balloons to score the big prizes. Then we moved on to the ring toss, which was obviously fixed but fun nonetheless, even if I didn't win a goldfish. Next, we headed to the Tilt-a-Whirl and stood in line for twenty minutes, catching each other up on our lives. Last summer, Sawyer had just graduated from high school and was working at his father's gas station a few miles out of town. Apparently, he'd really liked it because he'd chosen to keep working there instead of moving on to something bigger and better, like college or a more lucrative job elsewhere. Some people, Sawyer claimed, were never meant to leave Erwin.

After getting sufficiently scrambled on the Tilt-a-Whirl, we moved on to the more relaxing Ferris wheel. Once we'd reached the top, I scanned the ground for Harper and Emmett but couldn't spot them anywhere. They were probably at the bumper cars, Harper's favorite. She was vicious in one of those things.

"I think you've gotten even more beautiful since last summer," Sawyer told me as the wheel began to revolve. My hair whipped across my face from the breeze and he reached up to brush it back, tucking it behind my ear. I promptly stopped caring about what Harper and Emmett were up to and focused on the goose bumps Sawyer's fingers had raised on my neck.

Back on solid ground again, we pushed our way through the mob to the concession area, where Sawyer bought a bag of fresh-popped popcorn for us to share. I felt dizzy . . . from the rides and the speed at which we'd reconnected. It was like fall, winter, and spring had never even happened.

"You want to get out of here?" he asked once we'd demolished the bag of popcorn.

I wiped my buttery fingers on a napkin and tossed it in a nearby trash can. "I can't just ditch my cousin and our friend."

"Right." He took my hand and looked at me with an intensity that made my stomach quiver. I knew exactly what he had in mind, and I couldn't really say I was opposed to the idea. That was why, I suppose, I let him lead me to a quieter, less populated spot near the equipment trailers. Next to a bundle of cords that I wasn't entirely sure wouldn't electrocute us if we stepped on them, he drew me toward him and pressed his lips to mine.

I looped my arms around his neck and thought about the last time I'd seen him, how he'd kissed me good-bye in my driveway when my dads weren't looking. He'd been kind of scrawny then, and just a few inches taller than my five-foot-five. Now he towered over me, his hands big and strong as they slid up the sides of my dress.

"Whoa," I mumbled as he backed me up against the side of a trailer and started nibbling on my neck. I wondered how many beers he'd had and if he was too drunk to care that we were in a public place. I may have loved attention, but I wasn't an exhibitionist. "Not here," I said, pushing him back.

"No one's watching," he said, and then advanced on me again, his lips on my neck, his hands roaming freely.

I jumped when his fingers closed around my left breast. Sawyer and I had spent a lot of time together last summer, and we'd kissed a lot, but he'd never, ever tried groping me. He'd always been the sweet, conservative type. Apparently, those qualities had vanished right along with his scrawny frame.

"I said *not here*," I snapped, shoving his hand away.

He just laughed. "What do you think I brought you over here for, Kat?"

Not this, I thought when he came at me again, all hands and hot breath and unrelenting strength. Noah never did anything like that to Allie in *The Notebook*. The worst he'd done was hang off the Ferris wheel until she agreed to go out with him, and she'd never once regretted saying yes.

When you're in trouble, scream, even if you're not sure. That was what my dads had taught me. But I couldn't muster the breath to speak, let alone scream, so I did the next best thing. I pushed him as hard as I could and then delivered a swift uppercut to his chin.

Sawyer reeled back, a loud snarl escaping through his clenched teeth. His hand came up to cradle his jaw and he glared at me like I'd punched him in the face for no reason at all. I just stood there, speechless, clenching and unclenching my fist. Even though I'd had three years of training in boxing and knew how to throw a punch, Sawyer's chin must have been made out of extra hard bone because my knuckles effing *hurt*.

"Jesus Christ, Kat," he roared at me. "What the hell is wrong with you?"

"What the hell is wrong with *you*? If I'd known what a jerk you turned into, I never would've gone anywhere with you."

He moved toward me then, fury in his eyes, and I figured he was either going to hit me back or attempt another grope. But I never found out which because just before he reached me, someone appeared in front of me and blocked his path. Someone with wavy brown hair who smelled like soap.

"Touch her and I'll bust the rest of your face," Emmett said calmly.

"Dude, I wasn't gonna lay a finger on her," Sawyer said, spitting a glob of blood on the grass. "I don't hit girls."

"No, you just try to force yourself on them," an infuriated voice chimed in on my right.

Harper.

I tore my eyes away from Emmett's back and glanced over at her. She stood right next to me with her arms crossed, glaring at Sawyer like he was dog crap under her shoe.

"You should probably leave now, Sawyer," she said, "before I decide to practice my soccer skills on your balls."

Sawyer moved his lower jaw back and forth, testing its mobility, then shot me a glare as he passed. "Nice catching up with you, Kat," he said before disappearing around the trailer.

"Likewise," I muttered, suddenly wishing I'd knocked out a few of his teeth. He was yet another familiar summer thing that had changed without my knowledge.

Harper lifted my right hand to inspect it for damage. "Are you okay?" she asked when I flinched.

"Yeah, I just need to ice it."

"We saw you punch him," she said with a small smile. "It was awesome."

Emmett nodded in agreement. "It didn't look like you needed any help defending yourself, but I had to step in, Kat. I thought he was about to hit you."

I noticed then how pale he was, his eyes wide and glittering with anger. "I'm okay," I told him, and his shoulders dropped a little, like some of the tension had been lifted.

★ ★ ★

Back at the lake, Harper dropped Emmett off first and then came inside my cottage with me.

Pop was sprawled out on the couch, watching the local news on our clunky old TV that only got three channels. At least he wasn't writing. "How was the carnival?" he asked, sitting up.

"Very exciting," Harper said.

Pop raised his eyebrows, waiting for more, so I said, "Remember Sawyer Bray?"

"The skinny kid you ran around with last summer?"

I proceeded to tell him an abbreviated, PG version of the altercation. Still, in spite of my careful editing, his face turned a furious red.

"That little shit," he said when I finished. "I should have him arrested right now."

"Pop, he didn't hurt me," I said, sitting beside him on the couch.

"*She* hurt *him*," Harper added proudly.

I showed him my right hand, which had started swelling, and his eyes lit up with approval. "Good girl," he said, hugging me. "But if he ever bothers you again, I *will* have him arrested."

I hugged him back, remembering the expression of shock mixed with pain on Sawyer's face when I'd hit him and the quiet-but-deadly tone in Emmett's voice when he threatened to finish him off. Pop had nothing to worry about.

chapter 12

Dad had much the same reaction as Pop when he saw my swollen knuckles, but he wasn't the type to sit back and wait for a better excuse to act, like Pop. He didn't have Sawyer arrested, but he did disappear for about forty-five minutes on Friday night, shortly after he arrived at the cottage and heard about what had happened. He claimed he was going to the store for milk, but he returned home empty-handed and slightly flushed. I wondered briefly if there was a bruise in the shape of Dad's fist hidden somewhere on Sawyer Bray's body.

Our first night at the carnival may have ended on a low note, but the rest had been a total success. While I was off with Sawyer, Harper had managed to make some decent progress with Emmett.

"He spent twenty dollars trying to win me a teddy bear in the target shooting game," she told me Thursday night during an impromptu sleepover in my room. "He didn't, but it was fun watching him try. And when I hurt my neck on the bumper cars, he kind of rubbed it for me for a minute. God, he's adorable."

Hearing my cousin gush about a guy was such a rare occurrence, I couldn't help but giggle at her exuberance. She and Emmett were both so shy, summer would probably be half over before they even got around to holding hands. But even if it never went beyond that, I was happy to see Harper so happy. My last thought before I drifted off to sleep was that I still needed to thank Emmett for being so nice to my cousin and for standing up for me. Maybe he wasn't as grouchy and antisocial as I'd originally thought.

I didn't run into him at all on Friday, so early on Saturday morning, while Harper was off at soccer practice, I headed to his cottage to thank him and invite him to go to the carnival with us again later. This time, I'd stick with them instead of going off with some guy I thought I knew but clearly didn't.

As I knocked on Emmett's door, I mentally prepared myself for another wet-and-shirtless sighting. Instead, a very petite blonde in a bathrobe answered my knock and I was saved from acting like a blushing moron.

"Hi," I said to the woman who was obviously Emmett's mother. They had the exact same eyes—big and cobalt blue, the irises rimmed with black. "I'm Kat Henley. I live in the little beige cottage up that way." I pointed to my left, but her eyes didn't stray from my face. "I was wondering if I could talk to Emmett."

She smiled at me, and her grin was just like Emmett's, too—sudden and transforming. "So you're Kat," she said, opening the screen door to get a better look at me. "My, my. You *are* pretty."

The way she said it, with the emphasis on the *are*, made me think she was confirming something she'd heard someone else say. *Emmett?* I wondered, feeling my cheeks go warm. So I was going to act like a blushing moron after all.

"Emmett's not here," she went on. "He was gone when I got up this morning. Sometimes he runs at the crack of dawn." She reached up to cover her mouth as she yawned. "You're welcome to come in and wait for him. He shouldn't be long. Do you like coffee?"

She seemed too nice and friendly to be the same woman I'd heard participating in a screaming match with her husband just two weeks before. "I do," I said, "but my dad doesn't like me to drink it. He thinks it'll stunt my growth or something."

She laughed and peered down at her small frame. "Maybe he's right."

We made small talk for another minute or so and then I turned to leave. "I'll come back later," I told her. "It was nice to meet you, Mrs. Reese."

"Holly," she said, smiling again.

I nodded, even though it would be a while before I ever called her that. I'd been raised to address adults as Mr. or Mrs. Or Dr., in the case of Nate's father.

Speaking of Nate, I hadn't seen him all week except at a distance while sitting on my dock. I didn't *want* to see him, so I cut through the woods instead of taking the road so I wouldn't have to pass by his cottage. Besides, maybe I'd run into Emmett (figuratively this time) on my way through.

He was gone when I got up this morning, his mom had said. I wondered why he left the cottage so early when his parents were quiet and asleep, when running was what he did to escape their fighting, to clear his mind. Unless he'd left when they'd *started* fighting and stayed away all night, it didn't make much sense.

An idea hit me then. A memory. I stopped in my tracks and spun around, trying to get my bearings. When I did, I doubled back and headed in the opposite direction.

It took me a few minutes to remember exactly where I'd seen that small blue tent last weekend during my morning ATV ride. I knew it was near the brook, but I wasn't sure how far down. Maybe, I thought, it wasn't even there anymore.

But it was. Following my own tire tracks, I spotted a flash of blue through the trees after about twenty minutes of searching. I approached the tent cautiously and loudly, making sure its occupant heard me coming. Even if it was just Emmett in there as I suspected and not some machete-wielding weirdo, sneaking up on him seemed like a really bad idea.

I stepped out of the trees into the clearing, then moved toward the brook until there was a good ten feet between me and the tent. If it turned out to be a serial killer in there after all, I needed space to run. "Emmett?" I called softly.

There was a rustling sound inside the tent, and a few seconds later the entrance flapped open and Emmett's head appeared. "Kat?" he said, seeing me. "Jesus, I thought you were a bear."

I walked toward him, relieved that my hunch had proved correct. "Roar?" I said, grinning.

"What are you doing here?" He unzipped the opening all the way and climbed out. Luckily, he was fully dressed in shorts and a T-shirt. "And how did you know I was here?"

"Wild guess?" I said. Telling him I'd seen the tent on my ride last week and then put two-and-two together would mean admitting that I rode an ATV. And admitting that would surely lead to his figuring out exactly who the psycho was who'd almost run him down in the woods a couple weeks ago.

"Did you follow me here or what?" he asked warily.

"No, Emmett, I'm not a stalker. I went to your cottage first and your mom—she's really nice, by the way—told me you were gone when she woke up. Then I remembered seeing this tent here a few days ago and thought it might be yours." I peeked into the open tent and saw a sleeping bag, pillows, a blanket, a small cooler, a flashlight, and a large stack of books. From the looks of things, he spent quite a bit of time there. "Do you sleep here every night?" I asked.

"No, not every night. Only when it's . . . noisy."

I nodded in understanding, then looked around his little oasis. Halfway between the tent and the brook, at a safe distance from the overhanging trees, stood the charred remnants of a campfire. I pictured him sitting out here at night, the soft gurgling of the brook and the mesmerizing flames of the fire lulling him into a state of utter peace. No yelling, no bickering, no demands. No wonder he preferred this tiny space in the wilderness over being stuck in a cottage with his parents.

"Emmett, I wanted to—"

"Wait a sec." He ducked back into the tent and brought out the blanket, which he doubled up and spread out on the ground. "You can sit down, if you want. Sorry, I've never had company here before. Unless you count the squirrel who keeps trying to steal my snacks."

I smiled as I lowered myself to kneel on the blanket. It was soft and smelled like wood smoke. Emmett sat a couple feet away from me, facing the brook with his arms dangling off his raised knees.

"As I was saying," I said. "I wanted to thank you for the other night. At the carnival."

He glanced at me. "I didn't really do anything."

"Yes, you did. You hung out with Harper and then you defended me from Sawyer."

"You don't need to thank me for hanging out with Harper," he said, pitching a stone into the brook. "We had a lot of fun."

"She really likes you," I said without thinking.

"I know. Well, I suspected, anyway."

"Do you like her too? I mean, Harper's great, and I'm not just saying that because she's my cousin."

"She is great, and I do like her." Agitated, he shoved his fingers through his tousled morning hair. "Just not . . . that way."

My heart plummeted. How could I tell Harper this? And why couldn't I just come right out and ask him if he preferred boys?

"And as for defending you or whatever," he continued, turning toward me. "I just did what any guy would've done."

I dropped down on my butt and folded my legs criss-cross style. "Not any guy," I said. A lot of guys wouldn't have gotten in the way of someone who was bigger and possibly stronger than they were. He'd done it without even thinking about it, like it was second nature. Like it was his job.

I bit my lip, gathering the courage to ask what I'd been wondering ever since I saw the unyielding resolve in his stance that night, like he gladly would've taken the brunt of whatever Sawyer had in store for me. And how strongly he'd felt about trying to intervene. "I got the feeling you've done that before," I said carefully. "Shielded someone from possibly getting hit."

He picked up a small stick and started scraping it across the ground like he'd done at the last bonfire, the same night he told me about his parents. "Once," he replied. "But I wasn't big enough."

"How old were you?"

He threw the stick down and looked at me. The vulnerability in his face confirmed what I'd suspected: his parents' fights hadn't always been just verbal. "I was ten."

My mind flashed on an image of his tiny, delicate-looking mother. She was like a porcelain doll, easily breakable. "What happened?"

He faced forward again, his jaw twitching. "We had this neighbor, a single guy. Really friendly. My dad was paranoid and didn't like it when my mom talked to him. One day he came home and this guy was in our back yard, helping my mom move a heavy stone planter. That's all it was," he added, turning to me again, his gaze steady. "I was there."

I nodded and gestured for him to continue.

"Anyway . . . my dad waited until she came inside, and then he flipped. My brother was thirteen then and sometimes he was able to distract him. Snap him out of it. Dad never hit us. Only her." Emmett picked up the stick again, stabbing it into the earth. "But Wes wasn't around that day, so it was just me. I stepped between them like he always did, but it wasn't enough. My dad got to her anyway."

Picturing this scene made me shudder. "Why does she stay with him?"

"I don't know. She loves him, she says. Believes he can change." He tossed the stick in the water. "And he *has* changed, I guess. He hasn't hit her in years . . . not since my brother outgrew him and became an effective deterrent. Now that he's gone, it's up to me. My dad knows that if he ever hit her again, I'd kill him."

I studied Emmett for a moment, my gaze tracing the long line of his shoulders, the firm, taut muscles in his arms and legs. He may not have been as burly and intimidating as Sawyer, or Dad, or even his own father, but he could definitely hold his own. "You're big enough now," I said softly.

The corners of his mouth lifted into a small, tight-lipped smile and he shook his head. "What is it about you that makes me want to spill my guts? I mean, I practically just met you, and you already know more about me than some of my closest friends."

"I've been told I'm that kind of person. The one you want to tell your secrets to." I shrugged and smiled back at him, grateful to move on to lighter conversation. "And besides, summer friends are different from regular friends. Have you ever gone to sleep-away camp? It's like that. You're around each other all day, eat together, see each other in swimsuits . . . Familiarity bonds you faster. No secrets."

"No secrets, huh?" he said slowly. "Okay, then. You tell one to me. For instance, where did you learn to punch like that?"

I clenched my still-sore hand. "My dads made me take boxing lessons when I was twelve so I could learn how to defend myself. Turned out I really liked it, so I stuck it out for three years."

"So you can play soccer, box, and make pompoms out of a magazine. What other talents are you hiding?"

No secrets, was it? All right then, he asked for it. I hunched my shoulders and said, "I can ride an ATV."

He stared right into my eyes, and I could almost see the pieces clicking into place in his head.

"No," he said.

"Yes."

"You. On an ATV. Nope, I don't believe you."

"Believe it," I told him. "It's true. I usually ride early in the morning . . . in the woods . . ."

He shook his head again, quickly, like he was trying to dislodge the shocking revelation from his brain. "I'm going to pretend you didn't just tell me that."

"Okay," I said. "But it's still true. No secrets, remember?"

"Some secrets are never meant to be revealed."

The sun began poking through the trees then, and I took it as my cue to stand up. Emmett stood up too, and I helped him shake out the blanket and then fold it, each of us taking two corners.

"So, tonight," I said when our corners met up. "We're going to the carnival again. Do you want to come with us?"

He looked down at me. Our bodies were only inches apart, and I could smell the wood smoke on his shirt. "It depends," he said, raising his eyebrows.

"On?"

"Who'll be there."

I rolled my eyes. "I'm not going anywhere near Sawyer. Tonight or ever again."

"Good." He took the blanket from me and tossed it in the tent. "That means I won't have to either."

chapter 13

Our second visit to the carnival went by without a single Sawyer sighting. We did, however, bump into Nate McCurdy and his twin brothers at the target shooting booth. I think I'd rather have seen Sawyer.

"Well, well," Nate said when he turned away from his fake rifle and saw the three of us waiting in line behind him. "Where have you guys been hiding all week?"

"Wherever you're not," I said. I still hadn't forgiven him for how he'd treated my cousin.

"Cold." He watched Harper as she stepped up to the spot he'd just vacated and wrapped her fingers around the rifle. Then she wiggled it back and forth like she was checking to see if it spun far enough on its base to point at Nate. Emptying a round of BB pellets into his forehead *did* sound satisfying.

Zoe and Gabriella appeared then, each of them carrying bright blue Sno-Cones. Zoe smirked first at Harper and then at my dress—a short, sleeveless, floral-print A-line. She then proceeded to drape herself over Nate, while Gabriella's eyes zeroed in on Emmett.

Fueled by her distaste for the audience behind her, Harper pretty much annihilated the little star target, winning herself a stuffed banana (wearing sunglasses, of course). She did even better than the twins, which was impressive because Nate and his brothers were all experienced deer hunters. Emmett seemed especially surprised by Harper's excellent aim, seeing as how he'd tried and failed to win her a prize at that very game two nights ago.

"Let's go on the Orbiter," Zoe said when the twins finally got tired of shooting things.

"Do you want to come with us, Emmett?" Gabriella asked, tilting her head at him as she nibbled on her Sno-Cone. Classic flirt maneuver. I knew one when I saw it.

Emmett didn't move an inch from his position between Harper and me. "No, thanks."

A tense silence followed, punctured only by screams and laughter and the barkers' amplified voices around us. Then Nate looked at me, his smarmy grin slithering into place. "One of your gay dads invited us to your barbecue tomorrow," he said, wrapping his arm around Zoe's waist. "But I don't think I'm gonna go. Watching two dudes touch each other makes me want to hurl."

God, he was such an ignorant jackass. Still, over the years I'd learned to ignore comments like that. Growing up, there was always at least one kid in my class whose parents wouldn't allow them at my house because they didn't want their impressionable child exposed to my dads' "lifestyle." As if they were going to start randomly making out in the living room or something.

"Are you for real?" Emmett said, looking directly at Nate. "Why do you have to be such an asshole?"

Nate's smile slipped and he stared back at Emmett, his face reddening. "What's it to you, dude? So you're here like two weeks and suddenly you have me all figured out, huh?"

"You're not exactly complex."

I glanced at Harper and saw that she was biting her lip in an attempt not to laugh. I did the same, but a snort slipped out by accident. Nate's strange need to boast about his straightness at the expense of my dads had obviously rubbed Emmett the wrong way. Calling him out in public was usually an effective way to shut him up, and I was surprised Emmett had caught on so quickly. Then again, those quiet observer types seemed to pick up on a lot of things others didn't.

"What, did I hit too close to home or something?" Nate said, trying to laugh off Emmett's insult. "Is this your way of telling me you have a crush on me? Sorry, man, I'm not into dicks."

"Like I'd ever have a crush on you," Emmett said, totally straight-faced. "My standards are much higher than that."

Harper's eyes met mine and we broke up laughing. Fresh out of comebacks, Nate glared at each of us in turn, then grabbed Zoe's hand and started pulling her away. Gabriella and the twins followed, all looking slightly confused. Harper and I started laughing even harder, and we didn't stop until several minutes after they were gone.

"You," Harper said, still giggling as she elbowed Emmett's ribs, "are badass."

He shrugged, modestly pleased with himself. "I guess he definitely won't be at your barbecue now," he told me.

"Good," I said as we left the games area. "You'll come though, won't you? It's at four o'clock tomorrow. Bring your mom."

"What about his dad?" Harper asked.

Emmett and I exchanged a quick look, the memory of the morning's secrets passing between us. Harper didn't know much about Emmett aside from he was cute and

ran cross-country, and it wasn't my place to reveal anything more.

"He went back home for a few days," Emmett explained. "For work."

"Oh. Too bad. Kat's dads' barbecues are epic."

"What's the occasion?"

I stepped over a crushed corn dog. "No occasion, really. More like a kick-off party. My dad—the one you
haven't met yet—is on vacation from work this week and
doesn't have to commute back to the city tomorrow."

"What does he do?" Emmett asked. "For work, I
mean."

"He's vice president of an IT company, which means
he works nonstop. So his vacations are sort of like cele-
bratory events."

The Tilt-a-Whirl came into view, its lights twinkling
beckoningly. I gave Harper my puppy-dog eyes.

"Not a chance," she said. When I added a pout, she
said, "Remember the year I puked in the trash can in
front of those local boys? They took *pictures*, Kat. I'm still
traumatized." She nodded toward Emmett. "Maybe Emmett will go on with you. He doesn't have an aversion to
spinny rides."

I transferred my puppy-dog eyes to Emmett.

He smiled and said, "Come on, then."

While we waited in line, Harper took off in search of
a vacant Porta-Potty. As usual, being around Emmett
without her made me feel slightly guilty, like I shouldn't
enjoy spending time alone with him as much as I did.

"Thanks for what you did back there," I said after a
few moments of uncomfortable silence. "With Nate."

"Oh." Emmett rocked back on his heels. "I couldn't
resist. What he said was out of line."

"He's like that. I can usually ignore him, but I'm way
more used to his douchiness than you are." I silently ap-

praised him for a moment. "You know, I'm glad my hunch about you turned out to be right."

"And what hunch is that?"

I smiled with all my teeth. "You've never struck me as someone who has a problem with gay marriage."

"No," he said, grinning back at me. "I only have a problem with my parents' marriage."

When we reached the head of the line, we handed our tickets to the ride operator and I made a beeline for the nearest car. I had my seat belt all buckled before Emmett even climbed in. "It was nice seeing Nate so flustered," I said, continuing our conversation. "I wish there was some way we could get back at him for all the crap he's pulled so far this summer."

"Well," Emmett said as he fastened his safety belt, "when my brother and I were little, there was this neighborhood kid who liked to torture us. So one day we . . . nah, never mind. Too risky."

"What?" I hopped around in my seat like an overexcited toddler. I may have been a little hyper from the giant blob of cotton candy I'd consumed earlier. "Tell me, tell me."

He laughed and placed his hand on my leg to keep me still. It worked, but only because his fingers felt distractingly warm against my bare skin. As if he could read my thoughts, he quickly removed his hand. "A prank," he said, clearing his throat. "We played a prank on him. Something we saw on TV."

The ride jerked into motion and I had to brace myself from sliding against him. "What kind of prank?"

When he told me, I laughed so hard I had to hold onto the safety bar to keep from falling out. Emmett joined in, and his laugh was the last thing I heard before we started spinning.

★　★　★

Like Harper had said, my dads' barbecue parties were epic. They held at least three of them during the summer, inviting all the neighbors to join us. Sometimes everyone showed up, and other times, only a few made it over.

This time, however, *no one* bothered to come.

By four o'clock, it was still just me, Harper, our three parents, and way too much food. My dads tried to pretend they didn't care, that we'd have just as much fun on our own, but I think we all felt disappointed about the nonexistent turnout.

At four-fifteen, the festive mood picked up when our first and only guests appeared. Emmett brought his mom, just as I'd suggested. Mrs. Reese looked young and adorable in a filmy white sundress with her blond hair hanging in a braid down her back, and both my dads were immediately besotted.

"It's so nice to meet you all," she said, handing Pop the bottle of wine she'd brought over. "I was beginning to wonder if anyone around here was actually friendly."

"Well, the locals aren't, usually," Dad said, shaking her hand. "But we are."

"I can see that," she said, her cheeks coloring as she peered up at Dad. His effect on women was something Aunt Carrie razzed him about regularly. My dad was the very essence of *debonair*. "I can also see where Kat gets her beautiful green eyes."

Dad draped his arm around my shoulders and pulled me close. "You've met my girl?"

Mrs. Reese nodded and smiled at me. Again, I wondered how someone so nice could be embroiled in such a volatile marriage.

Harper, who'd been hanging back with Emmett, tugged him forward into our group. "Uncle Mark, this is Emmett." She beamed at him like she'd invented him herself.

"Nice to meet you, Emmett," Dad said as they shook hands. "What do you think of Millard Lake so far?"

"I really like it," Emmett said, glancing at me.

I could feel Harper's gaze on me as well, quietly assessing.

"When did you meet Emmett's mom?" she whispered to me after all the introductions had been made and our parents were sitting outside on the deck, drinking margaritas and getting along famously.

"Yesterday morning, when I went over to ask him if he wanted to go to the carnival with us again." It was the truth, but I still felt weird about skipping the part where I'd sought out Emmett in the woods afterwards. Harper and I had always shared everything, so keeping secrets from her—even someone else's secrets—made me very uncomfortable. Apparently, even something as solid and dependable as our relationship wasn't immune to change this summer.

When it was time to eat, my dads sent Harper and me inside to gather plates and check on the status of the ice trays Dad had filled and thrown in the freezer earlier. Emmett followed us, his gaze moving over the interior of our cottage as if he was comparing it to his own. I knew for a fact that the Cantings' cottage did not have gross fuchsia carpeting and ugly wall paneling. The Cantings, even as old as they were, had updated the place to a respectable level.

"Wow," Emmett said as he took in Pop's vast collection of kitchen appliances, all crammed together on the small counters. "Is your other dad a chef?"

"No, he's a writer," I said, exchanging an amused glance with Harper. That was something I *had* told her about Emmett, that he was a fan of my dad's books but had no idea he'd already met the author. That particular secret was too much fun not to drag out for a while.

"What does he write?"

I opened the freezer and poked a finger into the ice trays. Solid. "Oh . . . fiction," I said vaguely. I saw Harper's smile out of the corner of my eye.

"Like short stories or novels or what?"

"Novels . . ." Harper said with equal ambiguity. "He's really good. Maybe he'll let you read some of his stuff sometime."

Thankfully my head was still stuck in the freezer, because I didn't have a good poker face like my cousin.

"Harper, sweetie," Aunt Carrie called from the deck. "Run over to our cottage and see if we have any sour cream. Your uncles forgot to buy some."

"Because you're the only one who likes it," I heard Pop say.

Harper dropped the napkins she was holding and sighed. "Be right back," she said on her way out the back door.

Stack of ice trays in hand, I shut the fridge door with my hip and then jumped when I discovered Emmett standing right beside me. "So that thing we talked about last night," he said quietly. "The prank?"

"Yeah?" I was completely distracted by the ice cold trays in my arms and the clean sweat-and-sunscreen scent of him.

"I picked up the supplies this morning." When he grinned, I was pretty sure one of my ice cubes actually melted. "When do you want to do it?"

The back of my neck grew warm and I stepped away from him, setting the trays on the counter next to the fridge. "Um, tomorrow night? Nate's parents are leaving in the morning for some sort of conference and won't be back until Tuesday. That's what his dad told mine when he called to invite them to the barbecue."

"Is Harper in?"

I started dumping the ice into a giant bowl. "Nah," I said over the noise. "She's kind of the strict rule-following type. She'd be paranoid the whole time about getting caught." In truth, I hadn't even mentioned the prank idea to her. For one, breaking rules really did make her nervous and she'd probably freak out in the middle of it and get us all arrested for trespassing. Also, one of the reasons Emmett and I had decided to exact revenge on Nate in the first place was because he'd been such a jerk to her. If we ever got caught, she'd just feel responsible, like her honor wasn't worth defending and getting into trouble over. So it was better not to involve her at all.

"Tomorrow night, then," Emmett said, holding out his hand so we could shake on it.

I wiped my wet fingers on my shorts and then wrapped them around his. As we shook, I tried to ignore the prickle of heat creeping up my arm.

Later, after our guests had all gone home, my dads and I tackled the mess in the kitchen. Dad wrapped the leftovers while Pop and I worked our way through a tall stack of dirty dishes, each of us tired but content. The first barbecue of the summer had been a success.

"That Holly is a sweetheart," Dad said as he fought with the plastic wrap. "And Emmett seems like a good kid."

Pop handed me a dripping glass to dry. "Does Harper still have a crush on him?"

"Yeah," I said, rubbing my dish towel over the glass until it shone. "But he's not into her that way. At all. Actually, I think he might be gay."

Pop raised his eyebrows, considering this, while Dad made a scoffing sound behind us. I turned to look at him.

"That boy isn't gay, Katrina," he said, tossing the mangled plastic wrap on the counter. "I think that much is obvious after tonight."

"Why is it obvious?"

He reached over to ruffle my hair. "Because he could barely take his eyes off *you*."

chapter 14

"Come on, ladies! Hustle, hustle!"

I winced for what was probably the tenth time since the Erwin Eagles took the field. The bald, heavy guy sitting in front of us on the bleachers not only reeked of armpit, but he was also deafeningly loud. Even more so than me, and that was saying a lot.

"Wonder who he's here for," Aunt Carrie mumbled beside me.

"Whoever it is, I'm sure she can hear him clear as day," I whispered back.

"So can most of China," Dad said on the other side of me.

I sniffed and went back to watching the game. Dad and I were the only ones really paying attention; Aunt Carrie kept yawning and fiddling with her car keys, and Pop had spent the last twenty minutes stroking his chin as he stared off into space. He'd reached a pivotal scene in Book Six that afternoon and even Dad couldn't pry him off the laptop. He would've gladly kept writing into the evening if I hadn't played the father-daughter-bonding guilt card again. At least he was outside, near people. Even if some of those people had a staring problem.

I wished I'd remembered to bring my homemade pompoms. Not only was it a fun way to support Harper, but the spectacle of a summer person cheering for the home team would distract the locals from whispering about my dads. Erwin was a small town, and word had gotten around fast over the past few summers. Same-sex couples were somewhat of a novelty around there. Some people didn't care, but others couldn't seem to get over the shock of it. Sometimes I felt like I was in Oakfield all over again, surrounded by gossipy soccer moms.

"Pass it to thirty-three. She's open!" shouted the man in front of us, pounding his palms together for emphasis. The bleachers shook with his movements. "Christ, these girls aren't playing for shit tonight," he said at a lower volume to himself.

Unable to help myself, I cupped my hands around my mouth and yelled, "Great job, Eagles!"

Aunt Carrie buried her face in her hands while Dad laughed. The man in front of us turned to shoot me a look, his gaze landing instead on my dads, sitting side-by-side next to me with their hands just barely touching. Then he turned back around, muttering, "What is this, a frigging gay pride parade?"

Oh no, you didn't, I thought. When I bent forward to say something rude back to him, both Dad and Aunt Carrie shook their heads, stopping me. I leaned back, sighing, just as the halftime whistle sounded. The bald jerk got up and clomped down the bleachers to the field, probably on his way to berate the team up close and personal.

"Let it go, baby," Dad said, patting my knee. "Not worth it."

Pop surfaced from his haze long enough to agree with him. "Rise above," he said, raising a fist.

"I know, I know." And I did know, but knowing didn't help ease my guilt. Instead of drawing attention away from them, like I usually managed to do, I'd drawn it *to* them. Unintentionally, but still. Ever since I was little, I'd felt a responsibility to shield them from that kind of thing. It wasn't my job, I knew, and they'd been dealing with hate and intolerance long before I came along, but I still blamed myself when I failed to stop it from happening. They may have gotten used to the comments, but I never would.

To distract myself from Baldie, who'd wisely switched seats when he was through harassing the ref, I dug out my cell phone and opened my messages. Right away, my gaze zeroed in on last week's texts with Emmett, preserved for all eternity in my phone. Or maybe not. My thumb hovered over the EDIT button as I debated whether or not to delete them for good. I wouldn't have even bothered, but Dad's words from Sunday night still weighed on me. In fact, I felt so uneasy about the idea of Emmett possibly liking me, I didn't even consider inviting him to the game. I even thought about canceling our little caper later on, but my desire to teach Nate a lesson overrode any worries I may have had about potential awkwardness between Emmett and me.

Besides, maybe Dad had it all wrong. I hadn't noticed Emmett watching me with any particular interest. Then again, maybe the reason I hadn't noticed was because I always made a conscious effort not to watch *him*. Especially with Harper around.

God, I thought as I hit the BACK button, leaving the texts alone, *I'm a horrible daughter and a horrible cousin. And friend*, I added, thinking about Shay, who still hadn't replied to the half a dozen emails I'd sent her since the day she supposedly blocked my texts. Obviously, one thoughtless mistake on my part had been enough to ruin our friendship beyond repair.

Sometimes I wished I could be more like Harper and Emmett and even Pop. They held back, observed quietly, considered each possible consequence before proceeding. Me, I tended to rush right in, vocal and impulsive, focusing only on what was right in front of me.

Despite the fact that I prided myself in being a rebel, I'd never actually sneaked out of the house before. For one, it wasn't exactly easy to sneak out of a fourth-floor condo, and two, Pop was often awake at odd hours, writing. However, I was in a cottage with many viable exits, and both my dads were sound asleep by midnight.

At twelve-fifteen, I emerged from my room, tiptoed across the kitchen, and slipped silently out the sliding glass door to the deck. It was that simple. When I reached the yard, I paused and pulled on my shoes before continuing on to the road. I didn't turn on my flashlight until I was entirely out of view of the cottage.

Emmett was in the exact place we'd agreed upon— next to the big spruce tree with the knot on its trunk that looked like a creepy old man face. Harper and I called him Walter. The tree was a great meeting place as it was near the road and about halfway between her cottage and mine. Currently, Walter's weathered face was propping up Emmett.

"Kat?" he said, squinting against my flashlight's glow.

"No, I'm a bear. Roar."

"A bear with an extremely bright flashlight?" I heard a clicking noise and then his flashlight came on, blinding me. He lowered the beam from my face and aimed it on my body instead. "What on earth are you . . . oh."

I looked down at myself. "What? You said to wear black."

He clearly wasn't aware that when it came to fashion, I rarely skimped. Black wasn't a shade I wore often, but I had managed to rustle up some black leggings and a form-fitting black cami I usually only wore under sheer tops. Black flats and a sleek ponytail completed the undercover look I'd been going for. And red lipstick, of course, because it just seemed fitting.

"Yeah," he said, his flashlight still trained below my neck. "I did say that."

Good thing it was so dark because I was pretty sure we were both blushing.

I moved out of the light and started walking down the road. Emmett fell into step beside me. He was dressed in black too, and all I could make out were his teeth when he asked, "Sure you want to do this?"

"Yes." Our flashlight beams danced together on the gravel ahead of us. "Did you bring all of them?"

He jiggled the backpack on his shoulders, producing a muffled clanging sound. "Pretty much cleaned out the Dollar Store in town. The only color I couldn't find was purple."

"That's okay. We'll just have to do without it."

We turned off our flashlights before skulking up Nate's driveway toward his cottage, which wasn't as dark as I'd hoped. The porch light glowed, and muted blue light shimmered out from the living room window, indicating that the TV was on.

Emmett examined the lawn ahead of us, which was plenty big enough for what we had planned. "Do you think he's still awake?" he asked as we crept closer.

"He's home alone with his brothers," I said. "If I had to guess, I'd say they drank beer all night and then passed out watching a movie."

"I hope so."

The porch light flicked off and I ducked, yanking Emmett down with me. We crawled across the grass to the side of the cottage, out of view of the windows. My heart raced, and I felt torn between laughing hysterically and hightailing it the hell out of there.

"Do you think he saw us?" I whispered, huddling against the siding. I wasn't sure, but I thought we might have been crushing his mom's herb garden.

"I don't think so," Emmett whispered back.

We were panting from adrenaline and exertion and his breath smelled minty, like he'd just brushed before he left his cottage. I'd brushed too, but I still wondered if I smelled garlicky from the homemade salsa Pop had made earlier in his food processor.

"Should we wait a few minutes?"

I listened hard but couldn't hear anything besides crickets and the occasional rustling sound from the woods. "Yeah, but just a few. This is going to take a while to do."

We stayed put for about five minutes, crouched low with our backs pressed against the side of the house. All seemed quiet at the McCurdy residence.

"Ready?" Emmett asked. When I nodded, he un-hitched his backpack from his shoulders and unzipped it. I turned on my flashlight, aiming it at the opening. He reached inside the bag and pulled out dozens of transparent packages, each one containing forty-eight plastic forks. He'd done good.

It had been Emmett's idea to "fork" Nate's yard, which involved simply sticking a bunch of plastic forks, tine end up, into his lawn during the night. This was a common prank, apparently, one he and his brother had seen on TV when they were little and decided to recreate on their neighborhood bully's front lawn. But for me, *common* was synonymous with *boring*, so I'd put my own spin on it. Hence the multi-colored forks I'd asked Emmett to buy. This "forking" was going to have some meaning.

Two hours later, we were finally finished and it looked even better than I'd envisioned in my head. A large patch of Nate's lawn was now home to a fork portrait *(forkrait?)*

that would surely give me away as the culprit, but it was worth it.

"Nice," Emmett said as he took a picture with his phone.

I did the same, giggling uncontrollably at the image of Nate walking outside in the morning and finding *this* in his yard, visible to anyone who happened to drive by. It was the perfect revenge.

Saturday night at the carnival, after the Tilt-a-Whirl, when I'd asked Emmett to buy not regular white forks, but red, orange, yellow, green, blue, and purple ones instead, he'd immediately caught on to what I had in mind. A rainbow, at least four feet wide and blatantly unmistakable. The symbol of gay pride and diversity—*that* was what I wanted emblazoned on Nate McCurdy's lawn. I probably would've been content with randomly-placed forks had he not made that crack about my dads making him want to puke. And the incident at the soccer game earlier had only fueled me more.

Nate, and people like him, could do with a little dose of color in their lives.

Emmett and I took off for the road, tired and grass-stained and high on success. I so wished we could be there in the morning when Nate saw our creation, but our imaginations would have to do.

"I can't believe we pulled that off," Emmett said as we headed back to my cottage.

I grinned and raised my hand for a high-five, but he didn't slap it like he was supposed to. Instead, he touched his palm to mine and held on.

"Emmett," I said softly when our fingers entwined. This was bad. Really, really bad. In fact, holding hands on a dark road on a warm night when our blood still fizzed in our veins was possibly the worst idea in existence.

"What?"

I stopped walking and pulled my hand from his. He stood in front of me, mere inches away, his flashlight pointing toward the trees behind me.

"Harper really likes you," I said in a choked voice. Why did he have to smell so damn good, like soap and toothpaste and shaving cream and something else, something uniquely him?

"Do *you* like me, Kat?" he asked in a silky tone I'd never heard him use before. One that made me shiver in response.

Yes, yes, yes, everything in me screamed. But my mouth formed the words, "It doesn't matter if I do or not. Harper's my cousin."

"Yeah, I get it," he said, sounding a little sad. Resigned. "Family is important, right?"

"Very important. To me. So we can't . . . be like that. But you and Harper, you guys have so much in common. If you'd just try—"

He started walking again, cutting me off. I stood there for a moment and then hurried to catch up with him.

"Harper's nice," he said once I was by his side again. "But I can't force myself to like her as more than a friend." He looked over at me. "Sometimes people can't help who they're attracted to. I thought we both believed that."

An image of our beautiful fork rainbow popped into my head. No, we couldn't help who we were drawn to. But in our case we *could* deny it, if we had a good enough reason to. And we did. Family loyalty was the best reason of all.

chapter 15

A stream of humid air moved in on us overnight, and the next day turned out to be the hottest one yet. Harper and I spent most of the afternoon up to our necks in the lake, trying to keep cool. But after the almost-constant flow of warm weather we'd been having, the water temperature wasn't any more refreshing than the air.

"We should've tried to get summer jobs," Harper said as we floated on our backs a few yards out from my dock.

"Jobs? Here?" I turned my head to look at her. She'd been acting weird all day. Subdued.

"Yeah. At the ice cream shop or something."

I let my body sink until my feet touched rocks. "Harper, if a summer person took a job away from a local, there would be riots in the streets."

"I guess you're right." She twisted to the side and stood up straight. "I was just thinking about next year and college. All my friends back home are working right now, saving money. And here I am, relaxing at the lake like a lazy slob."

"Like they wouldn't be lazy slobs at the lake if they had the opportunity?" I said, splashing her. "It's your last summer here, like, forever. You can work next year."

"I know." She brushed some water drops off her face. "It's just I think I've outgrown this place."

I felt a twinge of hurt. Outgrown it? But Millard Lake was *ours*, the one place where time stood still, where we could reconnect and act like kids again. Spending the summer with her was something I looked forward to all year, this year more than ever. What happened to Operation Best Summer? Had it died along with the old Goody's and Nate's last shred of decency?

Harper saw the hurt in my features. "I didn't mean I've outgrown *you*, Kat. Just the lake." She sighed and shook her head. "I don't know. Maybe I just feel that way because of what happened with Nate and Emmett. Being here doesn't feel as fun and carefree as I remember, that's all."

"Wait, what happened with Emmett?" Just saying his name caused a rush of warmth to spread out from my stomach.

She snorted. "Nothing. That's the problem. He'll never see me as more than a friend."

"You don't know that for sure, Harper."

"Yes, I do," she said, skimming her fingers along the water's surface. "I tried flirting with him after our run this morning and nothing. Zilch. Either I'm really bad at it or he's just not interested."

"Your run?" Perhaps some lake water had seeped into my brain. Her words weren't making much sense.

"I've joined him on his morning runs a few times," she said, shrugging her sunburned shoulders. "It's almost impossible to keep up with him, but what a workout."

I wondered why I'd never heard about that. Obviously, Harper had a few secrets of her own. And Emmett hadn't mentioned it either. Then again, why would he? He was open with me, sure, but he didn't tell me everything.

"Anyway, I guess it makes sense that he's not into me. He's way out of my league."

"Harper." I hated it when she acted all self-deprecating and insecure, like she wasn't good enough for someone cute and decent like Emmett. Whenever she put herself down or doubted her awesomeness, I wanted to kick her dickhead father's ass. "That's not true."

"Sure it is. He's smart and funny and gorgeous. He could have any girl he wants."

Not any girl, I thought, remembering our long, tense walk back to my cottage last night after I'd shot him down. Things had felt so weird between us, I wouldn't have been surprised if he avoided me for the rest of the summer. Maybe it would be better if he did.

"You're all those things, too." Building her up was another responsibility I'd taken on over the years, though my success rate was spotty at best. Her parents' divorce had done too much damage.

"No, Kat," she said, sunlight glinting off her Ray-Bans as she looked at me. "*You* are."

My heart thudded in my chest. Did she suspect? Had Emmett told her? But no, her tone of voice was matter-of-fact, not angry. I was pretty sure she'd be angry if she knew how much I wished that I'd been the one to claim Emmett first.

That evening, Dad let me take his car to pick up some take-out at Goody's. He rarely let me drive the BMW so I made sure to take the long way, detouring down several streets in town before popping back out on the main road. The icy cold air conditioning felt nice.

Finally, I pulled into Goody's and parked in the deserted parking lot. Apparently, the renovations weren't doing much to pull in extra customers.

"Hey, Kat," Sherry said when I walked in. She was sitting at the counter, playing with her phone and looking bored.

"Hi." I leaned against the counter. "I'm here to pick up an order."

She glanced behind her at the kitchen. "Right. It'll be ready in a minute." Patting the stool beside her, she said, "Have a seat. Hot out there, isn't it?"

"Brutal." I sat down and scanned the empty diner. Even the tablecloths looked dejected. "Sherry, why don't you bring the jukebox back at least?"

"Nah." She waved her hand. "It wouldn't fit with the new décor. Besides, I sold it."

"To who?"

To whom, Pop corrected me in my head.

"Some guy from out of town who collects fifties memorabilia."

I sighed. Perhaps Mr. Collector Guy could be persuaded to sell it back. The place was in desperate need of some livening up. Plus, it was the first summer I hadn't pressed B6 for "Yakety Yak" even once.

"It's probably the heat keeping people away," Sherry said, nodding as if trying to convince herself as well as me. "Everyone's at home grilling hotdogs or eating ice cream for dinner."

Feeling sorry for her, I smiled and lied. "Right."

A bell dinged in the kitchen and Sherry jumped up. "Except for you and your dads, of course. Be right back with your food."

The moment she left, the heavy wooden door swooshed open, letting in a blast of heat and Nate McCurdy.

Wonderful. I swiveled in my stool and let out a loud sigh.

"Well, look who it is," he said, feigning surprise. "Hurricane Katrina."

I proceeded to ignore him, concentrating instead on the salt and pepper shakers in front of me on the counter.

The stool next to me made a squeaking sound, and a moment later I caught a whiff of deodorant and boy sweat.

When he spoke, his voice was close in my ear. "I ran into Sawyer Bray yesterday. He said you punched him in the face the other night at the carnival."

I turned to look at him. His expression seemed doubtful, like he didn't believe I had such violence in me. "I did."

He smirked. "He also said that your father—the big, ripped one—showed up at the gas station while he was working and threatened him with bodily harm if he so much as looked at you again."

"His name is Mark," I said emphatically. "You know my fathers' names, Nate."

"Whatever." He tapped his fingers on the counter. "Zoe says Sawyer takes steroids and that's why he got so big so fast. But who knows . . . I always thought he was a douche."

"Takes one to know one."

Nate glowered at me and then leaned in closer, invading my personal space. "I know it was you who left that gay fork rainbow in my yard last night."

I was still pissed at him, but I couldn't help but laugh at his words. *Gay fork rainbow* sounded like the name of an indie band or something. "I have no idea what you're talking about," I said, blinking innocently at him.

"Bullshit," he replied as Sherry came back with my bags of take-out.

"Nate!" she chirped, excited for another customer. "What can I get for you, honey?"

His scowl blossomed into a wide smile. "Just a milkshake. Vanilla."

She handed over my food and I slid a few bills across the counter, telling her to keep the change.

"Sure thing," she said, directing the comment to both of us.

When she scurried off to make the milkshake, Nate's smile became a scowl once again. "You made a bunch of holes in my grass, you know," he said petulantly.

"Just think of it as free aeration."

He didn't seem to appreciate my thoughtfulness. "My parents get home tonight and they'll want to know what happened. What am I supposed to tell them?"

I pretended to ponder that for a moment. "Hmm. How about, 'Mom, Dad . . . I'm a dumb, insensitive homophobe who got what he deserved.'"

He glanced over at Sherry, who was pouring milk into a stainless steel cup. "I'm not a homophobe, Kat. I didn't mean what I said that night at the carnival, okay? I was just . . ."

"Just what? Showing off for Zoe?"

"I don't give a shit about Zoe." He sighed and turned away, but not before I noticed the pink creeping up his cheeks.

"Why, then? Were you trying to get Harper's attention or something?" When he didn't respond, I let out a snort. "You think insulting her uncles and acting like an ass will make her hate you any less? Seems kind of counterproductive to me, Nate."

"What can I say?" he mumbled, shrugging his shoulders. "I'm not all noble and sensitive like Emmett."

I laughed. "So you're jealous because we like Emmett more than you? Oh my God." I stood up and grabbed my bag of dinner, all set to walk away and leave him there. But I only got as far as the cash register before I paused, turned, and walked back over to him. "Look," I said, my defenses lowering as I reminded myself of something I often overlooked. McTurdy had feelings too. "I'm sorry for ruining your lawn. I'll come over later and fill in the holes before your parents get home, okay?"

One corner of his mouth kicked up. "So it *was* you."

I rolled my eyes impatiently. My food was getting cold.

"Don't worry about it," he told me, smiling again as Sherry arrived with his milkshake in a to-go cup. "I'll just do what I always do when something gets messed up or broken." He handed Sherry some change and slid off the stool, shooting me his smarmy grin over the lip of the cup. "Blame it on Keaton."

chapter 16

"Do me a favor, would you, Katrina?"

I glanced up from the toenail I was painting and looked over at Dad, who was wedged behind our ancient fridge with a screwdriver in hand. It had conked out the day before, spoiling about a hundred dollars' worth of groceries.

"Okay," I said, expecting him to ask me to find the number of an experienced appliance technician. Dad was handy, but I still feared for his life when he messed around with electrical things. The fridge was unplugged, but still.

"Run over and ask Holly if she wants to come over for drinks tomorrow night. And her husband too, if he's around."

My nail polish brush froze a few inches above my pinky toe. "Emmett's parents?" I said hesitantly.

"Yes." His head popped out from behind the fridge. "Why? Do they not socialize together?"

No, they only scream at each other constantly and hey, guess what? He used to hit her, too. "I don't know," I said, going back to my nails.

"Well, can you go invite them? If I don't stay here and fix this, we'll be having peanut butter sandwiches again for dinner."

"Can't you just call? My nails are wet."

He pulled the fridge out another few inches, grunting with the effort. "I don't have their phone number. And it can wait until your nails dry."

"Fine," I muttered, capping the polish and clunking it on the kitchen table in front of me.

It wasn't that I didn't *want* to run the errand for my dad. I just didn't want to walk anywhere in the heat. Or see Emmett. Or invite his father over. Or possibly have Emmett *hear* me inviting his father over. *If only Harper was here,* I thought. She could go with me, maybe ease some of the tension. But she and her mom had gone to the walk-in clinic earlier to get Harper's ankle checked out by a doctor. She thought she might have twisted something during her last soccer game. Besides, she was still embarrassed by her post-run flirting fail with Emmett the other day and would probably refuse to join me anyway.

However, when I got to the Reeses' cottage a half hour or so later, I felt kind of grateful to be alone. World War Three was in full swing again, even louder than the first time I'd witnessed it. And on top of the yelling, it sounded like Mrs. Reese was crying. Now that I'd met her and seen how nice she was, how small and delicate, I wanted to run in there and shield her from potential harm, just like her son had done for me. Just like I tried to do in a different sort of way for my dads. But if Emmett—their own son—couldn't get them to stop, what made me think I could?

Just as I was about to head back to the road, I spotted a glimmer of movement near the shoreline beyond the cottage. I moved in that direction, my flip-flops crunching over the brown, parched lawn. When I reached the top of the steps leading to the dock, I could see Emmett crouched on the rocks near the water, pushing a piece of sandpaper over the surface of a worn-out canoe. For a moment I just stared at him, watching the muscles flex in his arm as he pressed hard against the boat, ridding the wood of its old, chipped paint.

"Emmett," I called, but he didn't react. It was then I noticed his earbuds, secured into place and blocking out the world. I walked down the steps and approached him slowly, then touched his tanned shoulder with my fingertips. "Emmett."

He jumped and whirled around, the square of sandpaper flying out of his hand. "Jesus, Kat," he said, ripping out his earbuds. "You almost gave me a heart attack."

"Did you think I was a bear again?" I asked, smiling.

"No, I thought you were a spider. I freaking hate spiders."

"Good to know." I crouched down next to him and examined the weathered canoe. "What are you doing?"

He picked up the sandpaper, testing its roughness with his thumb. "The previous owners left this here. Thought I'd try to fix it up and see if it still floats." He started sanding again. "I'm also hiding," he added over the steady scraping noise.

"Yeah," I said, glancing around for an extra piece of sandpaper and finding one on the rocks behind him. I started sanding a small splotch of paint near the bottom. "I can see why."

Emmett paused and looked at me, sweat dripping down his temples. "Not to sound rude again, but what are you doing here?"

Keeping in mind the context of the situation, I tried not to take offense. Screaming parents had to be humiliating. "My dad wanted me to come over and invite your parents to our cottage tomorrow night. For drinks."

"My father doesn't drink. That was one of my mom's

conditions the last time she agreed to take his sorry ass back." He turned back to the canoe, his mouth twisting derisively. "And as you may have noticed, he's not exactly the friendly-neighbor type."

"Right," I said, at a loss for anything more to say. Emmett seemed a bit off today. Snippy and short-tempered, like the first time we met. "Well, how about just your mom then? My dads think she's the greatest thing ever."

"Glad someone does," he mumbled, then went back to scouring the canoe. I joined him, and we worked in silence for a while until I got too overheated to continue. We were on day number three of an oppressive heat wave and it showed no signs of breaking anytime soon.

Feeling woozy, I moved over to the edge of the lake and splashed some water on my face. A minute later, I heard Emmett come up behind me.

"Let's cool off properly," he said, and I turned to watch as he stepped up on the dock. Then, without further comment, he took a running leap into the lake.

Grinning, I climbed up on the dock, kicking off my flip-flops near the edge. Luckily I'd been swimming earlier and still had my bikini on underneath my sundress. I quickly pulled the thin fabric over my head and tossed it aside. Then, acutely aware of Emmett's eyes on me, I jumped feet-first into the water.

The lake was colder at this end, and deeper too. I flailed a little, panicking when I resurfaced and couldn't touch bottom. Ever since I was a toddler, bobbing around in the public pool with one of my dads during Parent-and-Tot swim class, I'd hated being in over my head.

"You okay?" Emmett asked, grabbing one of my hands to steady me. Since he was only doing it to save me from drowning, I didn't resist the contact.

"I'm fine," I said, spitting out some lake water.

He let go of me and swam a few feet to the right. "It's not as deep over here."

I followed him and was relieved when my feet touched rocks. "I *can* swim," I told him, feeling embarrassed. "I just don't like deep water."

He smiled for the first time since I'd arrived. "Damn. I thought you were faking so I'd have to save you."

I glared at him. "No. And don't you dare make fun of me, Emmett. You're scared of spiders and they can't even kill you."

"Some can." He ran a hand through his hair, causing several wet strands to tumble across his forehead. I watched them fall, vaguely mesmerized.

"Um," I said, forgetting what we'd just been discussing. "So I was talking to Harper the other day." *Good job,* I told myself. *Redirect your focus to where it belongs.*

"Don't you talk to her every day?"

"No. I mean, yes. I mean . . ." What the hell was wrong with me? I never got flustered around guys. "She mentioned what happened between you two a couple days ago. After your run," I added when he gave me a blank look.

"Oh, you mean when she tried to kiss me?"

I started coughing, even though I was pretty sure I hadn't breathed in any water. "She tried to *kiss* you? *Harper?*"

"Yeah. When I dropped her off at her cottage after our run, she just stood there with this expectant look on her face, like she was waiting for me to do something. Then she sort of leaned into me like she was about to kiss me. I backed away and told her I had to go. It was really awkward." He raised his eyebrows at me. "She didn't tell you?"

"Not about that part." I suddenly felt irritated, but I wasn't sure if it was because Harper had kept this partic-

ular piece of information from me, or because she'd almost kissed him and I was jealous. In any case, that was
not what I'd been expecting to hear. Harper didn't usually go around trying to kiss people. *Bold* and *impulsive*
was more my territory than hers.

"She was probably too embarrassed to tell you," Emmett said. "I still feel bad for shooting her down like
that."

No wonder she'd been so solemn the other day.
Harper had a rough time coping with rejection.

"I'm sure she'll forgive you."

"She also asked me if I was gay." He grinned at me
again. "Is that the general consensus around here?"

I shrugged. "Well, you did help me make a gay fork
rainbow."

He laughed and flung some water at me, but I ducked
and splashed him back even harder, soaking his face and
hair.

"Big mistake," he said, lunging toward me.

I screamed and started swimming away, but he got
hold of my ankle and pulled me back, forcing me to
stand. Giggling, I pushed away from him and tried once
again to escape. He caught up to me a second time, but
instead of grabbing my ankle, he wrapped his arms
around my waist and pulled until my back was flat against
his chest. And then we were no longer laughing.

The water grew still all around us as we stood there,
skin to skin. His chest rose and fell against my shoulder
blades, and I could feel his quickened breath on the curve
of my neck, warm and steady. In fact, I could feel *all* of
him, and it took every ounce of willpower I had not to
face forward, wrap my legs around his waist, and bury
my fingers in his hair.

But I didn't, because I couldn't. Instead, I unlocked his
hands from around my waist and swam away. When I got

to the dock, I grabbed hold of the ladder and pulled myself up and out.

"Kat," Emmett called from the water. He hadn't moved. "I'm sorry."

Without looking at him, I nodded mutely, slipped my dress back on over my bikini, and shoved my feet into my flip-flops. "Ask your mom about tomorrow night," I said before pounding up the steps and into the yard. I had to get out of there, fast, before I jumped back in that lake and kissed him senseless.

My walk back home was hot and confusing. I didn't know what would happen between us, or what, if anything, I would say to Harper. I didn't even know if I'd make it back to my cottage without dying from heatstroke. There was only one thing I knew for sure in that moment as I sprinted through the woods toward home. Emmett Reese was positively, without a doubt, one-hundred-percent *not* gay.

When I burst through the door of the cottage a few minutes later, Harper was sitting on the living room couch, her ankle wrapped in black tape.

"Why are you soaked?" she asked me at the exact same moment I said, "How's the ankle?"

She looked at her foot. "Fine. Not sprained. The doctor just told me to stay off it for a day or so and keep it wrapped in KT tape. Why are you all wet?"

"Oh." I glanced down at myself like I hadn't even noticed. "I was swimming."

Her forehead crinkled. "Uncle Mark said you went to invite Emmett's parents over for drinks."

The glass door slid open and Dad came in carrying a roll of electrical tape. Behind him, I could see Pop and Aunt Carrie sitting on the deck, hiding from the sun under the giant patio umbrella.

"What happened to you?" Dad said, seeing me. "You've been gone for two hours. Did you invite them?"

"They weren't home," I lied smoothly. "Emmett said he'd ask them and let me know later."

Dad nodded and went back to the fridge, satisfied with my answer. My cousin, however, proceeded to study me so intently, I had to make up some lame excuse about needing a shower just so I could escape the weight of her gaze.

It didn't take two hours to extend a simple invitation, and we both knew it.

chapter 17

The next afternoon, my dads sent Harper and me to the supermarket to pick up the supplies for the appetizer-and-drinks gathering at our cottage later that evening. At first I thought my cousin was just being nice, accompanying me on a boring trip to the store, but as I soon discovered, she had ulterior motives.

"Oh look, it's Conner Dunford," she said with a nudge to my ribs as we turned our cart into the snack aisle.

"So?" I replied. The presence of Conner Dunford in Erwin's grocery store wasn't exactly noteworthy. He'd been stocking shelves there for the past two summers. At the moment, he was yawning as he halfheartedly replenished the Doritos supply.

"Soooo . . ." Harper said, drawing the word out. "I thought you might want to invite him over tonight."

I looked at her like she'd sprouted an extra head. Conner was tall and blond and kind of cute, but he had the personality of a wet paper bag. "Why would I want to do that?"

She tossed a tube of Pringles into the cart, avoiding my eyes. "You guys flirt with each other every time we run into him. It would probably make his week if you asked him out."

"I don't *want* to ask him out," I whispered as we drew closer to him. "And besides, I flirt with everyone."

She shot me a quick narrow-eyed glance and I immediately wanted to take back what I'd said, or at least add the caveat *Except for Emmett*. Ever since that morning, when Emmett had caught up to us on the road between our cottages and told us that yes, his mother would be happy to drop over for drinks, Harper had been struck with a renewed hope. Especially when, lured by the promise of s'mores, he had agreed to come over, too. Finally, after being deprived of them for weeks, s'mores were happening at my fire pit tonight whether Pop approved of it or not.

Luckily, I had that to look forward to. The prospect of spending an evening with Emmett totally stressed me out. When we'd spoken earlier, I could barely even look at him. All I could think about was what had happened in the lake, the intoxicating feel of his body against mine. Actually, I'd thought of little else since.

"So will you do it?" Harper asked me.

"Hmm?" I said, lost in thought. I sounded like Pop.

"Invite Conner," she said out of the corner of her mouth. He was only half an aisle away from us, well within hearing distance. "So we can both, you know, have someone."

Have someone. Was that what she thought? That she *had* Emmett? Harper was a wonderful person, and I loved her like a sister, but sometimes she had trouble taking a hint.

"Please, Kat." She unleashed the puppy-dog eyes that she'd learned from me and aimed them in my direction. "For me."

I sighed. How could I say no to that? It wasn't like I had to *make out* with Conner or anything, and I knew he wasn't the type to come on too strong, like Steroid

Sawyer. Conner wasn't the sharpest crayon in the box, and he wore way too much cologne, but he was sweet and basically harmless.

"Fine," I told her through gritted teeth. "But you owe me."

She nodded and shoved me gently toward him. He smiled hugely at the sight of me. As Harper had predicted, he was thrilled by the invitation and readily agreed to join us. He even offered to bring some pot. *Oh Lord*.

"Thanks, but no. My parents will be home," I told him, and he shrugged and continued to beam at me like he'd been into the pot already. Harper owed me, all right.

"You'll have to teach me how to do that someday, Kat," she said once we'd left the snack aisle and Conner behind.

I scanned the shelf in front of me until I found the graham crackers, then added two boxes to the cart. "Do what?"

"Turn on the charm like that. Flirt. Guys are like putty in your hands."

I snorted. She made me sound like some kind of magic sorceress, reducing men to drooling idiots with one simple glance.

"I told you," I said, deliberating over the chocolate display. "You just have to be confident. Ask them questions about themselves, compliment them, touch their arm, smile . . . that sort of thing."

Harper reached over and scooped up a few Hershey bars. They weren't Swiss, but they would have to do. "I feel like an idiot when I do those things. Maybe I need to start wearing makeup and dresses, like you. Guys like the whole 'damsel in distress' thing, don't they?"

"Just because a girl wears lipstick and dresses and cares about her appearance doesn't mean she's helpless, you know. My dads brought me up to be strong and independent."

"I know," she said, squeezing my arm. "I think that's what I envy about you the most."

Conner didn't show up at my cottage that evening until after Harper, Emmett, and I had already torn into the s'mores fixings and devoured four each. As he crossed my yard where the three of us lounged on the grass around the fire pit, Emmett watched him guardedly, like Conner was about to snap and lunge at me any second. Maybe he thought all Erwin guys were raging assholes.

Once I'd introduced the boys, Harper moved over so Conner could sit down beside me, putting her within touching distance of Emmett. He didn't seem opposed to the new development, but he didn't exactly look relaxed either. Not that I was hyper-aware of his body language or anything.

"Another s'more, Emmett?" Harper asked, offering him the marshmallow bag.

"Don't you mean 'some more s'mores'?" Conner said in his slow, lazy drawl.

They both ignored him.

"No, thanks," Emmett said. "I'm kind of full."

Harper tossed the bag to me, but I put it down on the grass. I was full too, bordering on nauseated. Maybe Pop was right about excess amounts of sugar. Or I could have been reacting to Conner's cologne; he smelled like he'd *bathed* in it.

"Yeah, I'd better stop too or I won't fit into my soccer shorts on Monday," Harper said, stretching out her long, toned legs for Emmett to admire.

Only he didn't. For the past few minutes, his gaze had barely left the fire. I thought of the night of our fork prank, how he'd trained his flashlight on my leggings-

and-tank-top-clad body way longer than was necessary. And yesterday, when I felt his eyes on me as I stood on his dock in my bikini. Clearly, Emmett preferred curvy girls.

"So, Conner," Harper said, slapping a mosquito off her neck. "You don't have a girlfriend, do you?"

"Not at the moment."

"Good to know." She shot me a smile. "Isn't that good to know, Kat?"

I stared at her, surprised. Harper wasn't usually so forward. Perhaps the quick makeup job she'd let me do on her earlier had emboldened her. What exactly was she trying to do? Last summer, she'd been incensed when Sawyer Bray kept pushing her off on other people in an attempt to get rid of her. Now she was doing the same to me—offering me up to Conner so I'd "have someone," a distraction so she could hang out with Emmett without guilt. Like I would've stood in the way, otherwise.

Emmett tore his gaze away from the fire and watched me, too, waiting to hear my answer. Waiting to see if I cared one way or the other that Conner was single. I didn't, but Emmett's close proximity to my cousin bothered me just enough to say, "Definitely."

Conner gave me one of his mellow smiles and started eating raw marshmallows straight from the bag. Emmett went back to his staring contest with the fire, and I jumped up suddenly, like I'd forgotten something imperative and had to go fetch it immediately. In reality, I just needed a little break from all three of them.

"Bathroom," I said by way of explanation as I took off for the cottage.

Inside, I leaned against the counter in the dimly lit kitchen, downing a glass of water and listening to the adults as they laughed and talked outside on the deck. As

I stood there, contemplating the fullness of my stomach and whether it could handle any more food without rebelling, the glass door slid open and Emmett's mom entered the cottage.

"Oh," she said, jumping slightly at the sight of me. "Hi, Kat. I thought you were outside."

"Hi, Mrs. Reese." I held up my almost empty water glass. "Just needed some water. S'mores make me so thirsty."

"Call me Holly." When she smiled, she didn't look nearly old enough to be the mother of two grown boys. "Are you guys having fun?" she asked, joining me by the counter.

As usual, I felt like a giant next to her. "Yeah," I said, wondering if I was going to say anything tonight that *wasn't* a lie. "How about you?"

She laughed and placed a hand on her chest. "Oh my God, your dads . . . they're adorable, Kat. I just love them."

"The feeling is mutual," I told her, grinning.

"And Carrie, too. She's just so strong, you know? Raising her daughter on her own . . . I admire her. I admire *all* single moms."

You could do it, too, I felt like telling her. She could leave her toxic marriage, survive on her own, and be a better, happier person for it. I didn't know her very well, but there was something about her—the same steely resolve I'd seen in Emmett—that made me think she could be strong too, if she let herself.

"You have a really nice family, Kat," she said, placing her small fingers on my forearm. "And you and your cousin have been so nice to Emmett. I appreciate that. We both do, actually."

I shrugged. "It's not exactly hard."

"It is, though, for some people," she said somberly.

"Emmett can be very . . . closed off. He's been through a lot growing up, and it's really affected how he relates to people. He can be difficult to get to know."

I nodded, unsure of what to say. Did she know I'd heard the fighting? That I knew about her and her husband?

"But you and Harper," Mrs. Reese went on. "You guys have really helped to bring him out of his shell this summer." She smiled. "He talks about you, Kat. Well, Harper too, but mostly you. You've made quite an impression on him."

My face flushed with embarrassment and pleasure. "Oh. Well . . ."

She touched my arm again. "Sorry, I didn't mean to embarrass you. Or keep you from your s'mores. I just came in to use the washroom."

"Please keep me from the s'mores," I begged, and she laughed and leaned in to give me a quick hug before sprinting to the bathroom. *Well, what do you know,* I thought, watching her go. *Emmett's mom is a hugger, too.*

When I got back outside, I found Conner sitting next to the fire pit, totally alone and munching on a graham cracker. I glanced around the yard for Emmett and Harper but couldn't see them anywhere in the vicinity. "Where did they go?"

"Down by the lake," he said through a mouthful of crackers.

I craned my neck in that direction, but all I could see was blackness. "Are they waiting for us to meet up with them down there or what?"

Conner swallowed. "Uh, I think they want to be alone."

A million different emotions bubbled in my stomach, but all I could do was plop down on the grass next to him and wait. *Maybe they're just talking,* I assured myself. *Right. Alone. In the pitch dark.*

"So you're glad I'm single, huh?" Conner asked, bumping my shoulder with his. His cologne was over-powering. "You wanna do something about that for me?"

I inched away from him. "Not particularly."

"Okay then," he said agreeably before diving back into the graham cracker box.

Harper and Emmett stayed away for a full twenty min-utes. When they returned, joining us once again around the fire pit, they were both unnervingly quiet. I tried to gain clues from their expressions, but it was dark and they both kept their eyes on the ground, revealing noth-ing. Either they had kissed and it was so amazing they'd both been struck mute, or they had kissed and it had been so disappointingly awful they couldn't even look at each other, or Harper had tried to kiss him and he'd dodged her, like last time. Each scenario came with its own tiny dagger that stabbed at my heart.

The atmosphere around the four of us felt kind of wilted, like all the fun had been sucked out of the evening. I think it was a relief to all of us when the night ended and it came time to go our separate ways. Conner left first, then Emmett and his mom. When it was just Harper and me, alone in the yard, I asked her what hap-pened between her and Emmett on the beach.

"Nothing," she said as she helped me douse the fire with handfuls of sand.

"Twenty minutes of nothing?"

She brushed sand off her hands and looked at me. "We don't have to tell each other *everything,* you know."

I pushed back a pang of hurt. "I know. I was just cu-rious."

Suddenly, her face softened and she threw an arm around my shoulders, pulling me close. "A girl is entitled to a few secrets," she said, smiling cryptically.

That didn't make me feel any better. In fact, it made me feel about ten times worse, but I smiled back at her anyway. As a girl with more than a few secrets of her own, I couldn't exactly disagree.

chapter 18

I still hadn't given up hope that Shay would eventually forgive me. She'd been my only real friend at school, and without her, without at least *one* person on my side, senior year would surely be hell. And lonely. It was probably too late to switch schools, and besides, I didn't want to start over somewhere else. In spite of everything that had happened, I liked my school and wanted to graduate there next year . . . even if some of my classmates thought I was a boyfriend-stealing whore.

Still, in spite of what people thought about me and said about me, I wasn't the type to back off and cower—which was why during the rare times I had a signal on my cell, I took full advantage of social media. Shay—along with a slew of others—had unfriended me on Facebook, and she still ignored my emails and calls and texts. But that didn't stop me from reaching out to her, pleading and apologizing, using several different methods until finally, one day, she got sick of it and responded.

It was Wednesday morning. I took Pop's car into Erwin to pick up a couple necessary items at the drug store. I wasn't sure he even knew I'd left; the minute Dad's car had disappeared down the road on Sunday evening, heading back to the city for work after his too-short vacation, Pop reached for his laptop and had barely come up for air since.

As I strolled through the drug store, I made sure to pick up a bottle of Advil for his inevitable eye strain (and my monthly cramps), and then headed back outside.

The stifling humidity had finally broken and the air felt cool and refreshing, raising goose bumps on my arms. The sight of them made me think of cold winters and snow and strolling down the icy city streets with Shay, the two of us bundled against the wind, mittened hands gripping paper cups of hot chocolate as we walked back to school before the afternoon bell. I felt an ache in my chest, missing her. Missing home. Fighting back tears, I sat on the bench in front of the drug store, dug my phone out of my purse, and clicked it on.

No new messages.

Were there ever? Everyone, friends and friends-of-friends, had all sided with Shay. For all my bright makeup and retro clothes and flashy audaciousness, I was still invisible to them. But I'd gotten way too used to the spotlight to fade away that easily.

I tapped Shay's name and texted her one word. **Hi.** Not **I'm sorry.** Not **Please forgive me.** I'd done enough of that already. Just **Hi.** Like Emmett had texted to me that day at the soccer game. No expectations. Simple.

My heart leapt into my throat a few seconds later when my phone chimed with a response.

What do you want, Kat?

There was nothing friendly or encouraging about those words, and I could almost hear the weariness in them, but still . . . at least she hadn't actually blocked my number like she'd said she was going to do. Maybe I still had a chance.

Nothing. I just miss talking to you.

I waited for at least ten minutes, staring at my phone as people passed by on the sidewalk in front of me, but her reply never came. Apparently, *she* didn't miss talking to *me*.

The bench I was sitting on creaked as someone sat beside me. A moment later, I felt fingers touch my arm, warm and gentle. I bristled, assuming it was Nate ready to pout some more about the holes in his yard or argue the fact that he was a jerk. But when I looked up from my quiet phone, all set to tell him to get lost, I saw a pair of blue, blue eyes, watching me with concern.

My reprimand died on my tongue. Emmett was next to me, a to-go cup from Erwin's one and only coffee shop in his hand. All of a sudden, my senses exploded with the scents of coffee and soap and the feel of his knee brushing mine.

"You okay?" he asked, glancing down at my hand, which was wrapped around my phone in a white-knuckled death grip.

"Yeah." I tossed the cell back into my purse and then sort of draped it over my drug store bag in an attempt to hide the bright blue box of tampons tucked inside. And Advil. One glance in there and he'd assume I was suffering from a raging case of PMS—which probably wasn't too far off the mark.

"What are you up to?" I asked him. We hadn't seen or spoken to each other since Saturday night in my yard, but I'd thought about him. Thought about how his body had felt in the lake and wondered about those twenty minutes he'd spent alone in the dark with Harper.

"Just getting coffee," he said, holding up his cup. "We ran out this morning."

"It smells good," I said with a sigh.

"Want a sip?"

Instead of telling him no, that my dad didn't want me drinking coffee and lectured me about caffeine addiction the few times I'd tried to sneak it, I held my hand out for his cup. Emmett gave it to me and I drank, letting the bitter heat of the coffee pool in my mouth for a minute before swallowing. *Heaven.*

"Want me to go get you one?" he asked when I handed it back to him. He immediately took a drink, as if trying to capture the taste of my lips before it got rinsed away.

He wants to share germy saliva with me, I thought, *even though he may have already shared some with my cousin.* Just the possibility of that felt wrong.

"No, thanks." I gathered my purse and bag and started to stand up. I needed to get away from him before I grabbed him and made him sample my mouth firsthand. "I should go."

"Wait," Emmett said quickly, and I sat back down, turning toward him. He took another sip of coffee. "Um, I was wondering if you wanted to do something with me later."

I raised my eyebrows at him, intrigued. "Like what?"

"I don't know. Swim, go for a hike, play another prank on Nate . . ."

I shook my head at the last suggestion. The gay fork rainbow had been a success, and a second round of lesson-teaching would surely drive the point home, but my pranking days were over. Vengeance, as fun and satisfying as it was, only felt right in the moment. Like my dads kept trying to teach me, I had to let it go and rise above.

"Go for a hike, huh," I said, tapping my nails on the bench seat. What could it hurt? I'd made it abundantly clear that we couldn't be anything more than friends, a fact he'd seemed to accept. And it *would* be nice to do something besides sit around my cottage, moping about Shay.

"Yeah. You up for it? Should we invite Harper too?"

"Nah," I said, feeling yet another surge of guilt. "Her ankle flared up again after her game the other day. She has to stay home and rest it."

He nodded, not looking entirely disappointed by the news. "You and me, then? Around six-thirty?"

"Did you have a final destination in mind?" I asked, reaching for his coffee again.

He smiled as I downed a huge gulp. "I know just the place."

"Shouldn't we stick to the trail?" I asked Emmett as we trekked through the woods a few hours later. Already, I was regretting my decision to do this. Not only was it a bad idea to spend time alone with him, but he was also about a thousand times fitter than me. Even walking, he was fast and sure, traversing the bumpy forest floor like it was smooth, clear asphalt. Meanwhile, I kept tripping every few seconds as I struggled to keep up.

"Don't worry," he replied, glancing back at me. Noticing how heavily I was panting, he slowed down a bit. "I have a pretty good sense of direction. And a compass."

"Great," I wheezed.

My choice of footwear probably wasn't helping either.

Earlier, when he had come by my cottage to pick me up for our hike, it was the first thing he noticed. "Do you have anything besides Converse?" he'd asked hopefully.

I'd thought about the large collection of shoes I'd brought: flip-flops, flats, espadrilles, heeled sandals, wedges, and one pair of light pink Converse sneakers. "But they look so cute with this outfit," I'd said, holding out one foot.

Emmett had shaken his head, dismayed.

I was regretting those damn sneakers the most. The pinky toe on my left foot felt like it had been taken over by a giant blister.

"Where are we going?" I asked for probably the third time since we'd started walking. It was after seven, and soon the sun would be dipping below the trees. I wasn't scared of the woods, but that didn't mean I wanted to get lost after dark. Just that morning, I'd heard a local news story on the radio about an upsurge in the area's coyote population. Deer and squirrels and even black bears were one thing, but I'd heard stories about people getting chased and even killed by wild coyotes.

"You'll see." He appeared to know exactly where he was going. Since he ran in these woods daily, he already knew them better than I did. I'd only been through there on my ATV, and half the time I barely paid attention to my surroundings.

Ten minutes later, I started hearing the sound of rushing water on my right. Soon after that, he led me into a small clearing much like the one he liked to camp in near the cottages. Instead of a narrow, gently burbling brook, the water was more extensive, channeling over and between the rocks at a much faster speed. The whooshing sound I'd heard was mostly the work of a small waterfall at the far end where the water fed back into the lake. The heavy rain we'd had overnight had increased its momentum. The sound filled my ears like a roar.

"When did you find this?" I bent down to immerse my hand in the water. It was clear and cold.

"A couple weeks ago." He crouched beside me and

dipped his hand in next to mine. "You've never been here?"

"No, never. I had no idea it was even here."

Emmett smiled, pleased to have shown me something new on my own turf. We stayed there for a while, just kneeling by the water's edge and listening to nature. I didn't know about him, but I felt more peaceful and content in that moment than I had so far this summer.

"We'd better head back." He glanced up at the sky, which had begun to cloud over. "It'll be dark in here soon and I didn't bring a flashlight."

On the way back, I asked him about his brother. He didn't talk about him much and I was curious.

"Wes is a good guy." Emmett was walking slower, matching my pace. "He calls us a few times a week. Well, my mom and me, anyway. He doesn't have much use for my dad."

No wonder, I thought. "So he never comes home to visit? And he's been gone how long?"

"Two years. He's been back twice so far, for Christmas. I don't mind. I mean, I wish he was around more, but I get why he stays away. I plan to do the same thing next year after I graduate."

"Move out west?" We could see the woods path through the trees, and the lights from what had to be the McCurdys' cottage. The sight made my stomach lighten with relief.

"No. Escape. I'm going away to college so I can live in a dorm. It would probably be quieter than my house."

I remembered his words from a few weeks ago, when we'd sat outside his tent together. Now that his brother was gone, Emmett believed it was up to him to keep their dad in check. "But your mom . . . ?"

"I know. I feel bad about leaving her alone with him,

but I can't handle being their mediator for much longer. Besides, I don't think he'll ever hurt her again. He knows what would happen."

I hoped he was right, even though constant yelling seemed almost as damaging as violence to me. "Where are you applying to college?"

He brushed back a hanging branch so it wouldn't smack us in the face. "A few places, but I'll probably end up at Kinsley."

My heart did a little cartwheel. "We live about ten minutes away from the Kinsley campus. I'll probably end up there, too."

He turned to me, about to say something, when a loud, crackling sound interrupted him. It seemed to come from somewhere behind us. Very close behind us. We both stopped walking and froze.

"Um," Emmett whispered. "Did you happen to hear the news this morning? About the coyotes?"

I gulped audibly. "Yes. I did. Should we . . . are we supposed to run or play dead or what?"

"I run better than I play dead." He grabbed my hand and started pulling me through the forest.

Laughing, we bolted for the cleared path, which was just a few yards away. It was hard to see the ground, but I trusted him and my own two feet to guide me safely toward more even terrain. Halfway to the path, we shoved through a thicket of bushes and Emmett dropped to the ground, yanking me down with him. At first I thought he did it intentionally, to hide us from a pack of hungry, stalking coyotes, but then he started cursing.

"What happened?" I whispered. The woods were fully dark, and I could just make out his silhouette, writhing on the ground beside me.

"I tripped over a rock or something," he gasped. "I'm okay."

"You sure?" I glanced around me. No glowing eyes or threatening growls. Emmett had injured himself for nothing.

"Yeah. Just skinned my knees. And my elbows. Maybe my chin too. Fuck."

I moved closer to him, feeling along the damp earth with my hands. *Why hadn't we brought flashlights?* "Let me see." It was a ridiculous thing to say because I couldn't see my own hand in front of my face, let alone his various skin abrasions. Still, I placed my fingers on his clean-shaven jaw and pulled him toward me.

"Here," he said softly, taking my wrist and moving my hand a couple inches to the left, closer to his chin. As he did this, I lost my balance and tumbled forward, landing on top of him.

It wasn't like in the movies where the girl lands effortlessly and lightly across the guy's chest, nothing more than a surprised squeak emanating from either of them. No, it was more like an attack, clumsy and painful. My elbow dug into his stomach, making him grunt, and my face ended up in the dirt beside him.

Jeez, I thought as I hauled myself off him and spit some dirt onto the ground. *Way to finish him off.* "Sorry," I said, my face burning in more ways than one. "The ground is a little uneven here."

He sat up, his face just inches from mine. "Are you okay?"

I nodded, then remembered how dark it was. "Yeah. It's just my cheek. I think I scraped it."

"Let me see."

Seconds later, I felt his warm palm on the side of my face, his thumb tracing the edges of the scratch. I closed my eyes and breathed in the tantalizing blend of earth and trees and Emmett, sucking it into my lungs like it was a rare brand of oxygen I needed to survive.

His thumb slid downward, grazing my lips like he was locating them on a map, plotting his destination.

He was going to kiss me, I knew, if I let him continue down this road. It was up to me to stop it, to veer him off course. "Emmett." When he didn't pull back or remove his hand, I did it for him. "We can't."

I heard him swallow. "Why not?"

"For one, I have dirt in my mouth."

"I don't care."

"It's not even that. It's . . ." I sighed and looked away, into the woods. The trees swayed in the light breeze, their branches nothing but smudged shadows against the gunmetal-gray sky. I turned back to Emmett. "You kissed Harper." Then I held my breath, waiting for him to deny it, to tell me I was crazy, that he would never.

But he didn't say any of those things, and his silence gave me my answer.

"You kissed her," I said again, with a hint of accusation.

"*She* kissed *me*, actually." His voice was harsh. "You wanted me to try, Kat, remember? So I tried. Yeah, we kissed for a few seconds. And you know what happened next?"

I sat perfectly still, my knees pressed into the gritty soil. I was afraid to hear what happened next.

"Nothing," he bit out. "Nothing happened, because that's what I felt when she kissed me—nothing. She knew it, too. It was pretty obvious that I wasn't into it. Into her. I don't want to kiss Harper. I never have. She's not the one I want to be with, and I told her that straight out. I told her I like someone else." He heard my sharp intake of breath and added, "She doesn't know it's you."

"Exactly," I said, my heart racing at his words. "She doesn't know, and she can't know, Emmett. She . . . she'd hate me."

His hand brushed my bare leg, making me shiver. "I'm not with her, Kat. She and I aren't together and we never will be. You haven't done anything wrong."

But I have, I thought. I *have.* I was treading on dangerous ground, being with Emmett. Hearing the things he said and feeling what I felt for him. Harper had liked him first, had claimed him first, and that meant he was off limits to me. He wasn't technically hers, but he was hers all the same. Family trumped everything, even this. *Especially* this.

Harper and I were blood, and Emmett was water.

"I have to go," I said, standing up so fast that I almost fell back down. Dizzy and disoriented, I picked my way toward the path, ignoring Emmett's protests behind me, his offers to walk me back to my cottage.

I didn't need him to see me home. Even in the pitch dark, I knew exactly which way I needed to go.

chapter 19

"Heads up!" I yelled, tossing the giant beach ball to Keaton, who was paddling in the lake a few feet from my dock. The ball bounced off his head and landed near the shore. He cut through the water like an overexcited little dolphin and went to fetch it.

We'd been doing that for the last half hour, shortly after his mom had dropped him off. Harper and I had agreed to babysit him for the afternoon while Mrs. McCurdy took the twins somewhere. She hadn't mentioned Nate's whereabouts.

As Keaton scrambled to retrieve the ball, I sat back down next to Harper on the dock, dangling my feet in the water.

"I can't believe summer's more than half over," she said, her eyes on Keaton as he waded back into the lake, beach ball tucked under his skinny arm.

"I know." It had been a weird first half of summer, the slow, hot days interposed with swimming and soccer and tension and Emmett. Always Emmett.

I'd been kind of relieved when Mrs. McCurdy called that morning, asking me to look after Keaton. Having him around would surely help diffuse the strange vibe that had been brewing between Harper and me since yesterday, when she finally brought up the night of the s'mores feast.

"I think Emmett has a girlfriend at home," she said as we walked to Goody's for ice cream.

"Oh?" I tried to sound noncommittal when what I really felt was burning jealousy. He would've told me, *I reasoned.*

"When we were on the beach the other night, he said he liked someone else. So it's either a girlfriend or Gabriella finally got her hooks into him."

My relief almost overpowered the guilt I felt in that moment, knowing that the girl Emmett liked was me. Not a girlfriend at home. Not Gabriella. Me.

"I'm over him," Harper said, tossing her long, blond pony-tail over her shoulder. "I can't compete with the kind of girls he's probably into. I give up." She glanced at me and I rearranged my features quickly, trying to look indifferent. "I'll understand if you still want to hang out with him though. I know you guys are friends."

She watched my face carefully, assessing.

Was it a trick? Did she know? *I wondered.* But no . . . Harper would never believe that I had it in me to betray her. Lie to her. She always assumed the best of me.

"We're friends," I agreed, nudging her arm. "But you're my cuz, Harpy."

She smiled and nudged me back. "And you're mine, Katty."

Our conversation had ended there, and it should've been so easy to say to her, "Since you're not going to date Emmett, do you mind if I do?" But she wasn't the type to step aside and just accept something like that. Even when we were little kids, she'd been possessive of whatever she felt was rightfully hers, whether it was Bar-bies or her mom or the last cupcake. She'd never liked to share. Emmett wasn't *hers*, of course, and he was free to date who he wanted to date. As long as it wasn't me. Even though she hadn't said as much, I'd read that part loud and clear. Nothing was going to come between us and Operation Best Summer, especially not a boy.

A day later, the slight tension between us still lingered. I had the same feeling I always got when my dads fought—like something had stabbed a hole in the safe, protective bubble surrounding us, exposing us to the kind of misfortune that was usually reserved for other people. The shift between my cousin and me made me feel unbalanced, like my relationship with her wasn't as impenetrable as I'd always thought.

"Heads up!" Keaton called as he flung the beach ball back at us.

Harper caught it seconds before it smacked me in the face.

"Nice one, Buster," I said, splashing him with my foot.

"I'm hungry," he said randomly.

We went inside where I made him a peanut butter sandwich out of Pop's famous oatmeal bread while Harper located some contraband Kool-Aid packs. I made a sandwich for Pop, too, even though I knew it would remain untouched as he powered through the conclusion of Book Six.

"I'm so close, so close," he'd been saying all week, like a mantra.

After lunch, we headed out to the yard to kick around the soccer ball.

Harper taught Keaton some moves, showing him how to kick and pass and dribble the ball. When it came time to demonstrate tackles, she beckoned to me. "Kat's gonna try to score a goal, and I'm gonna stop her."

Keaton looked on eagerly.

"Sure your busted ankle can handle it?" I jeered.

"My ankle is fine. Go."

I started dribbling toward the goal—two large rocks spaced evenly apart by the edge of the driveway—all the while bracing for what I assumed would be Harper's legendary back tackle. Instead, she performed a sliding tackle, hurtling feet-first at the ball while grabbing my shirt for leverage. I wasn't prepared, so my feet flew out from under me and I ended up sprawled on my back in the grass, blinking up at the cloudless sky.

"That was *awesome*," I heard Keaton say from somewhere behind me.

I turned my head to the side just in time to see Harper maneuver the ball neatly between the rocks. A flawless goal. She whooped and turned around, her joy deflating when she caught sight of me. "Sorry!" she called. "You okay?"

The wind still hadn't returned after being knocked so violently out of me, so I made a wheezing noise and sat up. "What the f—" I glanced at Keaton, who was two feet away and listening. "What the *heck*, Harper?"

She grabbed the soccer ball and walked over to me. "Sorry," she repeated, giving me a hand to help me up. "Got a little carried away."

I stared at her, my breath coming in puffs. She was never that aggressive when we were scrimmaging. We were competitive with each other, even ruthless, but not to the point of dirty moves.

"We're not on the soccer field, you know," I snapped, feeling the ache in my tailbone. "And I'm not the opposing team."

"I said I was sorry," she snapped back. "It's not my fault you're so out of practice that you can't anticipate my moves anymore."

"Are you guys mad?" Keaton asked.

"No," we both answered him at once, our eyes still

locked on each other. We stood there, seething at each other over Keaton's blond head, until footsteps sounded on the gravel driveway.

"Nate!" Keaton took off.

I broke eye contact with my cousin and watched Keaton run toward his brother, his mouth going a mile a minute as he filled him in on his unorthodox soccer lesson. Nate appeared to be only half listening, his gaze shifting between Harper and me as he approached.

"Just came to pick up the brat," he explained, taking in my messy hair and Harper's grass-stained knees and the fact that we undoubtedly looked like we wanted to kill each other. That was new to Nate. Usually we looked like we wanted to kill *him*.

"I'm not a brat," Keaton said. "And I don't want to go. I want to see Harper tackle Kat again."

Nate couldn't hold back a leer.

Jackass.

"Me too, brat, but we have to get back. Mom will be home soon and we still haven't cleaned our rooms." He gave his hair a self-conscious pat and looked at Harper. "Hey, do you guys want to come over tonight? Roast some marshmallows?"

"I'd rather die," Harper told him, then turned and walked toward the woods, soccer ball between her palms.

Nate's gaze swung to me, but all I could do was shrug at him. With one last glance at Harper's retreating form, he put his hand on Keaton's head and steered him toward the road.

Once they were out of earshot, I caught up to Harper at the edge of the tree line. "What is your *problem*?"

"Me?" she said, spinning around to face me. "I'm not the one with the problem, Kat. You've been acting weird for weeks."

"Weird how?"

She shook her head and sighed. "Never mind. You're perfect and wonderful, as usual. It's probably just me."

"Harper." When she turned to leave again, I grasped her arm, holding her there. "I want to know," I said firmly. "Tell me how I've been acting weird."

"You're just—" She let out another sigh. "You're not yourself lately. You're distracted and secretive and—"

Irritation prickled up my spine. She was right, of course, but how could she accuse me of something she was guilty of too? "*I'm* secretive? What about you? 'A girl is entitled to a few secrets.' Isn't that what you told me the other night?"

She shut up and dropped her gaze to the ground. I had her there, and she knew it. We'd both been acting weird and cagey lately, and it wasn't just due to Emmett. Maybe she *had* outgrown me. We'd always been different—total opposites, in fact—but sometimes that didn't matter in families. Sometimes sharing blood was enough to bond people, to connect them for life. And other times, it wasn't nearly enough.

"My ankle hurts," Harper said, and then she pivoted on her heel and continued toward the woods and her cottage, leaving me alone on the grass.

A few hours later, a knock on the door jolted me out of a dead sleep. I'd lain down after Harper had left, more to rest my aching back than because I was sleepy, but I'd ended up dozing off anyway. Groggy, I dragged myself off my bed and went to answer the door.

"Dinner!" Aunt Carrie stood on the other side, her arms loaded with plastic-wrapped plates of what appeared to be pasta, a huge loaf of bread balanced on top. As I held the door open for her, I caught a whiff of garlic. My stomach growled in response.

"I thought you guys might need a home-cooked meal

by now," she added, placing the bread and plates on the table. There were four . . . one for each of us and one to save in the fridge for Dad, who usually rolled in around eight p.m. on Fridays. No plate for Harper, but that wasn't surprising.

"Thanks," I said, glancing at the microwave clock. Five-thirty. I'd slept for almost three hours. *Crap.*

"Where's that brother of mine?" Aunt Carrie asked as she flitted around the kitchen, gathering napkins and forks. "Still attached to his laptop?"

"Shower." I'd heard him in there as I passed by the bathroom. He always waited until zero hour to pull himself together before Dad arrived.

"Well, let's start without him. This is getting cold."

Aunt Carrie was a great cook. The fettuccine alfredo she'd made practically melted on my tongue, and the garlic bread was soft and buttery. After subsisting on PB&J, bananas, smoothies, and ice cream all week, it was exactly what I needed. My energy returned the minute the first bite hit my stomach.

"Where's Harper?" I asked, severing a noodle with my fork.

"She wanted to stay home." Aunt Carrie picked up the pepper grinder and looked at me. "You two have a fight?"

"I guess."

"What about?"

"I'm not even sure," I replied with a shrug.

She smiled. "You used to do that when you were little, you and Harper. Have little fights over nothing and then forget about them a few hours later. I think that happens in all close relationships." When I didn't respond, she reached over and patted my hand. "Don't take it personally, Kat. She's always overly sensitive for a couple days after a phone call with her father."

"He called?" I asked, chomping into a piece of garlic bread.

"Last night. Told her he couldn't get together with her at the end of August after all. He'd promised to take her rock-climbing the weekend before she starts school, but apparently something came up with work and he had to cancel. Harper was upset."

The creamy alfredo felt like paste in my mouth. God, no wonder she'd been so antagonistic earlier. "She didn't tell me."

"Yeah, well, you know how she is when it comes to Lawrence. She doesn't want people to know that he still has the power to hurt her." Aunt Carrie let out a heavy sigh. "I wish she'd realize that most parents have that power over their children, even when they're fully grown."

I knew she was referring to her and Pop's parents, who had practically disowned Pop after he came out in college. Their father had eventually come around, but he'd died when I was eight. Their mother still hadn't forgiven him, or Aunt Carrie either, for sticking by him. Or Aunt Beth, for helping to create me. In my grandmother's mind, good God-fearing people didn't a) turn out gay, b) accept a gay sibling, or c) help that gay sibling become a parent.

But ostracizing one's own children was just fine, apparently.

Pop appeared in the kitchen then, scrubbed and shaved and wearing clean clothes. "What calorie-laden delicacies did you bring over this time?" he asked his sister.

Aunt Carrie pushed out his chair with her foot. "Sit. Eat. You're getting too thin anyway."

"He always forgets to eat near the end," I reminded her, scraping every last bit of sauce off my plate.

"I'm so close, *so* close," Pop chanted. "A couple more chapters to go and I'm done. Then I'll relax."

"What about revisions?" I asked.

"And promotion?" Carrie added.

"And book signings?

"And—"

Pop held up his fork, stopping us. "Okay, another few months and I'll relax."

"Or start Book Seven," I muttered.

Aunt Carrie laughed and gave us each second helpings of rich, fattening garlic bread.

chapter 20

The next twenty-four hours seemed to drag on forever. Hanging out with my dads was fine, but I saw them every day, year-round. Summer was for Harper, for swimming and walking and making messes in her kitchen or mine. July and August always went by so fast; I hated to waste even one day being pissed at each other.

By Saturday afternoon, I couldn't stand it anymore. I sprinted through the woods to her cottage, all set to make amends and get on with Operation Best Summer. With a quick warning knock, I let myself in their cottage and called out a greeting.

Aunt Carrie answered me from the kitchen where she was mixing up some sort of sauce or marinade at the counter. "She's not here. The Eagles are playing a tournament in Everton today."

I paused to take a deep breath. The entire cottage smelled like teriyaki. "Why aren't we there, cheering her on?" Everton was a mid-sized town about forty minutes away. The Eagles didn't play many away games—in fact, that was their first one—but I'd assumed we'd be in attendance for those, too. Harper hadn't told me about any tournament.

Aunt Carrie dipped a finger into the mixture and tasted it. "Mmm," she said, then glanced over at me. "She assumed we didn't want to go, I guess. Those tournaments can last for hours. I wasn't keen on sitting in the heat all day anyway."

I would have, I thought. I would've done anything to show my support, even bake for hours in the sun, shaking my homemade pompoms and screaming obscenities at the ref. Obviously, Harper didn't need me for that anymore. She didn't seem to need me for anything anymore.

"Oh," I said, trying to hide my disappointment. "Well, let her know I stopped by."

"*You* can let her know." Aunt Carrie covered the sauce with plastic wrap and stuck it in the fridge. "Later, when you come over for dinner. You are coming tonight, right? With your dads?"

"I wasn't sure if Harper wanted me to."

"Of course she does, Kat. You're her cousin."

I thought about the giant bruise I sported on my tailbone. "Right," I said dully.

I left Aunt Carrie to her dinner prep and headed toward home, taking the road. Just as I reached Walter, the old man face in the tree, I heard footsteps on the gravel behind me and then my name. I swiveled around to see Emmett jogging toward me, his pace steady and strong. He reached me in no time, coming to a halt a couple feet from where I stood. I couldn't help but stare as he leaned over and caught his breath, damp hair tumbling into his face. Once again he was shirtless, his skin deeply tanned after weeks in the sun, shorts hanging low on his slim hips. *Runners,* I decided, *are beautiful.*

"Thanks for stopping," he said, straightening up and tugging out his earbuds.

What did he expect me to do? I wondered. *Take one look at him and run in the opposite direction?* Maybe that was what I *should* have done, avoided him and his distracting body for the rest of summer, but that would have been almost impossible. His cottage was just a few minutes from mine, the town was small, and our parents had become BFFs. We were bound to run into each other at some point.

"Out for a run?" I asked unnecessarily, then chastised myself for sounding so stupid. My brain was still scrambled from the last time I'd seen him, three days ago, right before I left him in the woods near Nate's cottage. His scrapes had healed nicely, I couldn't help but notice. Mine had, too. Then I remembered his fingers on my face in the dark, tracing my cheek, my lips.

Focus, I told myself.

"Yeah," he replied like I'd actually asked a reasonable question. "Where are you coming from?"

"Harper's. She's not home. Soccer tournament."

He nodded and fiddled with his earbuds while I tried not to ogle his naked flesh. My own flesh felt warm and tingly and it was only partially the fault of the sun.

"Hey," he said suddenly. "I've been meaning to show you something."

I somehow managed to say, "What?" even though my imagination had begun whirling in all sorts of lurid directions.

He turned and started walking back where he'd come from, gesturing for me to follow.

Unable to come up with a reason why I shouldn't, I fell into step beside him. He led me all the way to his cottage, then we passed it, continuing down to the shore line. There, propped against a large rock, was the canoe we'd sanded together last weekend, the day of our "moment" in the lake. At least I *thought* it was the same canoe. It had been transformed. The outer surface was smooth and painted a shiny red. Even the inside looked clean and new.

I glanced at Emmett, who was grinning.

"Finished it Thursday," he said.

"It looks great." I ran my palm along the grain in the wood. "Have you tried it out yet?"

He shook his head and grabbed the canoe paddle, which looked like it had been restored as well. "I was waiting for you."

I swallowed. *He wants me to go in this old thing? Float around in the middle of the lake with nothing between my feet and the deep water but a few planks of cedar?* I'd been on a boat before, of course, but never one I wasn't quite sure wouldn't sink like a stone and take me with it.

"I'll do all the paddling," Emmett said, seeing the hesitation in my face. "You can just sit there, looking pretty."

That got me. In spite of my sweet-and-dainty appearance, I wasn't a helpless weakling. I'd get in that damn death trap of a boat, and I'd help paddle it, too. "What are we waiting for?" I took the paddle from him and placed it in the canoe. Then I gripped one end of the canoe and lifted, grunting with the effort.

Emmett smiled, kicked off his running shoes, and lifted the other end. Together, we got the heavy canoe into the water and climbed in, each of us settling on the hard seats at either end, facing each other. The canoe tipped for a moment, and we both grabbed the sides, steadying ourselves.

"Think we can make it to the island?" he asked as he dipped the paddle in the water and pushed, turning us around.

I squinted across the lake, judging the distance. It seemed far. "There's nothing over there," I said, adjusting the soaked hem of my sundress around my legs. "Harper and I went over on Nate's dad's fishing boat once. It's just trees."

We glided along in silence for a while, Emmett doing the paddling while I unobtrusively watched his arm mus-

cles ripple with the strain. Once again I felt like I was in
a scene from *The Notebook*, floating along in a boat with
a guy I tried to deny my attraction to but couldn't. Only
instead of hundreds of swans, we had bugs and the occasional duck.

"Want a turn?" Emmett asked, offering me the paddle.

"Nah," I said, stretching out my legs. "I'd rather just sit
here, looking pretty."

He gave me a sheepish look. "I was just kidding when
I said that. I mean, yeah, you're pretty . . . beyond
pretty . . . but there's a lot more to you than that."

I was suddenly grateful that my big sunglasses hid most
of my face. Guys complimented me sometimes, but
never with such earnestness.

"You don't have to act like that with me, you know,"
he went on, moving the paddle through the water again.

"Act like what?"

His gaze slid down my yellow sundress, stopping at my
white, flower-patterned flip-flops. "Like a girl who's
afraid to get dirty. I don't think that's the real you."

I laughed. "You know me so well, right?"

"All I'm saying is you don't have to pretend to be
some girly girl around me. Just be yourself."

"So, what? You think I dress like this to please other
people?" I asked, insulted. Maybe that had been true
years ago, but like most things repeated over a long period of time, eventually it became normal. Then preferable. "It just so happens I *like* wearing dresses and
makeup, Emmett. I like pink things, and fashion, and
sappy movies. This *is* me being myself. I can look like this
and still be okay with getting dirty."

He stopped rowing and looked at me. "Why did you
quit soccer, then? And boxing?"

"I quit boxing because I hurt my wrist. I quit soccer
because—" I clamped my mouth shut, knowing how pa-

thetic my excuse would sound. I'd quit because people assumed my lack of a mom had made me rough and aggressive. Looking back, I wondered why I'd ever let a few snide comments stop me from doing something I enjoyed.

"Because," I tried again, "I wasn't as serious about it as I should've been."

Emmett continued to peer at me, dubious. He didn't believe me. He thought I was a fake, manipulating people into thinking I was vulnerable and frail so they would what? Treat me that way?

I thought about last week with him in the lake, how I'd panicked in the deep water and he'd had to grab my hand to steady me. Had he really thought I'd done it on purpose? Acted the part of "damsel in distress" just so he'd have to save me?

Well. I couldn't have him thinking that, now, could I?

The canoe rocked precariously as I stood up, shed my flip-flops and sunglasses, and jumped clumsily over the edge. We were right in the middle of the lake, so the water was cold and seemingly bottomless, pulling me down for a few moments before my body's own buoyancy forced me back up.

When I surfaced, Emmett was in the water about a foot in front of me, a look of surprise mixed with panic on his face. "What the hell did you do that for?" he snarled at me. "Jesus, Kat. I thought you were going to drown."

I laughed, plucking some hair out of my mouth. "I can swim, Emmett. And I can throw a punch and kick a soccer ball and paddle a canoe. *And*"—I treaded closer to him and batted my eyelashes—"I can even ride an ATV."

He grabbed onto the canoe, which had started to float away, and smiled grudgingly back at me. "No, you can't."

"Yes, I can."

"Prove it."

I looked to my left toward the shore. We were pretty close to my dock. Meeting Emmett's eyes again, I said "Okay" and then started swimming.

He swam beside me, maneuvering the canoe between us just in case I needed to hold on to it. I wanted to a few times, but I pushed through my uneasiness and kept going, not stopping until my feet touched bottom.

"You can't prove it," Emmett continued to tease me as we dragged the canoe to dry land. "I bet you don't even *own* an ATV."

"Yes, I do." I hopped up on the dock, realizing too late that I was wearing a sopping wet, thin, light-colored sundress with a white bra and panties underneath. I crossed one arm over my chest while trying in vain with the other arm to loosen the skirt from its suction-hold on my thighs. Giving up, I turned back to Emmett and called, "Follow me."

Laughing, I ran up the steps and across the yard, my bare feet skating across the grass. I could hear him behind me, gaining on me easily with his strong runner's legs. By the time I got to the detached garage, he was right beside me, his eyes dancing with laughter.

"Stand back," I said, gripping the door lever and yanking it up. "And behold."

The garage was dark, especially to eyes that had been subjected to the sun for hours, but no one could mistake the sharp outline of my Yamaha Raptor Sport Quad ATV, the very one that came within several inches of hitting him a few weeks before. There it was, the indisputable, physical proof of my claim.

I moved closer to the ATV and turned to Emmett, flinging my arms out in a big, smug *Told you so.* Only he wasn't even looking at the stupid ATV. His eyes were on me, burning through the flimsy fabric of my dress, tracing the outline of my breasts, my hips, my still-dripping legs. When his gaze landed on my face again, I couldn't look away even if I'd wanted to. The unwavering force of it pinned me where I stood.

I'm over him, Harper had told me. At the time, it had made me feel better, but also a little envious. Because *I* wasn't over him. Not even close.

He must have seen something in my eyes, permission or acceptance or something else, because suddenly he was inches away, his breath washing over my forehead. I glanced up at him, biting my lip, and that was all it took for whatever was left of his restraint to completely evaporate. He held my face between his palms, tilted it upwards, and kissed me.

I'd been kissed by a lot of boys, in a lot of ways, but it had never once felt like this. My body was weightless, drifting toward his like it had no free will of its own. He pulled me closer, his fists closing around the fabric at the back of my dress, wringing drops of lake water down my legs and onto the cement floor beneath us. He had no shirt to grab onto so my fingers tangled in his hair, making the kiss deeper, more unrestrained, and infinitely more intense.

My hands dropped from his hair and skimmed over his shoulders, down his chest, touching the places I'd spent the last few weeks illicitly admiring. When my fingertips brushed the waistband of his shorts, he made a noise deep in his throat. The sound of it finally snapped me out of my lust-filled stupor. I drew back slightly, dropping my arms.

His hands were still twisted in my dress, and he didn't let go as he gazed down at me, questioning.

"What are we doing?" I whispered.

We were out of breath, our chests rising and falling together.

"I'm sorry," Emmett said hoarsely. He let go of my dress to brush an errant strand of hair off my face. "Actually, no, I'm not sorry. At all. I've wanted to do that for a while now."

I let out a long, shaky breath and buried my forehead in the space between his shoulder and neck. He smelled like lake water and sunscreen and *him*, and I never wanted to leave this spot. I still didn't know what we were doing, or what would happen, or where we'd go from there, but those worries seemed trivial now.

Right then, in that moment, I wasn't sorry either.

chapter 21

Harper may have been sensitive and more than a little hot-headed, but she was also quick to apologize. When my dads and I showed up at her cottage for dinner that evening, she immediately pulled me into her bedroom and shut the door.

"I'm sorry," she said, hugging me.

I hugged her back, trying not to think about the fact that a mere five hours before, I'd been wrapped in the arms of the boy she still liked but pretended not to. My stomach rocked with guilt as I stepped out of her embrace. "I'm sorry, too."

"You have nothing to be sorry for, Kat."

I bit my lip, which still felt slightly swollen from all the kissing. Emmett and I had stood in that garage for at least twenty minutes, completely absorbed in each other until the sound of a door closing echoed across the yard, breaking the spell. I'd almost forgotten that Pop was home. Luckily he hadn't seen us when he emerged into the sunshine to write on the deck.

Silently, I watched as Harper flopped back on her bed and twirled the end of her ponytail around her finger. "I was just upset about my dad bailing on me again. I shouldn't have taken it out on you."

"It's okay," I said, slumping down next to her on the ratty quilted comforter.

Harper's room looked much like mine—jars of rocks on the worn dresser, clothes flung everywhere, walls hung with posters that had been there since we were pre-teens. But while my wall art consisted of old actresses and the occasional modern-age celebrity, hers was all about soccer. The only poster that even came close to my tastes was the one above the bed: a shirtless David Beckham resting a soccer ball against his thigh.

"He wants to fly me home next week," Harper said.

Still preoccupied with Beckham's abs, I was momentarily confused. "Who?"

She laughed and nudged my foot with hers. "Dad. Supposedly he felt bad for canceling on the rock-climbing plan, so he wants me to stay with him for a few days and meet his new girlfriend. He met her at work. She's a nurse, apparently."

I nodded. Lawrence was a clinical pharmacist and it wasn't the first time he'd dated one of his hospital co-workers. At least he was no longer doing it while married.

"You're not going, are you." I said, phrasing the question like a statement. I hated how she accepted every measly little crumb of her father's attention, even when it was obviously a ploy to make himself seem like a doting father for whatever woman he happened to be seeing. "Harper," I said when she failed to respond. "This is our last summer together. Remember?"

She stopped playing with her hair and crossed her arms. "I know, but it's not like I'd be gone for weeks. It's just five days. I'd leave Monday morning and be back on Friday. What's the worst that could happen . . . I'd miss the two-for-one sundae special at Goody's?"

I felt that now-familiar twinge of hurt in my chest again, reminding me that things were still different this summer, even before our fight. However, this hurt was supplemented by a large dose of panic. How was I supposed to avoid being alone with Emmett if my trusty sidekick deserted me for five days?

The words *I kissed Emmett* had been on an almost constant loop in my brain since the moment I laid eyes on my cousin. Saying it out loud would be scary, yet freeing. If he'd been any other boy, I wouldn't have thought twice about describing our steamy make out session in detail. But he wasn't any other boy, and I knew Harper. Even though she was a year older than me, she'd always looked up to me. Depended on me. Trusted me to be one of the few people in her life who would never let her down.

So I knew, only moments after the kiss had ended, that it could never happen again. Once was a mistake, impulsive, a heat-of-the-moment decision. Harper might even forgive me for it if I ever felt brave enough to confess. But letting it happen again would be a deliberate betrayal in her eyes, and I already had one close friend in my life who hated me for overstepping boundaries. With Harper, the fallout would be even worse. She was my family.

"Will you be mad if I go?" she asked me.

I looked over at her hopeful, pleading face and felt myself soften. "No," I said, smiling. "It's just five days, right? We still have the rest of summer."

She scooted over and rested her head on my shoulder. "You're awesome, you know that? Even when you don't agree with my decisions, you still support me no matter what."

"Of course," I said, hoping I could say the same for her.

★ ★ ★

The next day, I called Emmett to let him know I planned to drop over later, after dinner, to discuss something important with him. Confused, he agreed.

At seven, I climbed into Pop's Volvo. It had been raining heavily all day, making the roads and woods paths slippery with mud. I knew if I attempted the ten-minute walk, I'd be soaked and filthy by the time I got there. As I drove, I thought about what I wanted to say to Emmett. I knew I couldn't just dodge him for the rest of the summer without some kind of explanation. He deserved to know why we couldn't be together in the way we obviously both wanted to be. He deserved to know where we stood.

I sped up as I approached Harper's cottage, even though I knew she was occupied, packing for her trip home tomorrow, and wouldn't see me pass by. The thought of her leaving still filled me with anxiety. I worried that without her around, distracting me and acting as a chaperone of sorts, I'd lose the focus of my willpower. Self-discipline wasn't exactly one of my strong points.

"Hey," Emmett said when he opened the door to my knock. "Come on in."

I stepped into the entryway and glanced around. I hadn't been in the cottage since the Cantings owned it. It looked different. All the doilies and knick-knacks had been cleared out, the ugly rugs disposed of to reveal the shiny hardwood underneath, and the gaudy flower-patterned couch and chair had been replaced with plush, neutral-colored ones. Mrs. Reese had good taste.

"Where's your mom?" I asked, not meeting his eyes. I could sense his gaze on me, drinking in every stretch of my exposed skin. Suddenly, I wished I'd worn sweatpants and a hoodie instead of a short skirt and cleavage-baring top.

"She and my dad went to Everton to see a movie."

"Really?" I said, as if the idea of his argumentative parents doing something normal and couple-y like going to a movie was just so astonishing. I had a flash of them screaming at each other over popcorn.

"Yeah." He raked a hand through his hair and I tried not to think about how soft it had felt between my fingers. "They've been getting along pretty well lately."

"That's good." I took another look around the empty cottage and said, "Hey, why don't we go for a walk?"

Emmett peered behind me at the driveway, which was currently about two inches underwater. "Um, it's pouring."

"Oh," I said, like I hadn't noticed. "Right."

Dammit. I'd been counting on at least his mother being home. Mrs. Reese was almost always around, working on something. She had a home-based business making gorgeous, homemade candles, which she sold through her online Etsy store.

"Is this a problem?" Emmett asked when I didn't budge from my spot by the door. "My parents being gone, I mean. Will your dads freak out or something?"

It *was* a problem, but not because of my dads. They trusted my judgment in these kinds of situations. Unfortunately, I wasn't sure *I* did. "It's fine," I said. "I'm just here to talk anyway."

Emmett seemed baffled again, and I couldn't really blame him. I was acting weird.

"Well, at least let me be polite and give you a tour first," he said, confusion dissolving into a smile.

"Is that just an excuse to get me into your bedroom?" I asked, smiling back. God, what was it with me and boys? When it came to flirting, I couldn't seem to help myself. It was like a sickness.

Emmett's response didn't exactly help matters either.

He rubbed the back of his neck and gave me this shy, oops-you-caught-me grin. *Harper was right,* I thought. *He is adorable.*

The layout of this cottage almost exactly matched ours—living room and kitchen overlooking the lake, bedrooms and bathroom along the opposite side. The square footage seemed a bit larger, but that could have been an illusion due to the light paint and warm lighting.

"I stole one of your light bulbs before you moved in, you know," I told him when the tour reached the kitchen.

He looked at me, eyebrows lifted, and I explained about the cranky blond lady who had swiped the range hood bulb for me.

"Sneaky," he said, going over to the stove and flicking the light switch on the hood. Nothing happened. "Maybe I'll steal it back the next time I come over."

If there is a next time, I thought as he moved away from the stove, toward me. As he passed, he held out his hand like he expected me to take it. Only I didn't. In fact, I immediately stepped back as if his touch might harm me. He paused to give me a long, searching look before continuing on to the hallway. Wordlessly, I followed him to his room.

The first thing I noticed was that he had obviously cleaned up in anticipation of my visit. Bed neatly made, surfaces dust-free, floor cleared of the usual bedroom clutter. It was possible that he was regularly this tidy, but I'd seen the jumbled disorder of his tent a few weeks ago, and his mother didn't come across as the type to clean up after him. If I had to guess, I'd say he lived like a typical teenage boy and had possibly shoved any mess into his closet before I arrived.

The second thing I noticed was that his room didn't seem like *his.* Harper and I and even my dads liked to bring things from home to make our summer space more personal and familiar. But the only thing in the room that appeared to belong solely to Emmett was the pile of books on the nightstand, one of which—oddly enough—was Pop's. Book Five of the Core Earth series. Other than that, his room had more of a guest room feel. I wondered what his room at home looked like.

Still feeling Emmett's probing gaze on me, I crossed the room and stood in front of the window, which faced the woods. I focused on the wet, swaying branches, trying to regulate my breathing and relax. But it was hard to relax when I was standing in his room with the scent of him everywhere and Emmett himself stationed just a few feet away, watching me. For a moment, I had to remind myself of the reason I was there in the first place.

"Emmett," I said, my back to him as I stared out the window. "We have to talk about what happened yesterday in the garage. I don't think—"

The floor squeaked and the next thing I knew he was behind me, his hands on my waist and his forehead resting against the back of my head. When he spoke, his warm breath fluttered against my hair. "Don't ask me to be just friends with you, Kat. It's not happening."

I shut my eyes and swallowed. "Why not?"

"Because"—his hands slid from my waist down to my hips and then back up again—"every time I see you, all I can think about is how much I want to kiss you."

The movement felt almost reverent, like he was memorizing my curves, worshipping them. My heart raced in my chest just like it had that day in the lake when he'd pressed me up against his body in much the same way. That time, I'd managed to summon up enough self-control to swim away and leave him behind. This time, however, I'd already experienced what it felt like to kiss him, and I knew exactly what I'd be missing if I walked away. So, when his hands found my hips again and squeezed, gently urging me around, I chose to stay.

I wasn't thinking about Harper, or my resolve to never do this again, or anything else outside of the moment. Every cell in my body was tuned in to Emmett as we kissed in front of his rain-smudged window, arms locked around each other. Soon we moved to his bed, where he sank down on top of me, making me suddenly grateful that I'd chosen to wear the short skirt after all. So much for just talking.

The kissing continued until the distinct sound of the front door opening filtered into the bedroom, causing Emmett to jolt away from me like I'd kicked him. "Crap," he said as we both scrambled into sitting positions. "They're home already."

I glanced at the digital clock on the nightstand and stifled a gasp. Nine-thirty. Had we really made out for two hours?

"Emmett?" his mom called from the other room.

"Yeah?" he replied while yanking his shirt back over his head. He tossed me mine and I did the same, making sure it wasn't inside out or backwards. Then I swung my legs over the edge of the bed and impulsively grabbed one of his books, which of course turned out to be my dad's. I pretended to skim through it, not really paying attention to the words inside. The last thing I wanted after making out with a guy was to be reminded of my father.

"You have company?" Mrs. Reese said, her voice louder as she approached the bedroom.

I had a fleeting urge to jump out the window, but she'd already seen Pop's car.

"Yeah," Emmett said again as his mother appeared in the doorway, dressed in a pair of white capris and a pretty lavender blouse. She took in the no-longer-neat bed and our tousled hair and then raised her eyebrows. "Kat, do your parents know you're here?"

"Yes." I knew my face was every bit as red as Emmett's was at the moment. It wasn't a lie, though. Pop did know I was there, but I hadn't told him about Emmett's parents' being gone because I didn't know anything about it until I got there.

"Well," she said, her gaze back on Emmett, who was staring at the floor. "Next time, make sure there's a parent here before you come over, okay?"

I nodded rapidly, my embarrassment making it impossible for me to manage a verbal response. Mrs. Reese gave us another sharp once-over before backing away from the door, leaving us to die of shame in private. A few seconds later, I heard her and Emmett's father murmuring to each other in the kitchen.

"I should probably go," I said, placing my dad's book back on the pile and standing up.

Emmett stood too, slowly, as if he wasn't quite sure his legs would hold him. "I'll, uh, walk you to the car."

My skin flushed even hotter when I had to face his father, who acted like he'd never seen me before in his life, even though we'd already met. To my relief, he seemed more amused than angry about the situation, and Emmett and I made it outside basically unscathed.

The rain had all but stopped, leaving behind warm, muddy puddles that were almost impossible to navigate in the dark. By the time we reached the car, my feet were drenched.

"Sorry about that," Emmett said when we stopped by the driver's side door.

I wasn't sure if he was sorry about the hooking up or that his parents had come home and caught us, so I just nodded again. I was a regular bobble head doll.

"I'll see you tomorrow?" he asked, his eyes searching mine.

He was worried, I realized, that I'd reject him. I might have, too, if I didn't like him so much. And if he wasn't such a damn good kisser.

"Sure," I said, and his features relaxed. Apparently, I'd left my self-control—what little I still had—back in his bedroom somewhere.

"I think we should go out sometime this week. Just us."

"What, like on an actual date?"

"Exactly. An actual date."

I opened the car door and looked up at him through my lashes. *Say no*, I ordered myself. "Okay," I said.

His smile was like a fist squeezing my heart. With one last quick kiss good night, he went back inside while I climbed into the Volvo and started it up. Once again, I hit the gas as I approached Harper's cottage. I'd planned to stop in there on my way back from Emmett's for a final good-bye, but there was no way I could do that after what had happened. Instead, I drove right past it, gripping the steering wheel until I was safe on the other side.

chapter 22

"Holly called me last night," Pop told me during breakfast on Tuesday morning.

"Oh?" I said through a mouthful of Multi-Grain Cheerios.

Pop took a long, fortifying sip of tea and I sensed what was coming next.

"She said she walked in on you and Emmett in his bedroom on Sunday night."

My mushy mouthful of Cheerios seemed to turn into a gum-like substance, impossible to break down and swallow.

When I failed to respond, Pop continued. "She thought I should be . . . *made aware* of the situation." He cleared his throat, and I noticed two red blotches forming on his cheeks. "I assured her that I'd discuss it with you."

"It's not a big deal," I said when I'd finally stopped chewing. "We weren't . . . you know. We were just kissing." We'd done more than kiss, but adding further detail would probably send Pop into cardiac arrest.

"Even so," he said, picking up his English muffin, "it's probably not a good idea for you to be over there—or over here, for that matter—without an adult present." He brought the English muffin to his mouth and then, changing his mind, set it back down on the plate. "And when you do decide to *you know*, please make sure you're safe."

I covered my face with my hands. It was too early for this. "I know, Pop. You and Dad have discussed this with me before. Many times."

"You're never too old for a refresher." The stern-parent business out of the way, he bit into his muffin. "I thought Harper was the one who liked Emmett."

"She does." I pushed my bowl away, no longer hungry. "We both do."

Pop's eyes widened as the complexities of the situation sank in, but I didn't even care that he knew. It felt good to get it out. In fact, it felt so good, I kept going. "She doesn't know I like him. Or that he likes me. I'm afraid to tell her."

He sighed. "Oh, Kat."

My eyes began to sting. If Pop was disappointed in me, I could only imagine how Harper would react.

"You can't keep something like that from her, honey," Pop said gently. "You know you have to tell her, right?"

I blinked a few times, forcing the tears back. "Yeah."

"Who knows . . . maybe she'll be okay with it." But his voice had a false ring to it. He knew as well as I did how delicate Harper's feelings could be. "How did all this . . . come about? You and Emmett?"

"I don't know. It just sort of happened. I didn't *mean* to start liking him."

Pop grabbed his mug and stood up. For a moment I thought he was disgusted with me and had to get away, but he came over to me and kissed the top of my head. "Well, sometimes these things are out of our control."

As he refilled his mug, I thought about everything he'd gone through to be with the person he loved. Dad had been "out" basically all his life, had never even dated a woman, but Pop had grown up in a different sort of environment, with people who would never accept him for who he was. For years, he'd denied his true self, even went through a slew of girlfriends during high school in an attempt to fit in. Then, when he met Dad in college and eventually came out, he said it was the first time he'd ever felt like *himself.* Happy. He'd been so sure of his feelings for Dad, he'd risked everything—even losing his own family—just to be with him.

My own issues paled in comparison to what he had endured, but I could understand the trepidation he must have felt, and how desperate he must have been for his family to accept his relationship with Dad and acknowledge how good they were together.

"You won't say anything, will you?" I asked Pop. "Even to Aunt Carrie?"

He sat down with his fresh cup of tea. "Of course not, Noodle. This is between you and your cousin."

"Thanks." I let out a breath. "So . . . am I grounded? For what happened on Sunday?"

His forehead wrinkled as he pondered my question. I could count on one hand the number of times I'd been grounded.

"No. I think the humiliation you undoubtedly suffered is punishment enough."

I agreed. "Good, because I have plans tonight."

He looked at me, a question in his eyes.

Now that some of the weight had slipped off my shoulders, my smile came easily. "I have a date. An actual one."

Although Emmett and I had spent nearly every waking moment together since Sunday night, I was still excited to see him when he arrived at my cottage that evening. There was just something about getting dressed up and having a guy pick you up in his parents' car that felt *different*. All official-like.

For the past couple days, between swimming and canoeing and making out in various hidden spots in and around the lake, Emmett and I had been formulating a plan for our first date. After much debate, we'd settled on the old stand-by—dinner and a movie. The closest movie theater was in Everton, a forty-minute drive away, but neither of us minded getting out of Erwin for a few hours. Mrs. Reese, who'd apparently recovered from what she'd witnessed when she got home from her own movie date the other night, was nice enough to let Emmett use her car.

Once Pop had thoroughly interrogated Emmett about his driving record, the state of the car's gas tank, and my curfew, we were finally allowed to leave on our date.

"You look amazing," Emmett said as we settled into his mom's Mazda.

"Thanks." I adjusted the hem of my white sheath dress, which I'd chosen specifically because it showed off my tan.

"I feel a little underdressed," he said, glancing down at his shorts and T-shirt.

He was a little *over*dressed, in my opinion, but I couldn't let my thoughts roam in that direction if we were going to make it through dinner and a two-hour movie. *Focus.*

Along with a movie theater, Everton also provided a decent selection of restaurants. No retro diners, unfortunately, but that was okay because we were both craving pizza. Luckily, we found a small Italian place right near the theater. Inside, a hostess led us to a cozy, private booth in the corner.

"So," Emmett said once the waiter had disappeared with our order, "your dad was pretty intense back there."

I rolled my eyes, remembering how Pop had quizzed him. "He's kind of overprotective when it comes to me. I'm surprised he didn't ask if you've ever run someone over."

"That's more your department, isn't it?"

The sip of Coke I'd just taken almost ended up spewed all over the table. I covered my mouth with one hand and looked over at him, relieved to see that he was smirking. "I was wondering when you'd bring that up," I said, removing my hand. "I didn't run you over, Emmett. I *almost* ran you over. There's a huge difference."

"All I know is that one minute I was running through the woods and listening to the Foo Fighters, minding my own business, and the next thing I knew there was an ATV headed straight for me. It got my blood pumping, anyway."

"You were a jerk, you know," I said, giving him a light kick under the table. "I know I scared the hell out of you, but you didn't have to yell at me."

His smile wilted and he fiddled with his napkin, folding the corners. "I felt bad about it afterwards. I was in a rotten mood that morning. My parents had been fighting since the moment we got to the lake and I just didn't want to be there. But that's no excuse for yelling at you. I try really hard not to be that guy."

"What guy?"

"The guy who takes out his anger on other people. I've always been afraid of turning out like my father. The whole 'learned behavior' thing. That's why I've never really had any serious girlfriends."

I regretted even bringing it up, even though, technically, he had. "There's also the whole 'break the cycle' thing," I said. "It's your choice."

"I know."

He stared into the flame of the small candle that sat between us on the table. An awkward silence descended, and I searched my brain for something to say that might break it. Finally, I decided to go with the two things I did best—diversion, and appealing to a guy's ego. "If you've never had any serious girlfriends, how did you learn to be such a good kisser?"

That got him. He sat up straighter and smiled. "A girl doesn't have to be your girlfriend in order to kiss her," he said, giving me a pointed look. "I've gone out with people before, but just casually. I guess I'm not the relationship type."

"Really." That made me wonder exactly how many non-serious non-girlfriends he'd been in a non-relationship with. Clearly I wasn't the first.

"Yes, really." He slid his arms across the table, one on either side of the candle, and grasped my hands. "But I might make an exception for you."

Fortunately, the pizza arrived then, saving me from a full-blown swoon. By the time the waiter had dropped everything off and left us to it, I had a handle on myself again.

"I'm a terrible girlfriend," I said in a casual tone as we each reached for a slice.

Emmett paused to look at me. "How so?"

Words probably would've gotten my point across adequately enough, but just to be sure, I decided to demonstrate first. Under the table, I let my knee brush against his, then ran my foot along his calf. At the same time, above the table, I fixed him with my patented full-watt smile.

His pizza slice slid out of his hand and landed on the table.

"I have a problem with flirting," I explained, taking my foot back. "Boyfriends hate that."

He cleared his throat and rescued his pizza. "You flirt with other guys like *that*? When you have a boyfriend? Yeah, I can see why they'd hate it."

"Well, no. That was an exaggeration. Usually I just smile a lot and get overly friendly."

"I've never seen you flirt with anyone."

I bit off some pizza and chewed, washing it down with a sip of Coke. "We're pretty isolated at Millard Lake. There's no one around to flirt *with*, other than you. And don't even think about mentioning Nate unless you want to see me regurgitate this pizza."

"What about that guy you invited to your campfire a while back?"

I snorted. "Conner? Harper forced me to invite him. I don't even like him."

Memories of that night came flooding back, the most prominent one being the kiss between Emmett and Harper by the lake. The one she'd never told me about. Suddenly, I felt like I had an ice cube lodged in my throat. I was out on a date with the guy she liked while she was hundreds of miles away with her asshole father, probably wishing she was back here with me. I wasn't sure which I felt guiltier about—that I was seeing Emmett behind her back, or that in the past two days, I'd barely even missed her. I was a selfish, horrible person.

"Anyway," I continued, my appetite gone, "I've never been in a serious relationship either because guys always dump me for flirting with their friends. Hell, even my best friend quit speaking to me after I paid too much attention to her boyfriend one night. That's exactly why I was so afraid to—" I broke off and lowered my gaze to the table. My stomach churned. Maybe I *was* about to upchuck my pizza.

"Afraid to what?" Emmett said, gripping my hand again.

"Admit that I liked you when I knew Harper did, too."

"Have you told her yet? About us?"

I shook my head. "I can't."

He slid his hand away from mine. "Harper and I were never together. Nothing happened between us aside from that one awkward kiss. She knows I don't like her that way; I've never once led her on. Why would she care if we dated?"

"Because she likes you, Emmett. She rarely even notices guys, but she likes you." I swallowed hard. "My best friend Shay? She was *furious* when she thought I was interested in her boyfriend. She still refuses to speak to me. With Harper, it would be ten times worse. For one, you and I have gone way beyond flirting. Two, she's my cousin. And dating the guy your cousin has a crush on is a shitty thing to do. What I'm doing right now would hurt her."

Emmett leaned against the back of the booth, his pizza forgotten. "So, what? We're supposed to sneak around for the rest of the summer? Hide it from her? How's that any less hurtful?"

A burst of laughter from a nearby table filled the tense silence that followed, saving me from having to answer. Good thing, too, because I didn't have one.

"You have to tell her, Kat. Like, soon. Tonight."

"She's visiting her dad," I reminded him. "I can't tell her over the phone."

Emmett continued to watch me, his gaze unwavering. He wasn't going to be satisfied with a just-friends status, or a secret relationship, or anything other than open, unflinching honesty. And I didn't blame him one bit.

"She gets home on Friday," I said, feeling the pizza's acidic sauce at the back of my throat. "I'll tell her then. Okay? Just let me have until Friday."

He nodded, accepting this, and then took hold of my hand again. We relaxed enough to demolish most of our dinner before heading to the movie, where we ate popcorn for dessert and pretended everything was perfect.

chapter 23

The remainder of the week floated by like a dream, one I dreaded the thought of waking up from. My days were spent with Emmett, mostly hiding from the rain in either his cottage or mine, whichever one had a "parent present." We watched movies, played video games, and sneaked in some alone time whenever we could. On Thursday, I helped his mom make some candles while Emmett, antsy from too much sedentary time indoors, went out for a long, muddy run.

One thing we didn't do was talk about Harper. Until Friday at five-ten, when her plane was scheduled to land, she didn't exist between us.

Friday afternoon, I spent a couple hours with him before leaving at two to meet my aunt Carrie at her cottage. Against my better judgment—which was how I did most things these days—I'd agreed to go with her to pick up Harper. The airport was located just outside Weldon, and the thought of a two-hour drive with my aunt, who had no clue about the secrets I'd been keeping from her daughter, filled me with anxiety. As a high school teacher for the past thirty years, Aunt Carrie had an uncanny intuition when it came to teenagers. Mostly, I was afraid she'd somehow draw the truth from me before I was ready to spill it.

Luckily, my aunt was far more concerned with Harper's impending emotional state after several days with her father. Even a five-minute phone call with Lawrence could unsettle her for days, she reminded me as we drove toward the city. Who knew how five days with him had affected her?

To our surprise and relief, Harper was all smiles when she spotted us waiting for her near the baggage claim. Her grin held as she approached us, hugging first her mom and then me. She looked tanned and well-rested and happy to see us, which for some reason only intensified my guilt.

"Where's Uncle Bryce?" she asked as we made our way to the exit.

"In the middle of a cliff-hanger, probably," I said. "He said he couldn't leave this close to the end."

Aunt Carrie glanced at her watch. "Kat, text Mark and let him know we're on our way, okay?"

I nodded and dug out my phone. We'd made plans to meet Dad downtown at a Japanese restaurant for dinner before the four of us headed back to Millard Lake together. It felt strange being back in Weldon. We rarely came back home during the summer, and when I stepped outside into a wall of smoggy heat, I remembered why. Summer in the city was hot, loud, and dirty.

On the drive downtown, Harper told us about her trip. "Dad's new girlfriend is actually really nice," she said with a quick, apologetic glance toward her mom.

Aunt Carrie looked more comforted than offended, however.

"They were on vacation from work so we were able to do the rock-climbing after all. And yesterday we went shopping and I got these." She lifted a curtain of blond hair and showed us her earlobes, which were home to a pair of dangly, yellow gold earrings with multicolored stones.

"They're gorgeous," I said from my spot in the backseat. It was true. They *were* beautiful, and so unlike the simple studs and hoops Harper usually wore. They were the kind of earrings *I* liked, flashy and noticeable. "Did your dad get them for you?"

She nodded, glancing again at her mom as she dropped her hair back over her ears. Aunt Carrie's face remained passive, but a slight thinning of her lips betrayed the irritation she worked so hard to hide. Lawrence often tried to buy Harper's affections, but never extravagantly. He must have really wanted to impress the new girlfriend.

When we reached the city center, Aunt Carrie asked me if I wanted to drop by my condo for a minute, but I declined. There was nothing in there I needed and truthfully, I just wanted to get back to the lake as soon as possible. Being home made me think about Shay, and thinking about Shay made me dread my upcoming tell-all conversation with my cousin. Would she scream at me like Shay had? Quit speaking to me? Ignore me whenever I tried to make amends? I wasn't sure if I could handle a second round of that.

Then I thought of sitting on my dock with Emmett as we watched the first rays of sunshine in days peek through the clouds, and I knew I had no choice.

"Did I miss anything exciting while I was away?" Harper asked me during dinner an hour and a half later.

Dad had shown up at the restaurant late, having gone home to change out of his suit first. He was picking wearily through his Thai barbecue chicken, looking exhausted and slightly disappointed that Pop hadn't come with us.

"Not really," I replied, popping a California roll into

my mouth so I wouldn't have to elaborate. God, I'd missed sushi. The only sushi to be found in Erwin was the packaged kind in the supermarket deli, which I feared might kill me if I ate it.

"So what did you do all week?"

Instead of answering, I shrugged and shoved another roll in my mouth. I couldn't talk about it over dinner in a busy restaurant with our parents present. I couldn't tell her about the countless hours I'd spent with Emmett, kissing him, observing him, getting to know him. I couldn't share the things I'd discovered about him, like that his beloved dog died of old age two years ago and he didn't have the heart to get a new one, or that his childhood best friend's name was Joel, or that he acted like two different people around his parents—sweet and solicitous with his mom, short and indifferent with his dad. I couldn't describe the way his hair changed color depending which way the light hit it, or the scuff of his jaw against my skin, or how his breath hitched whenever my lips found the sensitive spot beneath his ear.

And I definitely couldn't tell her about my feelings for him, how they expanded by the day and were unlike anything I'd ever experienced before. That, more than anything, would be the hardest to confess.

My dads' second big barbecue of the summer took place the next day, and everyone they'd invited showed up. Well, almost everyone.

"Excuse me," I said to Mr. and Mrs. Schaefer, who'd been regaling me with an amusing anecdote about their greyhound, Benson, who was stretched out on the lawn a few feet away. A childless forty-something couple, they owned the cottage on the other side of Harper's and only came out on weekends.

"Sorry," I added when they stared at me, taken aback

by my sudden disruption. "I just have to—" I motioned behind me at the convergence of neighbors in our yard, vaguely indicating that I had other things to attend to. In truth, I had just spotted Emmett emerging from the woods.

"Of course," Mrs. Schaefer said, waving a hand to dismiss me.

I gave them an apologetic smile and headed toward Emmett. Seeing me, he paused at the periphery of the yard and glanced around. His gaze landed on the deck, where I knew Harper was currently located, and then flickered back to me, questioning. I shook my head. *No, I replied with my eyes. I haven't told her about us yet.* His expression darkened slightly, and I felt the urge to defend myself. It wasn't that I was stalling, exactly. I just hadn't had a chance to bring it up. She'd gone straight to her cottage when we got back last night, and this morning she was at soccer practice. I couldn't very well break the news to her in the middle of a party.

"Hey." I reached him, careful to keep a respectable distance between us, even though I longed to wrap my arms around his neck and kiss him hello, like I'd done all last week.

"You haven't told her?" he confirmed. His eyes locked on mine, softening in a way that let me know he wanted to kiss me, too.

"Not yet." When I explained why, his expression lightened again, but not all the way. He seemed distracted. "Where's your mom?" I asked as we crossed the yard.

"She couldn't make it."

"Why not?" I'd invited Mrs. Reese myself on Wednesday, and she'd happily accepted. She jumped on any excuse to hang out with my dads and aunt.

"She just couldn't."

I stopped walking and seized his forearm, not caring who was watching. Something was going on. "Emmett," I said softly. "Tell me why."

He sighed and rubbed a hand over his face, not meeting my eyes. "She and my dad had a huge fight this morning."

I nodded. His parents' arguing wasn't exactly groundbreaking news.

"The worst one yet," he went on, the words halting.

"What was it about?"

He focused on my face again. "Your father."

Confused, I peered over his shoulder at the deck, where Dad was manning the grill while chatting with Dr. McCurdy. Harper was deep in conversation with Mrs. McCurdy at the patio table, their backs to us. She either didn't know Emmett was there, or was ignoring him in an attempt to stay true to her "I'm over him" declaration. She was also ignoring Nate, who'd been trying to get her attention for the past half hour.

"Dad?" I said to Emmett. "Why would they fight about him?"

"From what I gathered after listening to them yell at each other for an hour, they bumped into him in town last weekend and—well, you know how affectionate my mom is."

I nodded again. Mrs. Reese was like me, a toucher. Effusive.

"Anyway," Emmett continued, looking aggrieved. "My dad thought they acted a little too friendly with each other. I've mentioned before how paranoid he can be. He accused her of . . ." His sentence trailed off like it literally pained him to finish it. "God, it's so ridiculous, I don't even want to say it."

All I could do was stare at him with my mouth hanging open. "My father is *gay*," I said after a few moments.

"He has a *husband*." Even as I said it, though, I could understand a tiny bit why a certain type of guy might feel threatened by a tall, built, handsome, utterly masculine man acting chummy with his wife, even if the man in question wasn't into women. Illogical, but not entirely crazy.

"Yeah, my dad knows that. Like I said, it's ridiculous." Emmett sighed again, wearily. "He freaked out this morning when she mentioned the barbecue, so she told him she wouldn't go just to shut him up. She's going to call your dads later to apologize."

I shook my head. "That's insane."

"I know. I'm sorry you have to deal with my messed up parents."

"I'm sorry *you* do."

He reached up to stroke my face but I stepped back just in time, almost colliding with a lawn chair. Frowning, Emmett dropped his hand and tossed a glance over his shoulder. Harper was watching us, an inscrutable expression on her face. When she saw us looking at her, she lifted her hand in a small wave.

"This sucks," Emmett said under his breath as he turned back to me. "I can't even touch you."

"Just until I tell her," I assured him. My stomach lurched as if protesting the two glasses of lemonade I'd put in it earlier.

"And when will that be?"

"Soon." I slipped past him, gesturing for him to follow me up to the deck.

Instead, he turned toward the wide stretch of yard near the driveway where Nate and his brothers were tossing around a football. Apparently, Nate had given up on his pursuit of Harper. That she still hadn't forgiven him for something that happened weeks ago didn't exactly bode well for Emmett and me.

"I'll be over there," Emmett told me before heading in Nate's direction.

Nate seemed surprised to see him coming. They hadn't exactly gotten off on the right foot at the beginning of summer, and never did get around to becoming friends. Still, I guess even hanging out with McTurdy was preferable to being with me and pretending.

I spent the rest of the evening with Harper, eating and talking and watching the guys horse around on the grass. We talked about her trip, and soccer, and how big the moon looked . . . everything but what we should've been discussing. What we *needed* to discuss, and soon. I'd had a million opportunities to say the words, coax them from their hiding spot at the back of my throat, but they refused to surface.

Harper had returned to the lake brimming with renewed hope. She was happy. Almost confident. She deserved to enjoy the feeling for at least one more night before I came along and ripped it away.

chapter 24

After a short and restless sleep, I woke up early the next morning feeling tired but determined. Harper and I had made plans to hit Goody's for dinner, and that was where I would finally tell her. Or maybe I'd tell her on the walk back. Yes, that sounded better.

First, though, I needed to see Emmett. He'd acted so distant at the barbecue, barely even looking my way the entire night. I wasn't sure if his goal was to make Harper believe there was nothing between us or if he was simply pissed about my reluctance to expose our upgraded relationship status. In any case, I sensed his patience had hit its limit.

He usually ran in the early morning before it got too hot, so I hopped on my ATV and zipped into the woods to look for him. It didn't take long. After about five minutes, I spotted him up ahead of me to the left, running parallel to the path with his back to me. Since I'd noticed him well in advance, I had time to swerve in front of him and block his route, making sure he saw me. I cut the engine and slipped off my helmet and goggles, watching him as he advanced toward me. His form was graceful, fluid, and I found it impossible to look away. The fact that he was shirtless didn't hurt either.

"I don't know about you," he said when he reached

me and yanked out his earbuds, "but I'm experiencing major déjà vu right now."

I smiled, feeling a little self-conscious. He was used to seeing me in dresses and bikinis, hair styled and makeup in place. I hadn't even showered yet, my hair was full of static from the helmet, and my cosmetic-free face felt grubby and sweaty. Not to mention my dusty jeans and black jacket, which were far more practical than fashionable. Still, the look on his face as he studied me was the opposite of disgusted.

"What?" I asked, grateful that my cheeks were undoubtedly already flushed from wearing the bulky helmet.

"Nothing." He looked away, a ghost of a smile on his lips. "You just look insanely sexy on that thing."

I laughed and swung my leg over the seat, then propped my behind against it, crossing my legs at the ankle. "You don't exactly look unappealing yourself at the moment."

He moved a few steps closer and tugged the zipper on my jacket. "Does that mean I can kiss you now? Is it safe?"

I knew what he was really asking, and my answer was the same as the one I'd given him yesterday—shake of the head, remorseful expression. *No, she still doesn't know about us.*

Emmett let go of my zipper, and the playful mood between us abruptly shifted.

"I wanted you to tell her right away," he said, his eyes blazing. "Then you convinced me to give you until Friday, so I gave you until Friday. Now it's Sunday, and nothing has changed. Just be honest with me, Kat. Did you ever have any intention of telling her?"

I focused on a ray of sunlight on the toes of my boots, feeling another wave of déjà vu. He wasn't yelling at me like he had the first time we'd met, but the tone in his voice sounded the same—harsh and impatient. And just like that time, I found myself pinned to my seat, stung by his reaction. "Yes," I said, recovering quickly. "Yes. I'm doing it today. Tonight."

"I hope so. I have enough drama in my life right now. There isn't room for any more."

The implication of his words was clear. He was giving me an ultimatum. Either I came clean with Harper or he was done. Our relationship was too new to withstand such an obstacle. I didn't fault him. If I were in his shoes, I probably would've reacted the same way.

"It was unfair of me to put you in this position," I said, reaching for his hand. "I'm sorry."

His face softened as he laced his fingers through mine. "Me too. I don't mean to pressure you, I just"—he leaned in and planted a big, sweaty kiss on my lips— "need to be able to do that whenever I want."

I pulled him toward me again and we kissed under the trees, entertaining a large-but-discreet audience of birds and squirrels.

Harper didn't seem concerned when she realized I'd only eaten about a third of my dinner. "Not hungry?" she asked, polishing off her own burger with gusto.

I shook my head. My stomach was so tight, the few bites of food I'd managed to get down felt like they were inching back up my esophagus. I pushed my plate toward her and she snatched a handful of my fries, more than happy to help me out.

While she ate, I let my gaze wander to the back wall of the restaurant where the jukebox used to reside. So many wonderful summers had begun with that jukebox. The absence of it felt almost like an omen. Seeing Goody's transformation that first day had tipped the balance somehow, setting the stage for all the changes that followed. Maybe if that one little thing had remained the same, we wouldn't be in a mess right now. A long-shot, yes, but I'd always believed in the significance of tradition.

No, I thought. *This is my fault. All mine.* I'd tried to change my ways, tried to get myself into the habit of thinking before acting, and I'd failed. Catastrophically.

It wasn't until after we'd paid and stepped outside into the cool night air that Harper noticed my odd behavior. "Are you okay? You've been really quiet."

"I'm fine," I said automatically. My heart started racing in tandem with my brain, which kept generating ideas and then scrapping them just as fast. How was I going to tell her? What should I say? Where did I start?

Not here, I thought as we stopped at the edge of the road, waiting for our chance to cross. No way could I tell her near a place where cars came barreling toward us at a million miles per hour, oblivious to pedestrians. No, better to wait until we were safely on the other side.

As soon as we'd made it across, however, Harper sidetracked me by saying, "I ran into Nate earlier. What is up with him lately? He's actually being *nice.*"

"I noticed," I said, latching on to the distraction. "I think he feels bad for everything that happened."

"Good." She tipped her face up to the sky. Dusk had just begun to fall, plunging the gravel road into shadows. "Do you think I should forgive him?"

I pretended to weigh my answer, even though I had zero doubt. Nate was trying, at least. "Yes. I think he deserves another chance. He likes you, Harper."

"Hmm," she said noncommittally. "Maybe I will give him another chance. Start hanging out with him again. Who knows?" she added, laughing. "It might make Emmett jealous."

My body went cold. Here was my opening. I swallowed a couple times, aware of the thumping pulse in my
neck. We were past my cottage, almost halfway to hers.
Walter, the old man face in the tree, was just up ahead,
seemingly watching our approach. "Harper."

"Yeah?"

I stopped walking and clutched her arm, turning her
toward me. "I have to tell you something."

"Okay," she said slowly. When I hesitated, she raised
her eyebrows expectantly. "What? Is it about Nate?"

"No." I let go of her arm. "It's about Emmett."

"What about him? Oh my God, is he gay? I didn't
think so, but—"

"No," I repeated. "He's . . . with me."

She stared at me, and even in the falling darkness, I saw
the exact moment when the meaning of my words sank
in. Her eyes widened for a moment and then narrowed
as if she didn't quite trust her own hearing. "What?"

"Emmett and me," I said. "We're together."

"*Together.*" The word hung in the air, dense and heavy.
"You and Emmett are dating?"

When I nodded, she turned away from me, shifting
her gaze to the copse of trees beside us. "How long?" she
asked, her voice flat.

"What?"

"How. Long."

"Um." My mind whirled, trying to pinpoint the exact
measure of time. Did I go by when Emmett first admit-
ted to liking me? Our first kiss? First date? "A couple
weeks," I said, figuring that was the closest answer.

She turned toward me again, her eyes glittering as they
fastened on mine. She held my gaze for a long, tense moment before swiveling on her heel and walking away, toward her cottage.

At first, my body didn't want to move, but then it

sprang into action as if I'd been shoved. "Harper!" I called, following her. "Wait."

"Leave me alone, Kat," she said when I caught up to her.

"Please let me explain. I didn't mean to—"

She spun around and there it was—the look I'd been dreading. The same look that had flashed in Shay's eyes that afternoon when she'd yelled at me on the front lawn of our school. Disappointment. Regret. Betrayal. I'd done it again. Had driven away someone important. Someone who'd trusted me.

"I don't want to hear it," my cousin hissed at me. "Just leave me alone."

When she turned and walked away from me a second time, I didn't follow her. I waited until she disappeared down her driveway and then started walking again, passing by her cottage. It was fully dark, but I'd walked the route often enough that I didn't even need a flashlight.

I started hearing the fighting when I was still several yards from Emmett's driveway. By the time I got there, the argument had escalated into a full-blown screaming match, complete with what sounded like breaking dishes. Without even stopping to listen, I knew Emmett's parents were probably still fighting about whatever Mr. Reese had convinced himself was going on between my dad and his wife. *God,* I thought, *I bet they wished they'd never set foot near Millard Lake this summer.*

Somehow, I knew Emmett wasn't in the cottage, subjecting himself to the chaos, so I didn't even bother to go up and knock. I dug my phone out of my purse and pressed the flashlight app, letting the light guide me as I stepped into the woods. Ten minutes later, I was standing in the clearing next to the small blue tent, scratched up and shivering and on the verge of tears. Emmett, who'd been crouched by the fire, loading it with dry kindling, jerked to a standing position when he saw me.

"Kat?" He came over and gripped my shoulders. "What are you doing here? What's wrong?"

The heat from his hands only intensified my shivering. "I told her," I said, looking up at him.

His eyes swept over my face like he was trying to make sense of the expression on it, which must have been a mixture of shock and desolation, neither of which he'd seen there before. "How'd she take it? Is she okay?"

My mind flashed on the image of Harper's face, her features etched with hurt. She hadn't yelled at me the way Shay had done, but I almost wished she had. Yelling might have been easier to take than her quiet disappointment. "I don't know."

"Are *you* okay?"

I didn't know that either, so I focused on the only emotion I was completely sure of in that moment and leaned in to kiss him. After a short pause, he kissed me back, drawing me against his soft, wood-smoke-scented T-shirt. I kissed him like I wanted to crawl inside him and curl up there, secure in his comforting warmth.

"You're freezing," he said when my icy hands grazed the skin under his shirt. He led me over to the fire and told me to stay put for a minute. Then he reached one arm into the tent and pulled out his sleeping bag, which he placed on the ground next to the fire. "Climb in," he told me.

I did, then motioned for him to join me. It was a tight squeeze, but that was okay because I immediately pulled him on top of me and wrapped myself around him. After a while, I barely even noticed the firmness of the ground or the assortment of pointy rocks sticking into my back.

"Emmett," I whispered at one point. "Are you a virgin?"

He stopped nibbling at my neck and pulled back to look at me. "Yes. Are you?"

I nodded and he kissed my lips hard, one hand tangled in my hair while the other slid beneath the hem of my dress. For a moment, I was lost in the taste of him, the scent of him, the heat of his skin against mine. I shifted position and a particularly sharp rock dug into my hip, jolting me back to reality. As my mind cleared, everything that had happened came rushing back at once, overwhelming me. Barely an hour had passed since I'd shattered my cousin's trust in me and I was minutes away from sharing all of myself with Emmett, a boy I wasn't even sure I loved.

The thought stopped me cold. I'd chosen someone I'd known for only a couple months over someone I'd known all my life. Someone I shared a history with . . . and memories and blood. Someone I *knew* I loved, and who loved me. Or used to, anyway.

Family trumps everything, I reminded myself. When had I lost sight of that?

"Wait," I said, wedging my hands against Emmett's chest, easing us apart. "I can't do this."

He pushed himself off me, bracing his weight with his arms. "Are you uncomfortable? I know this isn't the best place—"

"That's not what I mean." I squirmed out from under him—which wasn't easy in the cramped confines of the single-person sleeping bag—and sat up.

The instant I emerged into the night air, the heat in my body dissolved into chills. The fire had burned down to a dim orange glow and the forest surrounding us seemed completely still, as if it was holding its breath, waiting.

"I mean I can't do this anymore. Us. Me and you. Any of it."

He scrambled into a sitting position beside me. "What are you saying?"

"She's my cousin, Emmett." I ran my finger along a seam in the sleeping bag, unable to meet his eyes. "I can't do this to her."

He didn't speak for a long time. When he finally did, the tone he used wasn't the rough, impatient one from that morning, the one I'd been expecting. He sounded hurt. Vulnerable. "Maybe you should've thought of that before we let it get this far."

"I did. I did think of it. You know how worried I was about hurting Harper. I just . . ." My voice broke and I looked away, hastily swiping a finger under my eyes. "I thought there was a chance she'd be okay with it."

"And it's our fault she's not? We have to be punished for it? Maybe you should stop worrying so much about protecting Harper and think about yourself for once."

"*All* I've been thinking about is myself," I shot back. I wiggled the rest of the way out of the sleeping bag and stood up, straightening my wrinkled dress. My eyes were dry once again.

Emmett watched as I shoved my feet into my sandals and gathered my purse. "I don't get you, Kat," he said, yanking his shirt back on roughly. "The reason you told her was so that we could be together without having to sneak around behind her back."

No, I thought. *The reason I told her was because I felt guilty. The rest was just wishful thinking.* "I have to go," I said, fighting back a second rush of tears.

Emmett climbed out of the sleeping bag, tossed a few handfuls of dirt on the fire, and grabbed his flashlight. Then, wordlessly, we headed for the woods together.

"You don't have to walk me home," I told him as we zigzagged through the trees.

"I'm not an asshole," he replied.

No, he wasn't. The only asshole in this situation was me, and I was on a roll. First Harper and then Emmett, both in the span of an hour. How many more relationships could I destroy before midnight?

It felt like hours before we reached my cottage. Emmett walked me right up to the door and then turned to me, his expression grave. "Like I told you before . . . I can't be just friends with you, Kat. It's this or nothing."

"Then I guess I choose nothing." I escaped inside before I had time to change my mind.

chapter 25

When I stepped into the living room, I discovered Pop sitting on the couch, eating leftover strawberry almond cheesecake squares right out of the pan. He only indulged in large quantities of junk food when he was rewarding himself for something, so I knew what that meant.

"You finished Book Six?" I asked, trying to muster up the appropriate amount of enthusiasm.

"That I did." He deposited the pan on the coffee table. "Wrote the last sentence an hour ago. Now it's time to let it marinate for a few days." He looked at me for the first time. "How was dinner with Harper?"

I shrugged, then burst into tears. Pop jumped up to hug me. He smelled like strawberries and sugar and for a moment I felt like a little kid again, being comforted over some silly little hurt.

"You told her about you and Emmett?"

I sniffled against his shoulder. "There is no me and Emmett anymore."

"Oh, Noodle," Pop said, patting my hair.

After a minute, I pulled away and wiped my eyes. He regarded me with a sort of panicked concern, like he wasn't quite sure how to fix me. Dad had always been better at handling my emotional outbursts and finding practical solutions to whatever it was that plagued me. Unfortunately, he was already back at our condo, prepping for his forthcoming week at the office.

"I'll be okay. I just want to take a bath and go to bed." Pop kissed my forehead. "Go ahead. I think I'll head to bed myself. I'm beat. Wake me if you need anything, all right?"

I assured him I would, even though it would be pointless. Even with both dads on my side, there was no fixing this one.

Forty-five minutes later, I was running a brush through my wet hair in front of the bathroom mirror when I heard a loud banging on the front door. My hand jerked, sending the brush flying into the sink. It was after eleven o'clock. Who in the hell could be paying us a visit at this hour?

Harper, I thought, throwing a bathrobe over my pajamas as I left the bathroom. *She's come to talk.*

I unlocked the door and swung it open, a small glimmer of hope igniting in my stomach. But it was quickly extinguished when I saw Emmett standing there, his face completely drained of color. He was panting like he'd just sprinted all the way over and there was a bloody scratch down the side of his face.

"What's wrong?" I demanded.

When he looked at me, his eyes were terrified. "My mom," he said between gasps. "I went inside and she was—there was blood and . . ."

My heart stuttered. "Emmett," I said, grabbing hold of his shoulder and shaking him firmly, trying to get him to focus. "What happened?"

He rested his palm against the door frame and tried to slow down his breathing. A few agonizing seconds passed before he answered. "My father. He hit her."

"Oh my God." I pulled him inside and shut the door behind us.

Emmett gave me a vacant look, as if he wasn't even aware he'd moved. "He hit her and I wasn't there."

I could see in his face that his shock was rapidly spiraling into rage.

"How bad is she hurt?"

"I don't know. She wouldn't wake up and her face was all bloody and I just—" He swallowed hard. "I didn't know what to do. There was no connection on my cell and I couldn't use the cottage phone, so I ran over here."

"Where's your father?"

"I don't know," he repeated. "He was gone when I got there."

I tilted his face to the side so I could examine his scratch. It didn't look deep. "Why couldn't you use your cottage phone?"

"He ripped it out of the wall."

I dropped my hand and stared at him for a few moments. It was then that I realized he needed more help than I alone could give. "Don't move," I told him before leaving the room.

Pop slept like the dead, so it took several shakes to rouse him. Luckily, he was always fully alert when he did wake. He took one look at my face and shot straight up in bed. "I'm up," he exclaimed.

"Pop, Emmett's here." I explained the situation.

Before I'd even finished, Pop was out of bed and throwing on the clothes he'd been wearing earlier. "I'm going to check on Holly. Emmett should probably stay here. He needs to steer clear of his cottage in case his father comes back."

I thought of Emmett's words from a few weeks ago. *My dad knows if he ever hit her again, I'd kill him.* Pop was right. He couldn't be there.

When we emerged from the bedroom, I was relieved to see that Emmett had obeyed my directive to stay put. He still looked half in shock. I went over to him while Pop called 911 to report the incident—something I probably should've done right away—then grabbed his car keys off the table.

"I'll take good care of her," he promised Emmett as he walked past him to the door and outside.

When Emmett made a move to follow him, I seized his hand and held him back. "You can't be in your cottage right now," I said gently. "You know why."

He wrenched his hand out of my grasp. "Then I'm going to go find him."

"No," I said, maneuvering myself between him and the door. "You can't do that either. Let the cops find him."

He glared at me, fists clenched at his sides. The shock had all but worn off, and anger rolled off him in waves. "Let me go, Kat."

"No," I repeated. I looked up at him, unblinking, until he realized the only way he was getting past me was if he physically removed me. And he'd never do that.

He backed away from me, his fury thawing into exasperation. He pushed his fingers through his hair and let out a frustrated sigh. "I can't just sit here and do nothing."

"You won't be doing nothing. You'll be waiting here with me."

His shoulders relaxed somewhat, and I could tell he was beginning to surrender. What had happened between us earlier seemed irrelevant. He needed someone, and I was there.

"Distract me, then," he said gruffly. He paced between the living room and kitchen a few times, fingers linked together at the back of his neck. "So I won't do something I might regret later."

Lucky for him, I had distraction down to an art form. I pulled out a kitchen chair and said, "Sit."

He stopped pacing and sat while I reached into the cupboard under the sink for the first aid kit Pop insisted we keep handy. I popped it open and extracted some sterile alcohol wipes and a tube of antibiotic cream. Then I went to work on Emmett's face.

"Jesus," he hissed when the alcohol wipe came in contact with his scrape. "That stings."

I eased up on the pressure, lightly dabbing the blood from the edges. "How did you get this?"

"Tree branch, I think. I barely felt it."

"Well," I said, opening a fresh wipe. "I bet you're feeling it now."

Once Emmett's cut was clean and disinfected, we tried to watch TV for a while. Each minute that passed felt like an hour, and I wasn't sure how much longer I could keep him occupied. Just as I was about to suggest a round of Crazy Eights, my dad walked in. Emmett bolted off the couch, his eyes glued to Pop's face.

"She's okay," Pop said before Emmett could ask. "I mean, she's regained consciousness, at least. The son of a bitch—" Pop stopped and cleared his throat, remembering who he was talking to. "Your father banged her up pretty badly. Loosened a few of her teeth and blackened both eyes. Her face is completely swollen so it was hard for me to determine the extent of her injuries."

Emmett winced, experiencing her pain secondhand. "Where is she?"

"The paramedics came and took her to the hospital." Pop motioned toward the door. "Come on. I'll take you to her."

Emmett nodded and then looked back at me, unsure.

The two of us had developed quite a knack for non-verbal communication over the past few weeks, so I caught on immediately. "Just let me get dressed."

Like most other establishments in Erwin, the hospital was small and dingy. When we got there, a woman directed us to a waiting room and told us to sit. "The doctor is in with her now. We'll let you know when she's done."

Pop and I waited with Emmett, positioned on either side of him like a human force field. No one spoke, but I could feel the tension radiating from Emmett's body. I wanted to take his hand, touch him, but considering I'd basically dumped him a mere three hours before, I didn't think he'd be very receptive to the contact. I just sat there, shifting occasionally in the lumpy padded chair and being quietly supportive.

Twenty minutes passed, and Emmett's anxiety peaked. "I'm gonna go call my brother," he said, and then stood up and left the room.

Pop and I looked at each other across the vacant seat.

"Should I go with him?" I asked.

Pop shook his head. "Just leave him be."

I averted my gaze to the window. From there, I could just make out the white flash of Emmett's T-shirt as he paced back and forth outside near the main entrance, cell phone at his ear.

"What a mess," Pop said softly. "Holly mentioned that she had some problems with her husband, but I never thought he'd *beat* her. He's twice her size, for Christ's sake. He could've killed her."

"This is all our fault," I told him.

He slid over into the empty seat beside me. "What makes you say that?"

"He beat her because of Dad. Because he thinks there's something going on between them. Emmett said they'd been fighting about it all weekend."

Pop didn't seem shocked, so I assumed Mrs. Reese had mentioned something about it when she'd called to apologize for missing the barbecue.

"How is that *our* fault? We're not responsible for the man's misconceptions. Or his temper, for that matter."

"It never would've happened if they hadn't met us."

"You can't know that for sure." He looked at me, his eyes bloodshot and tired. "You take on so much blame, Kat, even when it's not your burden to carry. You always have. When you were little and heard someone make a derogatory comment about your dad and me, you wouldn't get mad at *them*. You'd get mad at yourself for not being able to prevent it. As if you'd failed at your job."

I shrugged. I still felt that way.

"The only person who should be held accountable for what happened to Emmett's mother is Emmett's father," Pop went on. "It's not Emmett's fault, or Holly's, or yours. It's not your dad's fault either, even though it isn't the first time something like this has happened."

"What do you mean?"

"Well, it's never gone to this extreme, but we've had issues with jealous boyfriends and husbands before. Women have always loved Mark." He bumped me with his elbow. "Where do you think you got your charm?"

I smiled wryly. "Even when he's *not* flirting, he's flirting."

"Exactly."

Emmett returned then, sinking heavily into the seat next to mine. He looked utterly wrecked. Pop excused himself to go rustle up some caffeinated beverages, leaving us alone with the other waiting room occupants, which included a shady-looking man in a baseball cap and an old lady who kept coughing into a soggy tissue.

"How'd it go with your brother?" I asked.

He leaned forward, rubbing his hands over his face. "Not so good. I had to talk him out of booking a plane ticket and flying home to murder our father. Wherever the hell he is," he added bitterly.

"The police are looking," I reminded him.

Pop had updated us on the way to the hospital. Mr. Reese had taken his car when he'd left, but he couldn't have gotten very far.

"I know." Emmett's bleary eyes met mine. "And don't worry, neither one of us would actually kill him. Just rough him up a little. Or maybe a lot."

"You really hate him, don't you?"

"Yeah. I guess I do." He leaned back in the chair and sighed. "I should've been there tonight instead of hiding in the woods like a coward. This has been building between them all summer. It was only a matter of time before he snapped."

"You had no way of knowing this would happen."

"Yeah, but maybe I would've seen the signs if I hadn't been so damn preoccupied with you." His tone was brash, accusatory.

I felt like I'd been slapped.

"Sorry," he said, seeing my expression. "That came out wrong. I'm not blaming you at all. It's just . . . maybe you're right. Maybe our being together is causing more trouble than it's worth."

He was getting it, finally, but having him on the same page didn't make it hurt any less. And in spite of what Pop had said, I *was* partly to blame for everything that had happened this summer. It was *my* fault Harper hated me. It had been *my* choice to give in to my attraction to Emmett, even though I knew it was unfair not just to my cousin, but to him as well. It was also my fault—indirectly, anyway—that Emmett had been nestled in a sleeping bag with me tonight instead of in his cottage with his mother, shielding her from harm.

Maybe the reason I took on so much blame was because I knew, deep down, that I deserved at least some of it.

"Are you Emmett?" A tall, middle-aged nurse in navy blue scrubs stood in front of us, a kind expression on her face. When Emmett nodded, she said, "Your mom is going to be okay. She has a concussion and two broken ribs, so Dr. Mason wants to keep her here for a few days. You can go see her now. Room two-fourteen. She's been asking for you."

The nurse smiled thinly before disappearing back down the hallway. Emmett stood up, his strong, toned runner's legs trembling beneath him. My body ached with the urge to jump up and wrap my arms around him, but I didn't budge from my chair.

"Thanks, Kat," he said, looking down at me with those blue, blue eyes. "For everything."

I wasn't sure if he was referring to just tonight or the entire summer. In any case, there was an air of finality to his words.

"You're welcome," I said.

He turned and walked away, toward Room 214 and his mom. I knew he didn't want me to follow.

Pop returned a couple minutes later, bogged down with to-go cups of coffee and mini bags of crackers. To my surprise, he handed one of the coffees to me. I guess he figured his reservations about me and caffeine overdoses didn't apply tonight.

"Emmett in with his mom?" he asked, sitting next to me.

I waited until he'd finished balancing the coffee and

crackers on the empty chair beside him before saying, "Pop, I want to go home."

"Shouldn't we wait for Emmett?"

"No, I want to go *home*. To Weldon."

"What? Kat, we still have two weeks left."

"Only for a few days," I amended. "I just—I don't want to be here right now."

He stared at me, perplexed. He knew how much I hated the city in the summer, and how I counted down the days every year until I could breathe in the clean, pine-scented air of Millard Lake and finally feel free. What he didn't know was how tainted it had become for me, and how the thought of spending one more day surrounded by trees and water and this small stifling town made me feel like I was about to suffocate.

"Well," he said slowly. "There *are* a few things I should probably take care of at home. And your father would be pleased to see us. We'll leave tomorrow, okay?"

I nodded, relieved. I knew he didn't really have anything to do at home, that he was just saying he did to make me feel less irrational for wanting to leave, but I appreciated the lie. In a world overrun with crappy fathers, I'd somehow snagged two of the best.

chapter 26

In spite of everything that happened, I didn't feel right about leaving without letting Harper know. While Pop shut down our cottage, I walked the familiar path through the woods.

Aunt Carrie answered my knock. "Good morning," she said, looking me over.

I hadn't bothered with my regular beauty routine, opting instead for a messy ponytail, no makeup, and one of my dad's T-shirts over faded denim shorts.

"Come on in."

I shook my head. "I have to leave soon. Pop and I are going home for a few days."

"I know. He told me." She leaned her shoulder against the doorframe, propping the screen open with her foot. "He asked me to check in on Holly this week. Did they catch her husband yet?"

I nodded. Mrs. Reese had called from the hospital earlier to thank us and to give us an update. The cops had arrested Mr. Reese late last night at a gas station halfway between the lake and Hyde Creek. He'd remained safely behind bars until official charges were brought, and eventually he and Mrs. Reese would have to go to court. I'd assumed she and Emmett would close up their cottage early, but she'd decided she wanted to finish out the summer before heading home and filing for divorce. I hoped for both their sakes that she'd stick to her guns.

"Is Harper here?" I asked after I'd filled Aunt Carrie in on the latest news.

"Yes, but I think she's still—"

"I'm awake." Harper came up behind her mom, blond hair tousled from sleep. She met my eyes briefly before lowering her gaze to her bare feet.

"We'll see you in a few days, then." Aunt Carrie squeezed my hand and gave me a sad little smile, telling me without words that she still loved me but at the same time wanted me to get my act together and mend things with my cousin.

I nodded solemnly back at her, letting her know I'd do my best.

"Go ahead," Harper told me once her mom had gone back into the cottage.

"What?"

She stepped outside and closed the door behind her, then stood in front of me with her arms crossed over her chest. "Say you're sorry and smile and charm me into forgiving you. That's what you came here to do, right?"

I opened my mouth to answer, but nothing came out. She was at least partly right. "I *am* sorry, Harper," I said after a pause. "But I don't expect you to forgive me. There's no excuse for what I did. I knew you liked Emmett and I went and—"

"You honestly think this is about Emmett? No, Kat. It's about us. You and me."

That shut me up. I clamped my lips together and looked at her, waiting for her to continue.

"You didn't even consider coming to me and telling me how you felt. No. Instead, you went behind my back and hid it from me like I'm some kind of delicate flower." She pushed her hair off her face with an impatient hand.

"Why, Kat? Yeah, okay, so I had a little crush on Emmett. But did you really think I'd stand in your way if I knew how much you liked him? You think I'm that selfish?"

"No," I said quickly. *Where is this coming from?* "I just hated the thought of hurting you."

"I get that, and it *did* sort of bother me when I found out you guys were together. I'll admit it. But I can't say I was surprised. You're Kat Henley, after all." She gestured her arm toward me and laughed—a dull, joyless sound. "You have not just one, but *two* amazing fathers who adore you. Guys fall all over themselves around you. You're pretty and charismatic and everything I'm not. So of course Emmett would choose you over me. But you know what hurt me the most about all this?" She placed her palm against the screen door and pierced me with one last accusing glare. "That you assumed I wasn't strong enough to handle it."

And with that, she stepped back inside the cottage and shut the door in my face.

"*Written on the Wind* is on TCM tonight," Dad told me during dinner the next night. "Want to watch with me?"

"Um," I said. I didn't want to tell him that I was starting to lose interest in old movies, even the ones featuring Lauren Bacall in all her 1950s glory. The main reason I'd watched them in the first place was to get ideas for hair styles and clothes, and I didn't need any more. Ideas *or* clothes.

"Already have plans tonight?" Pop inquired as he dug into his baked potato—plain, of course. He was back to watching his weight again. "Seeing your friends?"

What friends? I thought. I'd alienated every one of them. "I'm kind of tired," I said, popping a big chunk of steak into my mouth so I could chew for a while instead of talk.

"Speaking of your friends," Dad said, eyeing me. "I called Holly last night to see how she was doing and Emmett answered the phone. He seemed surprised to hear that you're back home. You didn't tell him?"

"How *is* Mrs. Reese?" I asked, ignoring his question. I didn't want to talk about Emmett.

"Very sore, but she's healing." He reached for his beer and took a sip. "Physically, anyway. The mental part will take a bit longer." A cloud passed over his face, and I knew he was thinking about our conversation yesterday evening. He'd heard Pop's version of what had happened between Emmett's parents, but he'd wanted to hear mine, too.

I basically repeated what Emmett had told me at the barbecue about how his father had freaked out after witnessing Dad interacting with Mrs. Reese. "He feels threatened by you," I'd told him.

"I think he's more threatened by the idea of another man treating his wife with respect," Dad had replied. "It doesn't really matter who it is. He just doesn't want her to see that there might be something better out there."

He was probably right, but still. I could tell he felt somewhat guilty about his indirect role in it, just like I did. Even though Pop had told us a million times each that the only culprits in this situation were Mr. Reese's fists.

"Well, I'm glad she's going to be okay," I said as I gathered up my half-full plate and stood up. "And no," I added before heading to the kitchen, "I didn't tell Emmett I was leaving because he and I aren't friends anymore." *Or anything else.*

"That's too bad, Katrina," Dad said, his resonant voice following me out of the room. "Because he really needs one."

Irritated, I dumped my dishes in the sink and went to my room. I didn't mind having parents who genuinely cared and took an interest in my life, but sometimes they got a little *too* involved.

Alone in my room, I flopped on my bed and opened up my laptop. It felt strange being in our condo again. In past summers, I would've died before leaving my cousin's side for even a day. We'd never purposely avoided each other before, but then again, I'd never betrayed her before either. There had always been a mild competitiveness between us, a hint of unbalance, but I'd had no idea Harper thought those things about me, or believed I thought those things about her. Maybe these feelings had been brewing between us for years and we were both to blame. Or maybe it was just me, ruining yet another relationship with my short-sighted mistakes. No wonder Shay had been so angry and unforgiving. No, I hadn't set out to flirt with her boyfriend that night, and yes, I'd apologized for it a million times. But had I ever once tried to imagine my actions from *her* perspective?

Sometimes, a person needed more than apologies. The only thing that mattered, really, was to be heard and understood.

Impulsively, I logged onto Facebook and scrolled down my newsfeed. Shay had unfriended me months ago, preventing me from seeing her page and statuses, but that didn't mean she'd disappeared off the site completely. A couple of our old mutual friends hadn't bothered to unfriend me and one of them, Elissa Warren, had just posted a CHECK IN of her current location (South End Mall) and had tagged several friends who were there with her. One of them was Shay.

"I'll be back in about an hour," I said as I passed by the kitchen where my dads were cleaning up the dinner mess. Before they had time to ask any questions, I was out the door and in the elevator, heading to the lobby and outside.

South End Mall was at least fifteen minutes away by foot, but walking was usually quicker than contending with traffic and parking. I got there in no time and pushed through the glass doors into the blessedly cold air conditioning. After ten minutes of searching, I finally spotted Shay's glossy black hair outside the entrance to the movie theater. She was holding hands with Braden and laughing with her friends like she didn't miss me in the slightest.

Steeling myself, I walked up behind her and touched her arm. "Shay."

She whirled around, her dark brown eyes growing wide at the sight of me. I wasn't sure which had surprised her more, that I was wearing ordinary clothes and no makeup in public or that I was there at all.

"What are you doing here?" she asked, her shock over my presence overriding the anger that I knew was still there. "Shouldn't you still be at your cottage?"

"I came home for a few days. Can I talk to you for a minute? Alone?" I glanced over at my old friends, who stared at me with a mixture of discomfort and curiosity. They'd all taken Shay's side without question, and I couldn't blame them. My reputation didn't exactly make me a sympathetic figure.

"Uh . . ." She looked back at Braden.

He met her eyes for a moment and then shot me a suspicious look, like he wasn't entirely sure I wasn't about to maul him right there in the middle of South End Mall.

When Shay saw me look back at him, she stepped in between us protectively. She no longer trusted me anywhere near him. "I don't think so, Kat," she said coldly.

"Fine. Then I'll say this in front of everyone." I took a deep breath and caught the buttery scent of popcorn from inside the theater. On my left, Cassidy Boveri nudged Miranda Lipton's arm and tittered. *This should be good*, her expression said.

Ignoring them and everything else, I shifted focus to my former best friend. "I just wanted to tell you that I get it now. Why you refuse to forgive me. You're mad at me for what I did, but you're disappointed, too. You were nice enough to give me a chance, even after people warned you that I couldn't be trusted. And instead of proving you right, I let you down." My eyes started burning and I dropped my gaze to the floor, aiming the end of my speech at the speckled tile. "That's all I wanted to say. I won't bother you again." Then, too scared to venture even a glimpse of Shay's reaction, I turned and walked away.

When I got home, my dads were sitting in the living room together, watching TV. They both looked up as I entered the room.

"You okay, Noodle?" Pop asked, examining my face.

"Yeah." Surprisingly, I actually was.

"Where did you go?" Dad asked.

I reached up to smooth my windblown hair, which felt dull and flat from lack of product. "I'll tell you later, okay?"

He nodded, satisfied with my answer, and the two of them went back to watching TV.

I once again headed for my room, which was currently downright freezing. Dad had a habit of cranking up the air conditioning to "Antarctica" in hot weather. Shivering, I opened my closet and yanked a sweatshirt off its hanger. As I did, my eyes lit on something wedged in the corner of the top shelf. My old boxing gloves.

I flung the sweatshirt on my bed and turned back to the closet, standing on tiptoe to reach the gloves. It had been two years since I'd held them in my hands. The red leather was scuffed from the hundreds of punches I'd thrown while my grumpy old boxing teacher urged me on. I kind of missed Mr. Ogilvie. He'd been so disappointed when I quit. My sprained wrist was only part of the reason; I could have gone back after it healed. Instead, I just gave up.

No longer cold, I gathered up the gloves—along with an unused roll of hand wrap I'd discovered way back on the shelf—and left my room.

"Where are you going *now*?" Pop called as I passed the living room.

"To get some exercise," I called back, ducking out the door before they had time to inquire about my cagey behavior. A girl was entitled to a few secrets, after all.

I'd been in our building's top-floor gym only a handful of times in the past two years, and not to work out. Mostly, I'd just popped in to ask Dad something while *he* was working out. I hadn't actually used the equipment in ages, even though the gym was large, well-appointed, and just a short elevator ride away. The only piece of equipment I was interested in at the moment, however, was the free-standing heavy bag in the corner.

The gym was pretty deserted that time of night, so there was no one to see me sit down on one of the bench presses and wrap my hands and wrists, protecting them from injury. Once the wrap was secure, I shoved my hands into the gloves and approached the bag.

At first, I tapped it gently, getting a feel for the movement. Then, when that became comfortable, I started hitting harder, the muscles in my arms and shoulders settling into a rhythm they still knew by heart. My bad wrist ached, but I pushed through it, hammering my target until I felt exhausted and breathless . . . and finally, free.

chapter 27

Pop and I stayed in Weldon for the rest of the week, then on Friday evening after Dad got home from work, the three of us headed back to the lake to finish off the last two weeks of summer. I couldn't predict how the last weeks would play out, but I did know one thing for sure—even after everything that had happened, there was no place I'd rather be in the summer than Millard Lake.

"What did you say was wrong with it again?" Dad asked me on Saturday morning as we stood together in front of the garage, peering down at my ATV.

"The last time I rode it, I noticed it was making a weird noise," I explained, wiping a drop of sweat off my temple. At ten o'clock, the heat was already stifling. "Like a clicking."

Dad crouched down to inspect the tires. "A clicking?"

"Yeah." I demonstrated, emitting a series of high-pitched sounds that made the birds respond with chirps and my dad with uproarious laughter.

"Thanks for the demo," he said, still chuckling. When he straightened up again, something behind me caught his gaze and his broad smile drooped a few notches.

I spun around, expecting to see a wild coyote or something else equally as terrifying, but what I actually saw was my cousin, dressed in her customary Nike wear and walking toward us.

What now? I thought, my heart sinking as she drew closer. *Has she come to tell me off some more?* After Shay, I didn't think I could handle another awkward confrontation.

"I'll deal with the clicking later, Katrina." Dad squeezed my shoulder and walked away, pausing to give Harper a quick greeting hug before continuing on to the cottage.

Then it was just me and my cousin in the yard, eyeing each other warily over my possibly faulty ATV.

"Hey," she said after a long, tense silence.

"Hey," I replied. I searched her face for clues about what she might do or say next, but came up empty.

She did look significantly less angry than the last time I'd seen her, which was promising. As for her eyes, they just looked sad. "Can we talk for a minute?"

When I nodded, she cocked her head toward a shaded patch of lawn under the trees and then started toward it. I followed, sitting next to her on the prickly grass.

"How was your trip home?" she asked with just the barest amount of interest, like she couldn't quite manage being friendly.

I thought of Shay's face when she saw me at the mall and the many hours I'd logged at the gym, taking out my frustrations on a foam-padded bag. "Enlightening," I said vaguely.

"Funny," she said, wrapping her arms around her knees. "I could say the same about *my* week."

I kept quiet, waiting for her to elaborate. Clearly *something* had happened while I was gone, or she wouldn't be sitting with me, willing to talk.

"I went to see Emmett the other day," she told me.

"Oh?" I said, echoing her flat, barely interested tone. I hadn't seen or spoken to Emmett since Sunday night and

I didn't want her to hear how hungry I was for news about him. Or how desperately I missed him.

"Yeah. I wanted to talk to him about . . . everything. Hear his side of things." She shifted positions on the grass, the heels of her sneakers digging into the soft earth. "We talked for a long time about you. He told me how conflicted you were about dating him and how you resisted it for weeks before you guys actually got together. He said you never stopped thinking about me and worrying about my feelings. And that the reason you took so long to tell me is because you were ashamed of yourself for not being strong enough to stay away from him. You thought I'd look at you differently once I knew."

I nodded. It was all true.

"He also said you broke up with him."

I nodded again, then dared a peek at her. She was fiddling with the laces on her shoe, not looking at me.

"You're my cousin," I said. "Even though I haven't exactly proved it to you this summer, you're more important to me than some guy."

She looked at me then, assessing me the way she did when she knew I was holding something back. "Is that all he is to you, though? Just some guy?"

I turned away, examining the grass for four-leaf clovers so I wouldn't have to answer.

"Emmett and I talked about something else, too," Harper continued. "How he feels about you." When I still didn't say anything, she kept going. "He told me he thinks he might be in love with you."

My hand stilled in the grass and I couldn't stop my head from swiveling toward her. I studied her face, searching for any sign of dishonesty. "He said that?"

"He did. You know, I kind of suspected there was something going on between you and him. The way you looked at each other . . ." Harper leaned back on her palms, stretching her long legs out in front of her. "I guess I didn't want to admit it to myself. Just once, I wanted the cute guy to like me instead of you."

"I wanted that, too, Harper."

"I know. You even tried to push us together at first, even though it was useless. Emmett never saw anyone but you."

"I'm sorry," I said, leaning back with her. "I didn't mean for it to happen the way it did."

She shrugged. "It is what it is, right? I'm not like you, Kat. I don't light up a room when I enter it. I can't flirt. God, I'm eighteen years old and I've only kissed two guys. *Two*."

That made me think of Nate and their almost kiss in his kitchen. "Nate's into you," I reminded her. "I know his douchiness often overshadows all his other qualities, but you have to admit he *is* kind of cute."

Her lips twitched into a tiny smile. "Yeah, I guess he kind of is."

We lapsed into silence again, but it felt significantly less tense. Our relationship would probably never go back to the way it was before this summer, but then again, would anything? Like any other family, we fought and scratched and drew blood and then kept on loving each other in spite of it all. The bonds we shared were strong yet elastic, like ligaments connecting bone—easy to injure and difficult to heal, but ultimately resilient.

That evening, after much inner debate and even more stalling, I gathered my nerve and walked over to see Emmett. My progress was slow as I meandered through the forest I knew and loved. Soon I'd be back in the city, dodging people and cars instead of rocks and trees, so I wanted to take my time.

The Reeses' cottage seemed eerily still when I

emerged from the woods. No more fighting or screaming. Even the birds in the trees were quiet, as if grateful
for the respite.

Mrs. Reese answered my knock, a stiff smile on her
still-healing lips. "Oh! Hi, Kat." The multiple bruises on
her face had faded to a patchy yellow-gray, and her eyes,
usually so bright and expressive, held a foggy wariness
that would likely take months to go away.

It hurt my heart to look at her. "Hi, Mrs. Reese. How
are you feeling?"

"Oh, I've been better, but I'll be okay." She stepped to
the side and held the door open, her left arm curling
around her battered ribs. "You're looking for Emmett,
I'm guessing. He went to the store for me, but he should
be back soon. Come on in."

"Um, if you don't mind, I think I'll wait for him down
on your dock."

She regarded me for a moment, her eyes conveying
the thoughts behind them. *Please be gentle with my boy;
he's been through enough.* "Sure, go ahead. I'll let him
know you're down there."

I thanked her and made my way down to the shore.
On the dock, I kicked off my flip-flops and sat down,
dipping my feet in the water. Morning may have been
my favorite time of day at the lake, but twilight ran a
close second. I liked to watch the sky as it evolved from
blue to gray to black, seemingly in the span of seconds.

About fifteen minutes passed before I felt the dock
tremble beneath me, followed by the sound of footsteps.
Moments later, Emmett dropped down beside me, keeping his body a few deliberate inches from mine. "Hi," he
said quietly.

Looking at him tore at my heart even more than seeing his mom's bruises. Every line of his body sagged in
exhaustion. He looked downright defeated.

"How are you?" I asked.

He shrugged, not bothering to answer. Obviously, he'd been better too. "Why didn't you tell me you were going home for five days?"

Even though I hadn't been away from him for long, I'd almost forgotten how direct he was, and how much I liked that about him. Still, I stumbled over my answer. "Because I didn't think I needed to. I mean, we're not . . . we don't hang out anymore."

"Really?" He glanced down at himself and then at me, indicating that we were, indeed, hanging out right now.

"You said you couldn't be friends with me. Just friends. 'This or nothing,' you said. Remember? Those were the choices you gave me." I swirled my feet around in the water, creating tiny waves. "And then you said good-bye to me at the hospital, so I thought—"

"Wait," he said, holding up a hand to stop me. "I said good-bye to you?"

"Well, not in those exact words, but that's what I assumed." I thought about the finality in his voice that night when he thanked me, the sadness in his eyes. "You agreed that our being together was more trouble than it was worth. I thought you were done with me."

"Done," he mumbled, shaking his head. "If I was done with you, Kat, I wouldn't be sitting here right now."

And you also wouldn't be telling Harper that you think you might be in love with me, I added in my head. I wondered if he still felt that way, or if he'd even meant it in the first place. "So what happens now?" I asked after a lengthy pause.

"Well, in two weeks I'll go home and make sure every single thing belonging to my father is gone from our house while my mom tries to figure out if we can even afford to still live there. Then I'll finish my last year of high school and hopefully score a decent enough GPA to go to college. Other than that, I have no idea." He let out a breath and looked at me. "Or were you talking about us?"

I swallowed. "I guess that depends on if there still *is* an us."

He looked away, tilting his face toward the sky. The dim moonlight illuminated his skin, making him look pale and almost ethereal. "My life's too messed up right now to handle being jerked around like that again. I have a lot on my plate with my mom. She's gotten past this before and she will again, but I'm not so sure about me. I'll never forgive myself for not being there that night."

"I'm sorry for jerking you around. And the reason you weren't there that night was because you were with me instead. So let me shoulder some of the blame on that one, okay?"

"Are you kidding? If I hadn't walked you home that night, I never would've stopped by my cottage in the first place. She would've been there until morning, bleeding on the floor. Who knows what might have happened?" He cringed at the memory.

I couldn't stop myself from taking his hand. I understood how it was to feel that inherent duty to prevent and protect. I was also familiar with the guilt that came with it when I inevitably failed at my job. Even when that job wasn't my burden to carry in the first place.

Emmett didn't try to let go of my hand. In fact, he held on and squeezed. "So what happens now?" he asked, repeating my question.

I knew it was time to talk about us. If we *were* an us. "You're right, you know," I said, scooting closer to him. "You and I can't be just friends. But I don't think we can be nothing, either."

He nodded in silent agreement and then lifted our entwined hands to his lips. His warm breath washed over my knuckles, provoking a full-body shiver. I realized that when it came to Emmett Reese, I was helpless to resist.

"I spoke to Harper this morning," I said, feeling shy all of a sudden—a foreign emotion for me. I nervously cleared my throat. "She told me about your conversation the other day. And, um, she also mentioned what you said to her about me. That you think you might be in love with me?"

He lowered our hands, resting them on the rough wood between us. "I was wrong about that," he said solemnly. "I don't think I'm in love with you, Kat. Not anymore."

My stomach dropped, and all of a sudden I felt exceedingly grateful that I hadn't said out loud what I'd been pondering almost nonstop for the past week—that I thought I might be in love with him, too. That maybe we *were* worth the trouble. "No?"

"No." His ankle wove around mine, linking us together beneath the water's surface. "I know I am."

chapter 28

Closing up the cottage for winter usually took longer than opening it at the beginning of summer. In the week before we left, my dads and I spent countless hours cleaning and storing and trying to use up all the food in the cupboards and fridge. A certain heaviness always clung to the ritual. For most people, end of summer was signified by cooler weather and back-to-school sales. For me, it was washing beach towels and cooking that last frozen chicken breast so it wouldn't go to waste.

Because Harper and Aunt Carrie had an eight-hour drive home, they planned to leave on the Sunday of Labor Day weekend instead of stretching vacation until Monday like everyone else. As was tradition, summer with my cousin always ended in the same way it had begun, with hamburgers at Goody's.

This time, we decided to bring along some dates.

"You look pretty," Nate told Harper as she slid into the back seat of my dad's BMW, which he'd let me borrow for the occasion. And because it was raining and we didn't want to walk.

"Thanks," Harper said with a trace of surprise. Nate wasn't one for sincere compliments.

I peered into the rearview mirror at my cousin's reflection and saw that she was blushing, her mouth relaxing into a small, pleased smile.

"You look pretty, too," Emmett said, appraising me from his spot in the passenger seat. "In case I haven't told you enough already."

"You have, but thank you again." I leaned over the gear shift to kiss his cheek, then used my thumb to wipe off the lipstick smudge I'd left behind. For tonight, I'd gone all out—full makeup and perfectly-flipped hair and a snug pink mini-dress that showed off my legs. This, I'd realized, was how I felt most comfortable. Sweatpants and hoodies weren't exactly intolerable, but still. I felt most like myself in a dress.

My mind flashed back to a conversation I'd had with Emmett a few weeks before, when I'd finally explained to him the reasons I'd traded soccer balls and boxing gloves for makeup and dresses, transforming myself from a sporty tomboy into what I'd presumed was a "typical girl." His only response was to give me a strange look and ask, "Why can't you be both?"

Exactly, I thought as I drove. *Why can't I?* After all, I'd been fortunate enough to have been born into a place and an era where people were free to be who they wanted to be, believe what they wanted to believe, and love who they wanted to love.

Unlike the first time the four of us dined together at Goody's—or in other words, the night of the Most Un-successful Secret Setup Date Ever Attempted—the mood felt relaxed and festive. Nate scored even more points by being completely sober *and* for not trying to spike our drinks with forbidden vodka. Even Harper seemed impressed, and I sensed that if he made another attempt to kiss her later, he might actually succeed. As for Emmett and me, we planned to spend our second to last night of the summer together—and maybe our last—wrapped up in that cramped sleeping bag of his, finishing what we'd started the night everything blew up. This time, we wouldn't have that wedge of guilt between us, driving us apart.

"I'll see you kids next summer," Sherry said after we'd paid our bill and wished her a good night. She seemed kind of sad to see us go.

I was, too. I'd gotten kind of used to the new Goody's, especially those smooth, pretty chairs that didn't fuse to the backs of our legs like the old vinyl booths used to do. It would never go back to the old way, but maybe the new way could work just as well. Not all changes were bad. The only thing I still missed was that jukebox, which was definitely gone forever. Luckily, though, I'd come prepared with a suitable replacement.

Outside, it had finally stopped raining. The four of us piled into the car and I revved up the BMW's quiet engine.

"What are you doing?" Emmett asked, watching as I plugged my phone into the USB port and scrolled down the screen.

I found what I wanted, then hit the start arrow. "You'll see." I kept my eyes on Harper, anxious to see her reaction to what was coming next.

We'd come a long way over the past couple weeks, but we weren't entirely back to normal yet. Traces of tension still lingered between us, and I found myself second-guessing everything I said and did around her. But, to my relief, when those familiar opening lines blasted through the speakers, she smiled and then burst out laughing. "Yakety Yak" by The Coasters. Selection B6 on Goody's jukebox. Our summer anthem. The song we'd been bopping around to since we were preteens, enchanted by the silly lyrics and catchy, upbeat tempo. I'd downloaded it from iTunes during a fit of nostalgia and knew I had to share it with her, one last time.

"You guys are weird," Emmett declared as Harper and I sang along with the words we'd spent years memorizing, our shoulders wiggling to the beat.

"Dude, this is nothing," Nate said from behind me. "They used to do the same thing in public."

Weirdness aside, I felt about ten times lighter when the song finished. And going by the grin on my cousin's face, she did too.

The carefree atmosphere didn't last. That heavy end-of-summer feeling descended once again a few minutes later when I parked the car in front of Harper's cottage. She and her mom planned to leave at dawn the next day. Aunt Carrie and I had already said our good-byes earlier, but Harper and I had agreed to save ours for after dinner.

Nate mumbled an excuse and he and Emmett got out of the car and wandered off, giving us some privacy. When they were gone, Harper moved up into the passenger seat.

"Well," I said, tracing the steering wheel with my finger. "Operation Best Summer was kind of a bust, huh?"

She snorted. "It wasn't the greatest summer we've ever spent together, that's for sure. But at least it wasn't boring."

"Yes," I agreed. "There is that."

We sat quietly for a minute, each of us peering out the windshield at the cottage where Aunt Carrie was undoubtedly still cleaning like mad to get the place ready to be put on the market. Sherry had been wrong—she wouldn't see *all* of us next summer. Not Harper, who would be at home, working to save money for her second year of school. Nate would probably be back, but I wasn't sure what Emmett's mom was going to do with their cottage. She didn't even know if she'd be able to keep their house.

So, all things considered, there was no way to predict who would or wouldn't be around next summer. The only person I was one hundred percent sure of was myself.

"Mom and I will be back to visit in December," Harper said, her voice cracking. Then she turned to me and smiled. "So. Operation Best Christmas?"

I laughed through my tears. "Sounds like a plan."

She reached over to hug me, locking her slender arms around my shoulders. "Have fun with Emmett tonight," she said between sniffles. "You deserve it, Kat. And him."

I nodded, my throat aching too much to respond. "You have fun with Nate, too. Kiss the poor boy, would you?"

She pulled back, wiping her eyes. "I guess I should. I might never get another chance to make out with the biggest douchebag at Millard Lake." We laughed, and then she leaned in for another long hug. "Bye, Katty."

"Bye, Harpy."

Five minutes later we were still saying good-bye, but we weren't in any hurry. The boys could wait.

"I think that's all of it," Pop said, shoving the last box of kitchen appliances into the back of the Volvo. They seemed to have multiplied over the summer, even though he hadn't bought any new ones. "Hey, what are you doing? Leave that there."

"Bryce, there's way too much stuff back here." Dad rearranged some boxes, Tetris-style, and sighed wearily. "You won't even be able to see out the back window. Why don't you leave some of these here?"

Pop looked stricken at the thought of abandoning his precious appliances. "I'll just move some to the back seat. It'll be fine."

"There's no *room* in the back seat."

I glanced over at Emmett and rolled my eyes. I'd warned him that my parents bickered like this every time we were packing to go somewhere, but he still looked slightly taken aback at witnessing it firsthand. He wasn't used to seeing adult couples fight in a normal, healthy way.

Finally, my dads stopped squabbling and went back inside the cottage for whatever was left to pack, leaving Emmett and me alone by the car. If they had any compassion at all—and I knew they did—they'd stay in there for a good long while. I didn't need an audience for this good-bye.

"When are you and your mom leaving?" I asked, trying to stall the inevitable.

"Right after you do," he replied. "I told her I wanted to stick around as long as possible."

I turned toward him, and the next thing I knew, his arms were around me, his cheek pressed against my hair. My eyes stung with tears, but I blinked them back. This wasn't a *real* good-bye. He lived only an hour away by car, and we'd already figured out a visitation plan for the coming year. We'd give each other a couple weeks to get settled in at school and then we'd start spending Saturdays together, alternating between his house and mine until winter arrived and the snow made the hour-long drive unpredictable. In that event, we'd have to settle for lots and lots of texting.

I'd miss not seeing his face every hour of every day, but once-a-week visits would have to be enough to sustain us until we started college and he moved to the city for good. Until then, Saturdays belonged to us.

"I'll miss you," he said when we finally stopped hugging. "And I'll miss waking up each morning and wondering what you're going to look like when I see you that day."

I laughed. I was rocking one of my quintessential retro looks—black polka-dot shirt dress, pearl earrings, finger-waved hair. "I'll keep you updated with pictures," I promised.

He pulled me close again, his hands settling on my hips as he lowered his face to mine. Kissing him next to my dad's Volvo reminded me of this time last summer, when I'd kissed Sawyer Bray good-bye in the very same spot. But Emmett's kiss was different in every way that counted. His kiss was carnival rides and fork rainbows and bonfires and sweet, awkward firsts in a too-small sleeping bag. His kiss was one I wouldn't forget a day later.

"Oh!" I said when we broke apart. "I have something for you."

"Something better than that?"

I smiled mysteriously and stuck my arm into the open car window, grabbing the large manila envelope I'd stored on the passenger seat. Silently, I handed it to Emmett.

"What's this?" he asked, confused.

"Open it."

He lifted the flap and reached inside the envelope, sliding out the thick sheaf of paper. His eyes scanned the title page, slowly widening in comprehension. "This is freaking Book Six of the Core Earth series," he said, looking up at me in disbelief. "How in the hell did you get this? It hasn't even been released yet."

"Oh," I said coyly. "I just happen to know the author."

"You know K. B. Marks?"

"Very well, in fact." Unable to stand it any longer, I burst out laughing. "He's my dad."

Emmett stared at me like I was crazier than he'd originally believed. "K. B. Marks," he said slowly, "is your dad."

"Yep." I took the pages from him and stuck them back into the envelope before placing them on the roof of the car. "It's only the first five chapters. He'll give you the entire thing when it gets closer to publication. You'll be the very first fan to read Book Six."

Emmett shook his head, completely flabbergasted. "And you've never told me this . . . why?"

I shrugged and hit him with one of my flirty, full-watt smiles. "A girl is entitled to a few secrets."

chapter 29

I stood at my locker after the last bell of the day, trying in vain to ignore the nervous rumbling in my stomach. The hallway behind me was emptying quickly; I'd probably be late if I didn't get going soon.

My phone chimed with an incoming text. Welcoming the disruption, I dug it out of my backpack and checked the screen, smiling when I saw the message from Emmett.

Good luck today!

I texted back a quick thanks, but that was all the conversation I had time for. I'd see him tomorrow, anyway, when he arrived for our first Saturday visit. We were both looking forward to it, even though at first, he'd been reluctant to leave home. His mom had filed for divorce earlier in the week, a move he feared might send his dad into another rage, but he calmed down when my dads suggested that his mom spend the day in Weldon, too, a solution that pleased us all. Mrs. Reese would hang out with my dads while I escorted Emmett around the city, showing him all my favorite spots.

Planning our first post-summer day together had been a great distraction during those first three weeks of

school, when loneliness almost crushed me. My old
friends weren't acting hostile toward me, but they
weren't exactly friendly, either. Evidently, school hadn't
been in session long enough for them to recognize the
changes in me that I'd struggled so hard to make.

Oh well, I thought as I shut my locker and headed toward the stairs. *Rise above.*

Outside, the soccer field was overflowing with girls of
various shapes and sizes, all wearing shorts and T-shirts.
They gathered in clusters beneath the still-hot sun,
stretching stiff muscles and waiting patiently for Mrs. Hyland, the coach. I took a deep breath and then joined
them, staking out a vacant spot in which to loosen my
own sluggish muscles.

"Kat?" said a familiar voice from behind me, jolting
me out of my warm-up. "What are you doing here?"

I turned around and waited patiently while her dark
brown eyes took me in from my tied-back hair right
down to my brand new soccer cleats—pink ones, of
course. Then I said, "Hi, Shay."

"*You're* trying out for the soccer team?" Her tone
sounded more surprised than snotty, so I let myself relax
a bit. Shay was aware of my athletic past and the reasons
I'd quit sports, but like me, she'd assumed my resignation
was permanent. Also like me, she was shocked to dis-
cover that it clearly wasn't.

"Yeah," I replied, and then went back to stretching my
hamstrings.

I expected her to walk away then, return to wherever
she'd been before she spotted me and settle right back
into ignoring my existence. But instead, she fell in beside
me on the grass and wordlessly copied my movements.
When I glanced over at her, she looked back at me with
the tiniest shadow of a smile. I responded with a bigger
one of my own.

Mrs. Hyland showed up then with her clipboard and immediately started organizing the first warm-up drill, which involved directing a moving ball between two cones. "Okay, girls," she bellowed after she'd set up the goal and had us form a line. "Let's see what you can do."

My nervousness had all but disappeared by the time I reached the front of the line. My turn. I tightened my ponytail and sprinted onto the field, my new cleats digging into the soft earth. Just like with boxing, my body seemed to fall back into the right rhythms all on its own. When the ball rolled in my direction, I didn't even have to think. I just ran forward and kicked.

ACKNOWLEDGMENTS

Kat's story never would have made it off my computer without the help and support of a lot of people. I would like to thank:

Carly Watters, for your tireless support, gentle pushes, and thoughtful edit notes that always make me see my manuscripts in a whole new way. Your hard work and determination helped get me to this point, and I'm so grateful to you.

Alicia Condon, my editor, for your enthusiasm and for patiently answering every question I threw at you. And to the rest of the wonderful team at Kensington, for bringing my books to life in a way that exceeded my wildest expectations.

Shannon Steele, my friend, faithful first reader, and unofficial President of my nonexistent fan club. You kept me on point as I sent you the first draft, chapter by chapter, and you were *never* demanding or impatient when I failed to write fast enough (I actually typed that with a straight face). Thank you for the seedling of an idea that blossomed into this book, and for your help with the last line.

Cara Bertrand, my talented author friend, critique partner, and the first person I turn to for writing advice. Your helpful insights and spot-on suggestions are invaluable to me. ABNA may have connected us, but it's our shared love of words that makes us friends. Thank you for always reminding me to keep the drama on the page.

The readers, reviewers, and bloggers who do so much

to support authors and spread the word. Your passion and dedication amaze me.

My parents, family, and extended family, for being so endlessly supportive and proud. Enroll a little girl in a mail order book club and this is what happens; she falls in love with words and makes a career out of it. Thank you, Mom and Dad, for surrounding me with books all my life.

My children, for willingly sharing my attention with a laptop and for understanding how important books and writing are to Mom. I love you both.

And lastly, a million thanks to my amazingly generous husband. Creating a happy marriage for the parents in this book was easy because I live one every day with you (and your many, many kitchen appliances). Thank you for holding down the fort all those Sundays while I shut myself up in our bedroom to write. Without you, we all may have starved. Without you, this book would not exist. I love you.

Don't miss *Faking Perfect* by Rebecca Phillips, available now in bookstores and online!

**"Edgy and honest, *Faking Perfect* is the real thing."
—Huntley Fitzpatrick**

When Lexi Shaw seduced Oakfield High's resident bad boy Tyler Flynn at the beginning of senior year, he seemed perfectly okay with her rules:

1. Avoid her at school.
2. Keep his mouth shut about what they do together.
3. Never tease her about her friend
(and unrequited crush) Ben.

Because with his integrity and values and golden boy looks, Ben can never find out about what she's been doing behind closed doors with Tyler. Or that her mom's too busy drinking and chasing losers to pay the bills. Or that Lexi's dad hasn't been a part of her life for the last thirteen years. But with Tyler suddenly breaking the rules, Ben asking her out, and her dad back in the picture, how long will she be able to go on faking perfect?

**"Poignant, edgy, and real, *Faking Perfect* is an honest look at the courage and strength it can often take simply to be yourself."
—Julianna Scott, author of *The Holders***

When I seduced Tyler Flynn at the beginning of senior year, I never imagined he'd still be sneaking in and out of my bedroom window six months later. Then again, nothing about our relationship had ever been conventional.

"Shh," I said. "My mom's upstairs."

"She never hears anything," Tyler said with a frustrated grunt.

My window was stuck again. I lay on my stomach on the bed, my eyes on his slim silhouette as he banged his palm against the latch, trying to loosen it. A string of profanity followed each thump. Tyler had zero patience for things that didn't yield easily.

I rolled over and pulled the covers up to my chin. He was right—my mother never heard anything. Not even the strange noises coming from her daughter's basement bedroom in the middle of the night. Just like she never smelled my cigarette smoke or saw the roadmap of red lines that snaked through the whites of my eyes after a particularly wild party. She probably wasn't even aware that my bedroom window opened up to the side of the house where a person could slip in and out, undetected in the darkness.

After a few more minutes of abuse, the window finally

creaked open. The faint, crisp scent of winter filtered through the stuffiness in the room. Tyler shoved his feet into his sneakers and turned to the window, bracing his arms on the sill and steeling his body in preparation to boost himself out. Then, changing his mind, he spun back around to face me.

"You really need a new window." He raised his voice as if he was *trying* to alert my mother to his presence. He loved to goad me, see how far he could push me before I got mad and started locking him out. "I can't risk getting stuck in here for the night."

My insides recoiled at the thought of spending the entire night with him. "I'll just grease the hinges again or something. Good night."

"Anxious to get rid of me, Lexi?"

"You're letting all the heat out," I replied.

He reached behind him to shut the window again and returned to the bed, where I was still snuggled up under the multicolored quilt my grandmother had made for me when I was a baby. I wondered what she'd think if she could see me now.

"What are you doing?" I asked when Tyler kicked off his shoes and crawled onto the bed.

He settled on his back on top of the quilt's patterned squares, eyes closed, arms crossed over his chest. "I'm not ready to go yet."

I squinted at his profile. Usually, he was out of here before his heart rate and breathing even had a chance to slow down. He never stayed with me, never lay next to me while my cheeks still burned from his prickly stubble and my own secret shame.

"We're going to get caught, Tyler."

"We're not going to get caught," he said with utmost confidence, like the petty criminal he was. "You said your mom never sets foot in your room."

This was true. She'd avoided my room for years, and not because she respected my privacy. Six years ago, when I brought Trevor home from the pet store, I quickly realized that owning a corn snake came with some unexpected perks. For one, people thought I was weird, which I didn't mind much back in sixth grade. And two, my mother's deathly fear of snakes afforded me hours of uninterrupted alone time in my room, which I didn't mind either.

I wasn't sure why she was so afraid. Trevor (named after a boy I had a crush on at the time) lived in a tank on my dresser and rarely escaped anymore. He spent most of his time either hiding or eating the dead mice I stored in boxes behind a stack of ice trays in the freezer. Mom avoided the freezer too.

"So," Tyler said, wrapping one of my strawberry-blond curls around his index finger. "You wanna do it again?"

"No." I reached down to retrieve my T-shirt and slipped it on under the blankets. Once was enough. Once was always enough to release the pent-up frustration inside me, if only for a little while. Twice wouldn't happen unless I initiated it. I needed to be the one in control, which was why I'd chosen Tyler, Oakfield High's resident badass/burnout/man-whore. His type dodged commitment and never fell in love. He didn't care about being used, and he knew how to be discreet. And even though he was failing most of his classes, he wasn't stupid. He'd never risk the good thing he had going with me. Also, the sneaking around turned him on.

Tyler gave up on trying to tempt me with an encore and lit up a cigarette. He wedged a couple pillows behind his head and took long, lazy puffs as if relaxing in the park.

Annoyed, I sat up and flicked on the lamp.

"Hey," he said, shutting his eyes against the light.

I looked over at him, noticing that his perpetually tousled dark hair was even messier than usual, likely because I'd been running my fingers through it earlier. His shirt was inside out, his zipper half down, his neck mottled with what looked like a bite mark. Was this what he looked like afterward? I'd never actually looked closely at him after the fact. Usually, all I saw was his back and then his legs as he shimmied out my window.

"Why are you still here, Tyler?" I asked, waving away his smoke. "It's one o'clock in the morning. I want to go to sleep."

He smirked. "And have sweet dreams about Mr. Wonderful?"

"Don't push me," I warned.

"Oh right. Sorry, I forgot. It's a Lexi Rule."

I shot him a look. Okay, so I did have a few rules, but nothing unreasonable or difficult to follow. One, he had to avoid me at school. Two, he had to keep his mouth shut about what we did together. And three . . . under no circumstances was he ever allowed to tease me about my friend Ben, who I'd had an unrequited crush on for two years. Ben, with his integrity and values and golden boy looks, did not belong in this room with us. He wasn't like us.

Tyler finished his cigarette and dropped the butt into the half-empty can of 7-Up on my nightstand. As he did this, I heard a cough coming from upstairs and then footsteps plodding across the floor. My mother was walking from her bedroom, where she stayed up late every night watching the Game Show Network, to the kitchen, which was right above my room. Next, she would pour herself a glass of iced tea or white wine if there was any left over from the weekend, and then trudge back to her bedroom and shut the door. *Family Feud, Press Your Luck,*

Match Game, Password, The Price is Right . . . she watched them all for hours on end, her expression never changing aside from a raised eyebrow now and again when a contestant was being particularly boneheaded. She gave me the same look sometimes.

"Okay, it's time to go now," I said, elbowing Tyler in the ribs. It freaked me out that he was beside me and not evacuating the house like it was on fire, which had been the case most other nights. Having him here while my mother was awake went way beyond my comfort zone. "I have a math test first period tomorrow. Come *on*." I poked him again, and he finally started to get up.

"Oh yeah, I guess I do, too." He looked down at me and smirked again. "Thanks for helping me study again. I never knew vectors and shit could be so interesting."

"You're welcome," I said, even though we hadn't studied at all. The last time we really studied together was back in late September, when I used our upcoming math quiz as an excuse to get him into my room for the first time. He needed a tutor, I needed an outlet. It was all very practical and casual. Clinical, almost. Devoid of emotion.

Lately, though, I could feel something changing, the way animals can sense when a storm is near. A subtle shift in the air between us. A possessive look burning into my back as I passed him in the hall at school. A touch so gentle it made my breath hitch. And now this, sticking around as long as he dared, not quite ready to leave.

This was bad. It seemed Tyler was on the verge of breaking the one rule I'd left unspoken. Do not get attached.

I needed to squash this problem immediately.

"Let's not do this anymore," I said to his bare back as he took off his shirt and turned it right side out. I kept my eyes on the tattoo on his left shoulder blade—the grim reaper in his black cloak, smiling and holding a scythe. The harvester of souls.

Tyler pulled on his shirt and glanced back at me with a flickering of a smile. I tried not to let it get to me. All my life, I'd suffered such a weakness for boys like him. In the first grade, I'd had a massive crush on Cody Hatcher, who pushed kids at recess and regularly spit on the teachers. By middle school, I felt myself drawn to the troubled boys with bad home lives who cut class and sneaked cigarettes behind the convenience store. Then, in the tenth grade, when I started cultivating my good girl image and making new friends, I gave up on the bad boys and set my sights on the nice, well-adjusted ones. Like Ben Dorsey, for instance, track star and honors student and way too good to be true. Too good for *me*, anyway, which was why I'd strayed back to the bad boys again.

But nobody could ever know about that.

"Do what?" Tyler said, even though he knew full well what I meant. He'd heard those words from me before.

"This." I gestured to the tangled sheets and my half-nude body and then to him, the ultimate bad boy with his tattoo and cigarettes and close, personal acquaintance with the entire Oakfield police department.

"This," he repeated, leaning over the bed toward me, his hands sinking into the mattress. I pulled away from him, but not before I caught the warm, smoky scent of his skin. He saw my reaction and laughed, which infuriated and excited me. "You really want to stop this. You want me to leave and never come back. Right?"

"Right."

We stared each other down. From above, I could hear the faint applause of a live studio audience.

"Right," Tyler said, lowering his face to mine. He kissed me and I let him, even though once had been enough and he was the one in control and my mother was upstairs and awake.

I knew I was supposed to refuse him, to squash this problem once and for all and become the girl most people saw each day—the smiling, confident girl who'd secured a place at the top of the high school food chain. But I could never truly be her, at least not permanently. So I turned off the lamp, wrapped my arms around Tyler's neck, and pulled him closer. I shut my mind to everything else, including the intrusive thoughts of Ben. Ben, who I possibly could have loved if only I was brave enough to love someone like him.

I didn't love Tyler Flynn. I didn't even like him.